The Book of Collateral Damage

The Book of
Collateral Damage

SINAN ANTOON

TRANSLATED FROM THE ARABIC BY JONATHAN WRIGHT

YALE UNIVERSITY PRESS ■ NEW HAVEN & LONDON

A MARGELLOS
WORLD REPUBLIC OF LETTERS BOOK

The Margellos World Republic of Letters is dedicated to making literary works from around the globe available in English through translation. It brings to the English-speaking world the work of leading poets, novelists, essayists, philosophers, and playwrights from Europe, Latin America, Africa, Asia, and the Middle East to stimulate international discourse and creative exchange.

The author wishes to thank The Lannan Foundation for a residency in Marfa, Texas, in June 2014.

Yale University Press books may be purchased in quantity for educational, business, or promotional use. For information, please e-mail sales.press@yale.edu (U.S. office) or sales@yaleup.co.uk (U.K. office).

Printed in the United States of America.

Library of Congress Control Number: 2018955516
ISBN 978-0-300-22894-6 (hardcover : alk. paper)

A catalogue record for this book is available from the British Library.

This paper meets the requirements of ANSI/NISO z39.48-1992 (Permanence of Paper).

10 9 8 7 6 5 4 3 2 1

He left many blank pages in it.
—*On al-Fihris (The Index) by Ibn al-Nadim (d. 990)*

They speak for the dead and translate the speech of the living.
—*Al-Jahiz (d. 868), on books*

Every passion borders on the chaotic, but the collector's passion borders on the chaos of memories.
—*Walter Benjamin*

Time is the substance I am made of. Time is a river which sweeps me along, but I am the river. It is the tiger which destroys me, but I am the tiger; it is a fire which consumes me, but I am the fire.
—*Jorge Luis Borges, A New Refutation of Time*

We are our memory,
we are that chimerical museum of shifting shapes,
that pile of broken mirrors.
—*Borges, Cambridge*

Beginnings

I can still remember the first time I flew.

"Come on. It's time!" my father said firmly before flying off. My mother pushed me gently with her beak toward the edge and whispered, "Don't be frightened, my little one. You'll fly. We all fly. I'll be right behind you."

My three siblings were flying happily in the sky, oblivious to me. My heart was pounding, as if it, too, were also worried its wings might let it down. As if, like me, it was torn between the fear inside, which kept me in or close to the nest, and an overwhelming desire that compelled me to be like the grown-ups.

I moved forward warily to the tip of the branch, which dipped a little with my weight and that of my mother behind me. I didn't look down. I looked up, where my father was circling in a clear, cloudless sky. I spread my wings, then looked back toward my mother. She didn't say anything this time but her eyes gave me courage and she kissed my head with her beak. I remembered how she had often told me that we have strong wings and that mine would one day carry me to distant lands. I looked ahead and summoned all my courage and flapped my wings with vigor.

And I took off.

I couldn't believe myself. I flew with confidence, as if I had often flown before. The cold air swept past my white feathers. The whole sky was mine and the whole earth was laid out below me. With a flip of a wing I could twist and turn, rise and fall. I kept flying till the sun bade us farewell. I was the last to return home that day.

I laugh now, and I'm embarrassed too, when I remember that moment and the fear that later left me. Here I am now, flying with the grown-ups for days on our journey to the warm lands.

☙❦❧

A drop of sweat fell on the edge of the piece of paper and I stopped reading. His handwriting was neat and confident. The ink was black, maybe from a ballpoint pen. The words were perched like birds on lines that looked like small sky-blue threads running across small brown pages. I probably thought of this because he had written about the sky and flying. The passage reminded me of the storks' nest I used to see in Shorja on the dome of a building when I was young. I turned the page. The title of the passage that followed also began with the word *colloquy*.

The air-conditioning unit in the room was panting and sputtering, and the pores of my skin were oozing sweat from the heat. I wiped the drop of sweat off the page with my finger and caught another one that was rolling down my forehead and about to drop. I left the pages on the bed next to the buff-colored notebook, stood up, went to the air-conditioning unit, and turned the dial counterclockwise as far as possible. I went to the bathroom and washed my face in cold water. I dried it with the towel and went back to stand in front of the air-conditioning unit for thirty seconds. I thought about the long, tiring journey to Amman. I had to pack and sleep a little, because we were scheduled to leave Baghdad at six a.m. I went back to the bed and read his letter a second time:

Dear Mr. al-Baghdadi,

I hope you had a productive day in the arms of your fatigued Baghdad. Apologies for intruding and daring to disturb you. But I've thought long and hard about the happy coincidence that brought us together and about your sincere interest in my project and your kind offer to translate it (although I'm not in a hurry to have it translated or even published, as I mentioned, at least not for now). I decided to take a risk and lay claim to more of your generosity and kindness. I sat down waiting for you at the hotel reception until half an hour before the start of the curfew so that I could deliver this part of the manuscript to you personally, but you didn't come back. That's why I'm writing this letter. I attach the first chapter (it's the history of the first minute, which has yet to be completed, and I do have my own opinions on whether texts end or not and I might tell you about them in the future). I hope you like it and I hope you'll give me your opinion with the candor and rigor of a critic and a writer, even if it is negative.

With this letter you'll find a simple gift, because books are all I have in this world. I'll try to obtain an email account so that we can communicate across the continents and the oceans. Thank you in advance and I apologize again if I was a little rude at the beginning of our meeting. I'm not usually much good at dealing with people and I prefer books, because they never hurt or betray.

With affection,
Your brother,
Wadood Abdulkarim,
Baghdad,
July 29, 2003

He's not interested in being translated or published. So why is he sharing his manuscript with me so readily? Does he care that much what a stranger thinks? He's strange, this Wadood. I folded the letter up and put it in the notebook I had bought specially to record my impressions during this visit. It had large pages that were slightly tan. The edges were stitched and trimmed unevenly to look like an old book. It had a thick cover of buff leather and a thin red ribbon attached to the top of the spine as a place marker. The marker was still on the first page, where I had written just one word since arriving: *Baghdad*.

I envied Wadood his productivity. I can't even begin. And all this concern, or rather obsession, with writing rituals and instruments only ends in blank pages and silence. This visit had of course been hectic and hurried, and the pace of the work and daily travel exhausted me physically and mentally, leaving no time to write or even to think in peace. I have yet to start processing the whirl of scenes and people and ambivalent emotions. Nevertheless, I should have written something. One sentence at least. Every night I came back exhausted and sat on the bed. I picked up my pen but didn't manage to write anything. The first night was the only night I wrote anything—that one word, *Baghdad*.

I went back to thinking about his manuscript and his gift, which wasn't simple at all. Yes, it wasn't the first edition, only the second, but it was the first part of the collected poems of Abbud al-Karkhi, and it does date back to 1956 and I think it's rare. The book is in excellent condition. I browsed through the first few pages. There was a dedication to King Ghazi and a photograph of him on the next page, then one of al-Karkhi. The introduction was a collection of tributes and essays: there was a poem by al-Rusafi entitled "To the Poet of the Nation" (*What a fine man you are, Abbud/With your rhymes you raise the banner of zajal*), another poem by al-Zahawi, an essay by Raphael Butti on the use of colloquial Arabic in poetry and prose, one by al-Rusafi on *zajal* poetry and popular forms of literature, another one by Mohammad Bahjat al-Athari on colloquial and classical Arabic, and then, finally, the poems themselves. As I expected, "The Crusher," al-Karkhi's most famous poem, was the first in the collection. I fell asleep before I was halfway through and dreamed that al-Karkhi was our driver on the journey to Amman. All the way he recited his poems and explained their context and how they came about, but Roy kept insisting that I translate them. I lost my temper with him and said, "Poetry can't be translated that way. We're not at a press conference!" And I kept repeating, "*One hour and I'll break the crusher/And curse this damned life of mine.*" Al-Karkhi roared with laughter and said, "How did you get stuck with them?"

I woke up to loud banging on the door of my room and Roy's voice saying, "Come on, Nameer. We have to leave in half an hour. Don't you want to eat breakfast?"

I had a shower in record time, dressed hurriedly, and stuffed the rest of my clothes and other things into my bag. I hadn't bought anything other than the books from al-Mutanabbi Street. My bag was big enough for them and the box of cookies that my aunt had given me. I put Wadood's envelope, my notebook, and the al-Karkhi poems in my backpack with my passport. I hate to be late for a departure or for any appointment, but I had another, much more important reason for hurrying. I wanted to savor one last time the Iraqi-style clotted cream and the hot *sammun* bread that arrived fresh every morning from a bakery close to the tiny hotel in Karrada. When I went down to the ground floor, Roy was going over the bill with the receptionist, who spoke enough English for them to understand each other, and I was already sick of translating. "Do you need any help?" I asked him anyway. "No, everything's cool. You have some time because Laura's still packing and needs twenty minutes. The driver hasn't arrived yet either."

I put my bag next to Roy's big bag close to the front door and went to the hotel restaurant, a small room with four tables and a door that led to the kitchen. Abed, the waiter, saw me from inside the kitchen and we exchanged greetings. I sat down at a table on the right, turned my cup over, took a Lipton teabag from the plate in the middle of the table, and put it in the cup. If it had been real tea, from a teapot and flavored with cardamom, the breakfast would have been perfect. In America I had stopped drinking tea, especially after I moved out of my family's house and switched to coffee. Two minutes later Abed arrived, carrying a tray with a small bowl of clotted cream, another with date syrup, and a blue plastic basket holding two loaves of sammun bread. He put the tray on the table in front of me, then went back to the kitchen to fetch the hot water for the tea. He hadn't said much, except for the first day we had breakfast, a week earlier. He asked me at the time about my traveling companions.

"Excuse me, sir, but the group you're with, what's their story?" he said.

"They're married and they've come to shoot a documentary," I replied.

"Really? A month ago there was a group of French people staying here who were making a film too. Very well, and you would be the director?" he asked.

"No, I just came with them to translate for them and help them."

"Do you live abroad?"

"Yes."

"Where?"

"In the U.S." I said.

"How long have you been away?"

"Since 1993."

I asked him about his work.

"I've been working in this hotel for four years," he replied. "Our house is in Camp Sarah but for the last few months, since the fall of Baghdad, I go there only once a week. I sleep here."

We didn't speak after that. He was always busy with his work, and over breakfast Roy, Laura, and I had discussed the day's schedule and the places we were going to film. As he poured the hot water into the cup, he asked, "It looks like you're leaving today, sir?"

"Yes, that's right."

"Hope you have a safe trip. Which city do you live in, sir?"

"In Boston," I said. "But in one week I'm going to move to a state called New Hampshire," I added for accuracy.

"I've never heard of it, to be honest."

"It's on the border with Canada. Very cold," I said.

"The cold's easier to take than this damned heat. What do you do there?"

"I've got a job at a university," I replied.

"Congratulations. I hope it goes well." I expected him to ask what my discipline was, but a voice called him from the kitchen. "Excuse me, sir," he said politely.

I put two spoonsful of sugar in the cup of tea and stirred it. I took a sip that almost scorched my tongue and put the cup back. I took a loaf of sammun, split it open along the side, and spread the cream inside, adding two spoonsful of the date syrup. Abed didn't come back. I ate slowly to enjoy my last breakfast. I had tasted this *gaymar* back in America on a visit to San Diego, where many Iraqis live, but it tasted different there. This cream reminded me of Umm Jalil's cream, which she used to leave in a bowl on the stoop of our house early in the morning. I remembered how a stray cat rubbed its nose in the cream one morning and made off with some of it. Would Umm Jalil still be alive? I examined the sole painting hanging on the wall opposite. It was an attempt to draw a traditional Baghdadi backstreet. There were women in abayas carrying baskets with the dome of a mosque, a minaret, and a sunset scene in the background. The colors were garish and there were unintentional mistakes in the perspective and the proportions. An attempt to reproduce a sense of authenticity, but it fell into the trap of self-Orientalism. I reproached myself silently for the way I was over-analyzing. There I was—thinking like an academic even before I officially started my new job. I had seen many of these paintings in the city, sold to journalists and newcomers. I remembered that the department chair had asked me in an email to decide what course I planned to teach, apart from Arabic, so that it could be added to the curriculum, and I had to decide quickly. The woman who had held the position before me had taught a class on Andalusian literature. The chair suggested I teach that too, and then I could propose another course for the following year. I didn't have enough time to prepare a new course, and Andalusian literature would be an opportunity to reduce the number of questions on terrorism and jihad, which had intruded on every class and lecture since 9/11.

I began the rituals of preparing another piece of sammun and cream, but Roy's voice called from the reception. "Hey, Nameer. Laura's ready and the driver's waiting." I finished making the sandwich, wrapped it in a paper napkin that was on the table, put it in one of the pockets of my backpack, and drank the cup of tea, which wasn't quite so hot.

Mullah Abbud al-Karkhi wasn't in the driver's seat, just Abul-arif, the Jordanian driver who had been with us throughout the visit and who worked on the Amman-Baghdad route and knew Baghdad well. Roy and Laura sat in the front seat next to the driver, while I took the back seat so I could stretch out and sleep.

Baghdad was still sleepy and yawning. Most of the shops had their eyes shut. There were some people on the sidewalks, but the streets were semideserted. A car drove past us from time to time. American tanks and armored vehicles were lurking at the junctions. Someone had written "US Army Go Home" in red paint on a wall. I was the one going back to the country that the U.S. Army came from, while it looked likely to stay. I was going back to a country that was not yet "home" even after a full decade. I had read expressions of gratitude to the Americans on other walls that made me sad. I wanted to see the Tigris and say goodbye to it. I didn't know when I would come back, or whether I ever would. The Tigris looked so pale on this visit. It no longer looked the way I remembered it. But did anything still look the way I remembered? Nothing had managed to escape turning pale. A pigeon fancier had awakened early to let out his flock and watch the pigeons circle in the city sky. Seeing the birds in flight suggested an answer to my question—an answer that gave wing to a simple joy. The doves were still as they were—beautiful and free . . . free at least for this fleeting moment.

The doves reminded me of the stork in Wadood's manuscript. I thought about him coming to the hotel and leaving his manuscript for me. It struck me as a rather strange and impulsive gesture. Or was I exaggerating and being too hard on him? Hadn't I asked him to write to me? Hadn't I offered to help? My sudden return to Baghdad with these Americans was also strange and impulsive. Had I come to rediscover something, or to make sure it was lost? Wasn't I ill at ease in this city and in a hurry to leave? Had I come back to examine the wounds I had left behind, or what? I wanted to read the rest of the manuscript, but not now because I was exhausted and sleepy. Later. It was a long way to Amman.

I woke up after about two hours to find desert stretching away on both sides of the road. I asked the driver where we were. "We passed Ramadi an hour ago. The others are sleeping too." I looked at them. Laura's head was in Roy's arms, and his was resting on the small bag that he used as a pillow.

"Didn't they stop us along the way?" I asked.

"No," he said, "only at the first checkpoint at Abu Ghraib."

"How long to the border?" I asked.

"You've got al-Rutba in an hour and a half and then about an hour after that we get to the border." He paused and then, looking at me in the big rearview mirror and half smiling, he added, "What? You're in a hurry to get out of Iraq, Mr. Nameer?"

He took every opportunity to make bad-tempered and malicious remarks. Twice I had argued with him angrily and I raised my voice so loud that I upset Roy. On one occasion I had confronted him, saying, "You love Saddam."

He was evasive, saying, "No, but I'm not with the Americans."

"And what makes you think *I'm* with the Americans?" I replied, but then I decided there was nothing to be gained by arguing with him. "No, Abularif," I said. "That's unfair. Did you ever have a passenger who didn't ask where we are and when we'll arrive?"

"Just joking," he laughed.

I was going to tell him that I missed being myself and on my own. I was tired of translating everything that was said. I had spent six whole days with them: Roy, Laura, and Abularif too. From early morning to sunset we had gone everywhere conducting interviews and filming. They were pleasant and working with them was easy, but six days was enough. The day before had been the only day when I was able to breathe and move around freely. Abularif took them to al-Nahr Street and the copperworkers' market to buy gifts, walk around the markets, and then have some traditional grilled fish to eat. I had gone to al-Mutanabbi Street to wander around and buy books. After that I went to our old house and then my aunt's, who had prepared a meal of stuffed grape leaves for me and invited relatives for me to meet. She pressed me to invite "your American friends that you're filming with," but I told her I preferred to come alone.

"They don't speak Arabic, auntie," I said, "and if they come I'll have to keep translating for them and I won't be able to enjoy being with you. Besides, they're busy tomorrow."

"As you wish then. Okay, do you remember our house? Can you find the way on your own?"

"Of course I can, what do you mean?" I said.

I used to go there as a child in the summer and play with my cousins and sleep there days at a time.

I walked a little, then took a taxi from al-Rusafi Square to our house in al-Amin al-Ula, which was later changed to al-Khaleej. I wanted to take a look at it and say hello to any of our neighbors who were still there. When we were about to approach the al-Amin bridge, I asked the driver not to cross to the other side of the canal because the street that led to the house was directly on the right. The cars slowed down and we saw a traffic jam in front of the street that led to our neighborhood. Some of the cars were turning and driving back toward us in the opposite direction. There were some Hummers and American troops waving the cars back. The driver wound down the window and shouted at one of the drivers who were coming back.

"What's going on?"

"The street's blocked," the other driver replied, "and they're not letting anyone in."

He looked at me with a sigh.

"I know another way," I said. "We can go back and get in near the courthouse and through the backstreets."

"Are you sure?"

"Yes."

He turned the car around and we went back. We turned at the traffic circle and took one of the streets leading to our street, but then we saw a Hummer parked at the end of the street. There was a man standing outside his house with a child and I asked him what was going on.

"They've been sealing off the area for an hour," he said.

I thought of getting out of the taxi and walking.

"Are they letting pedestrians through?" I asked him.

He shook his head and said, "No. No pedestrians and no vehicles."

The driver was looking at me and expecting me to pay the fare, so I asked him, "Can you take me to Beirut Square?" and he agreed.

I felt a lump in the throat. I had wanted to have a look at the house and the street I had played and run around in. I had thought I would knock on the neighbors' doors and ask about my childhood friends. The taxi driver didn't speak throughout the ride.

I wiped my sweat away with a handkerchief I was carrying after he dropped me off in front of my aunt's house. I saw three cars parked on the pavement. I pressed the bell outside, then pushed the metal gate, which was a little rusty and had flaking white paint. The garden wasn't as lush as it used to be. My aunt's husband, who had died three or four years earlier, had treated the garden as sacred ground. I noticed they had added some rooms to the second floor. There was a separate entrance with a staircase. My aunt came out through the front door and started ululating. Her face was still the same, except for the wrinkles. But most of her hair had disappeared beneath a black hijab that she hadn't worn before I left Baghdad. Wiam, her eldest son, came out behind her. I later learned that he and his wife and children were the ones living on the second floor. She cried as she hugged and kissed me, and started to scold me, of course.

"Shame on you. You've been here a whole week and you only come on the last day," she said. "We haven't seen you for ten years. Don't you love your auntie any longer, you rascal?" "The man's a doctor now and you still call him a rascal?" Wiam told her. I gave him a kiss and said, "I'm not a doctor yet. My dissertation isn't finished yet." He laughed and said, "All but a doctor." The others were waiting inside: my cousins, my other uncle and his wife, and their children and their wives and children. I greeted them one by one and tried to remember the names of the children and the people I hadn't met before. As for the grown-ups I had known before, time seemed to have crushed them like a steamroller, as if they had had to live through the last ten years several times over, back and forth, and had endured massive doses of pain.

"Why don't you stay here with us for a few days, my dear?" my aunt asked me as soon as I sat down.

"Unfortunately, I have to go back to Amman tomorrow."

"You mean you couldn't put off traveling for a few days?"

"No, auntie, I have to go back. I have a stack of responsibilities. I have to move to a new state and get ready to teach."

When I had called her to tell her I was in Baghdad, she had wanted me to leave the hotel and stay at her house. "It's a shame to come to Baghdad and stay in a hotel. Bring your American friends to stay at our place. We can make room for them. Bring them over," she said.

I told her that the filming schedule wouldn't allow it and they had to charge the batteries for their equipment every night and so we had to be in a place where there were no power cuts. "We have a generator, dear," she said.

My uncle, a retired engineer, was the only one to ask about my dissertation and the academic work I was about to start. The others bombarded me with questions about America and life there and what would happen in Iraq in the future, as if I knew or were in direct contact with Bush. Like the people whose words I had translated on camera for the past six days, my relatives were divided over what had happened. There was no consensus, even on the right term to use: *occupation* or *liberation*. There was an acrimonious argument between the men while my aunt supervised the preparation of the table. One of my cousins turned to me to ask me what I thought. He didn't like what I said and asked, "So you came out too to protest against the war?"

"Of course," I said.

He laughed and said sarcastically, "You are so spoiled, man. If you'd been living here with us all these years, even if the Angel of Death had come to liberate you, you would have welcomed him."

"America is the official agent of the Angel of Death," I said.

"Oh really! So why do you live there?" he asked in a loud voice.

"Enough," his father rebuked him, "you've gone too far!"

My aunt called from the guest room, "That's enough arguing. Come and eat."

I asked her about the tablets I'd seen her putting in the water jug. She told me it was to sterilize the water because otherwise it would cause diarrhea. She put plenty of dolma on my plate, especially stuffed onions because she knew how much I loved them. Then she said, "Is there food like this in America?"

"Where I live there aren't any Iraqi restaurants," I said.

"You've been living as a bachelor all these years, so why haven't you learned to cook?" she asked.

"Sometimes I cook, but not dolma."

After lunch we went back to the living room. I felt quite exhausted and could hardly keep my eyes open, but I pretended to follow the discussion against a background of clinking teacups and the sound of drinking. My aunt saved me by suggesting I take a siesta on the sofa in the guest room under the opening of the air-cooler "where you used to sleep in summer when you came here, remember?"

I smiled. "Of course I remember. Yes, please."

I took off my shoes and socks, put my head on the pillow she brought, and slept for an hour and a half. Then I woke up, washed my face, and went back to the living room. We chatted at length and drank tea again with the *klaicha* cookies that my aunt had made specially for me. She gave me a full box of them to take with me.

Before I said goodbye to them, my aunt pulled me by the arm and asked to speak to me alone. When she was alone with me she told me off for cutting off my father and not speaking to him for years. I asked her whether she knew the reason, what he had done to my mother.

"It doesn't matter," she said. "Whatever happened, he's still your father. Be magnanimous and don't break his heart. For my sake, Nameer. When you get back, speak to him. Please."

I didn't want to disappoint her so I promised to think about it. That was a white lie, like my promise that I would soon come back for a longer visit without work or other commitments. She made sure she sprinkled water after me so that I would come back. My cousin Midhat drove me to the hotel and gave me his phone number and email address before we said goodbye. The outer gate was locked, but the guard recognized me and opened it for me. I greeted the receptionist, who was watching television in the room next to the front desk.

"My friend," he shouted, "there's a package for you."

He got up from his chair, came to the reception desk, bent down looking for something, and then handed me a brown envelope. "Your friend Wadood," he said. "He waited here an hour and a half, and then he went, but asked me to pass this on to you."

I was surprised. I thanked him, took the envelope, and went up to my room.

Preamble (draft)

How can I write what happened?

(This "how" kept me up at night for many years.) And how can what I write escape the traps of distortion and domination of official history? I realize there's something paradoxical and ironic about it. Is it reasonable to worry about the fate of what I write before my pen even begins to bleed ink onto paper? There's a wonderful African proverb in Chinua Achebe's novel *Things Fall Apart* that goes "Until lions have their own historians, the history of the hunt will always glorify the hunter." The idea isn't new, of course, but the metaphor is a gem. The victors are always the ones who write history. By the time someone who wants to revise, question, or change it comes along, it's already too late. But what about the history of the victim? Or the victim's victim? That's what I am concerned with. The first time I read that proverb I empathized with the lion, of course. But then I thought hard about the matter and reconsidered, to discover, or rather remember, that I should be in solidarity with the lion's victim. I imagined, even felt, that I was inhabiting the gazelle (or any other prey) in this equation because it represents me and I represent it. I even feel I am it. I am the one who's been marginalized and disappeared at least twice. I'm the prey's prey. As for numbers, they don't serve the purpose. Statistics may count us, but at best they diminish our lives and our deaths. They dehumanize us. Assuming there's someone to count in the first place, because the historians of the hunt count the number of dead hunters! Numbers turn us into numbers. Dead signs and symbols in comparative studies designed to improve the hunt and make it more efficient. Our details disappear—our features, our color, our voices, our memories, our skin, our eyes, and so on. Once we've been skinned, our skins might be tanned and hung on the wall in the hunters' homes. Or photographs of the hunters, standing next to our dead bodies to celebrate a new record, might be hung on museum walls.

But where should I begin, and how? Can I enter time through a hole or through the window of one moment in time? I believe so. As soon as I get inside time, I can take the moment and analyze it as if it's a tear or a drop of blood under the microscope and discover the bonds and interactions that produce it. But how can I describe the moment when it isn't a moment, but in fact more like a tree? So I have to get down to the roots and listen to the earth's conversation with the tree and what it drinks from the earth. Then there's the trunk and everyone who has ever leaned on it or carved their name on it. And the branches and their memory and everything the wind has picked up and scattered far and wide. And all the birds that have perched on it on their way to distant places. And the ones that have nested in it and so on. It's a labyrinth. And which particular moment are we talking about? Is the moment the same moment everywhere? Or is each moment associated with its own place in the universe? If this last possibility is the case, then there is more than one time. There are times that might intersect but never coincide. But in this project I'm interested in one time in one place. First, I'll write down the history of the first minute of the war, which wasn't the first war I've seen. Most of the people who tackle history record centuries, decades, and years. I'm interested in minutes, especially the first minute.

The minute will be a three-dimensional space. It will be a place where I snipe at things and souls as they move. The juncture where they meet before disappearing forever, without saying goodbye. Humans say goodbye only to those they know and those they love, whereas things say goodbye to each other and to humans too. But we rarely hear their voices, their whispers, because we don't try. We rarely notice things smiling. Yes, things have faces too, but we don't see them. Those who do see them, after making an effort and training themselves to do so, and those who talk to them are labeled mad by your standards.

I'm the one who saw everything, and I see what they don't see.

There's always a moment in the life of every being and every thing in which their whole truth is manifested. A moment when the past intersects with the future. Those who can see and hear can discern the truth about that being. You no doubt sometimes see a photograph of a famous person, or even an ordinary person. And you realize that this photograph/moment preserves the whole existence and history of that person. I'm not sure, but many of these condensed moments come just before death. I know I contradict myself sometimes. Is there any way around that?

Time is a black hole. A hole into which things fall and disappear. Even the beginning of this whole universe, according to one theory, was an explosion. And the universe is just fragments and debris, and here we are, living the consequences and effects of it. I'm going to pluck this minute out of the black hole. But why? There are people who write in order to change the present or the future, whereas I dream of changing the past. This is my rationale and the rationale of my catalog.

I liked the preamble, the idea of a history of the prey and a catalog of the first minute. These were wild ideas that were not afraid to take risks. He could elaborate further of course and set his mind to arranging the sequence of ideas. I jotted down some notes in my notebook. I kept reading as we waited at the Iraqi border post at Traibil and again as we waited at al-Karama on the Jordanian side. I thought of writing about Wadood and his project. It could be intertextual with his catalog, including excerpts from it. Why not? But I had to find out more about his background and his life. I scolded myself for getting carried away with an idea that was wonderful but totally impractical. (Are wonderful things ever practical?) I had to finish my doctoral dissertation to secure my job, and I had to turn it into an academic work, and after that I might be free for novels. That would be logical, but it's not my logic.

Abularif drove me to the airport because my flight was due to take off in three hours. Roy and Laura planned to stay in Amman and visit Petra and Wadi Rum. "We need a holiday after all that pressure. It was so intense," said Laura, who overused the word *intense*, often for things that didn't deserve to be described as such. We hugged and I thanked them for the opportunity they had given me and re-minded them that my offer to help them translate the film when it was finished still stood.

I don't know what came over me when I agreed to go to Bagh-dad after all those years. It would have been better to go alone. At least to ensure that I had freedom of movement and could choose what I wanted to see, instead of being hostage to the team and its schedule, to which I was committed. But what was the point of all these recriminations now? There wouldn't be another trip. I had gone without expectations and thought I had immunized myself against any additional disappointments. I had read a great deal about what happens to emigrants who go back after a long absence and, consciously or not, search for what is left. I had read about selective memory and nostalgia and its snares. But the texts didn't help much.

THE COLLOQUY OF THE CALIPH

Harun al-Rashid's features were distinctive, and anyone who saw him could not easily forget his face. His eyes were black, often staring into the void. When he was angry, and he often was, they glared. His eyebrows, mustache, and beard were gray. They were bushy and longer than necessary. He didn't have much hair left on his head, except around the temples. He had a dark complexion, wore a gray dishdasha over a pair of pants and walked barefoot most of the time.

No one knew where the caliph lived. From his appearance, he didn't look as if he even had a home or that he owned many things other than what he wore. The street was his home, his palace in fact, as he used to shout emphatically at the top of his voice. He would scold the passersby for daring to walk on his sidewalks without obtaining his permission or paying taxes. "This is al-Rashid Street, my street, the caliph's street, you motherfuckers, not your mothers' street," he would say. This shocked many people and they kept their distance out of fear. But those who knew the street grew used to him and knew that he wouldn't attack anyone physically, but would only shout and argue. The shopkeepers humored him and paid him a pittance in tax—some dinars or a cigarette for temporary relief from his shouting. He would go up and down the street shouting at the cars too. Sometimes he ventured farther afield, went to the al-Shuhada' Bridge, where he stood in the middle, looked at the Tigris, and shouted at the fish. Or he would look at the sky and shout, "Your god is full of shit." This latter expression upset many people, and they would ask for God's forgiveness. Some of them would rebuke him. But he would respond with another such expression in a loud voice.

There were several stories about the history of the caliph, and it isn't possible to verify any of them. One version was that he was a rich merchant who had lost all his money after several bad deals and unwise decisions that had forced him to sell all his possessions within one year. He had gone mad after that. The other version said he had been driving his car at breakneck speed on the road to Mosul and had collided with a truck. The truck's load killed his wife and three children, and he was the only survivor. The third version said quite simply that depression and madness had run in his family for generations. He had been placed in the al-Rashad Hospital for many years. It wasn't known how he had ended up in al-Rashid Street. But his real name probably was Haroun.

Haroun was inspecting the street corners, looking for one of his subjects or his ministers who, whenever they saw him, pretended that he wasn't the caliph. He wanted to rebuke them. He couldn't understand why his kingdom was uninhabited this morning.

When I got back to Cambridge I had to meet my adviser before moving my stuff and going to Hanover in New Hampshire to prepare for the coming semester at Dartmouth College. I had told him by email that I had got the job and thanked him for the letter of recommendation he had written for me two months earlier, but I hadn't told him about my trip to Iraq. I liked him very much and was in awe of his encyclopedic knowledge of Semitic languages and everything related to classical Arabic literature, especially poetry. Apart from writing dozens of articles and papers, he had been one of the editors of the vast *Encyclopaedia of Islam*. But my one-on-one sessions with him were strange. He was painfully shy, and in conversation with him one had to work hard to overcome the moments of silence, whereas in his emails he seemed more easygoing and relaxed. Maybe he felt most free to interact with others when he was handling their research papers and dissertations. He would write astute comments, incredibly useful suggestions and references, and sometimes sarcastic comments.

When I reached his office on the third floor of the department building the door was open and I saw him trying to arrange some books and academic journals on the shelves. I knocked and went in. We shook hands.

"How was your summer?" he asked as I sat down. "Fruitful, I hope?"

"I don't know if you'll like the kind of fruit it produced," I said with a smile.

He laughed.

"I wanted to thank you again for your letter of recommendation," I said.

"Ah, yes. Congratulations on getting the job."

"Thank you. I know I wrote you to say that getting the job would give me an incentive to finish the dissertation quickly."

"I hope so," he said.

"I was supposed to submit the fourth chapter, but for the last month I've been busy with a project I hadn't planned for . . . I went to Baghdad as a translator with a team filming a documentary."

He raised his eyebrows. "Really?" he asked. "How was the trip?"

"To be honest, it was disturbing and psychologically draining."

"I'm sure," he said, looking through the window at the sky. "You know," he continued, "I was four years old when the Second World War ended, but I grew up with its ghosts and with the memories that adults in Cologne had of it."

This was the first time he had spoken to me of anything personal.

"Sometimes you have to do what you have to do," he added. "The important thing is to get back in the saddle and grab the reins again, as they say."

I was surprised at what he said and relieved that he was so understanding. I had thought he would express some disappointment.

"As you know, I lived in Beirut for more than a year when I was young," he continued. "I was helping Fuat Sezgin with his encyclopedia. I visited Cairo too, but I've never been to Baghdad, unfortunately. And how are your relatives? Most of them are here, aren't they?"

"Yes, my family's here in Virginia, but I do have relatives there. They're well."

"I read that the libraries have been damaged and many manuscripts have been destroyed."

"Alas, yes. We didn't go to the National Library or the museum, but I went to the Faculty of Arts, where I studied, and the library there had been burned down."

"It's a crime. People are more important of course, but . . ."

"But."

"*War is nothing but what you know it to be and have experienced, / What is said of it is not conjecture,*" he said. "Didn't we read Zuhair's *Muʿallaqa* together in the pre-Islamic poetry seminar three or four years ago?"

"Yes, four years ago."

"But politicians don't read pre-Islamic poetry."

I laughed derisively and said, "They don't read any poetry."

"Some of them read poetry, but they might not understand it." He always insisted on academic precision and avoided generalizations, even in casual remarks.

He stopped talking. This was the first time we had spoken with such familiarity, and I wanted the conversation to go on longer. But more than a minute passed without him saying anything and I decided it was time to leave. I stood up, thanked him for his patience and promised to send him the overdue chapter as soon as possible. He stood up, shook me by the hand and said, "I look forward to reading it."

I called to mind the first lines of Zuhair's *Muʿallaqa* as I went down the stairs:

Are there still black traces in the stone-waste of al-Darraj
and al-Mutathallam, mute witness to where Umm Awfa once
　　lived?
Her abode in al-Rakmatayn appears
like tattoos on the sinews of a wrist
Herds of wild cows and white antelopes wander there
Their young ones spring up everywhere
There I stood after twenty years
At pains to recognize the abode
Blackened stones marking where the cauldron was slung
and a trench like the debris of a cistern

When I recognized the abode, I said to it:
A good and very merry morning to you!

I couldn't remember any more. I repeated "A good and very merry morning to you" twice as I went into the department office. Jenny the secretary wasn't behind her desk, and there was nothing important in my mailbox, just ads about student grants and new courses in the fall, and an invitation to a party welcoming new students. I threw the papers in the recycling bin. I wanted to tell the secretary that I was moving and give her my new address so that she could forward all important papers there. I waited five minutes but she didn't come back, so I decided to write her an email later.

On my way back to the apartment I was approaching Divinity Avenue and Kirkland Street and suddenly felt like going to the Adolphus Busch Courtyard. It was the most beautiful spot on the Harvard campus for me. It's a secluded garden hidden behind the museum of Germanic art. Although it was on the way to the department and the library, I discovered it only in my last year there. Thanks to Rebecca, who pointed it out to me when I complained there were no quiet spots on campus. I started going there to read when the weather was mild. Sometimes we would meet to have a brown bag lunch there.

The garden was deserted, as usual. The semester hadn't started yet, and anyway it was half-deserted even when school was in session. I sat down on one of the benches and looked at the statue of the Brunswick lion, which now has a light green coat because the bronze has oxidized over the years. Although leaning forward and about to jump, it was peaceful enough to allow birds to nest in its open jaws, which the sculptor had frozen in a roar. The nest looked empty and still. The red ivy was climbing up the walls of the gray building as though it wanted to reach the roof. The glass in the enormous windows reflected the walls of the building opposite, the statue and a piece of sky. There were four gargoyle faces at the top of the columns, like the ones placed on churches and other old buildings to ward off evil spirits. I realized I hadn't spent enough time in this enchanting spot. It was normal to feel that, as I was about to leave the city and knew I would miss it when I was two and a half hours away. I could visit, of course, but it isn't the same as living there. I should call Rebecca. Our last conversation had been very short. I hadn't missed her much when I was in Baghdad. I had thought about her only once since my return. My heart was uneasy, preoccupied with conjugating the volatile emotions that swirled inside: the present and the past continuous. More like commotions than emotions! But at the end of the emails I sent from the Sheraton, the only place where we found an Internet connection in

Baghdad, I exaggerated and wrote "I miss you too" in reply to her "I miss you." I didn't know how long our relationship could last when it was sustained only by phone calls, Yahoo Messenger, and a short visit every six months. I wanted to sit on the bench and doze off for a while. But I had to return dozens of books I had borrowed from the university library and finish packing my books and other stuff into boxes before the movers came in the morning to take them to Dartmouth.

When I went back to the apartment I looked for the commentary on the *Mu'allaqat* to read the rest of that section on war:

> War is nothing but what you know it to be and have
>   experienced,
> What is said of it is not conjecture
>
> When you stir it up, you stir up something ugly
> When you provoke it, it will roar and rage
>
> Then it will grind you like a millstone
> It gives birth unexpectedly and produces twins
>
> And yields you a harvest very different from the bushels
>   or silver
> That villages in Iraq produce for their people

It took me four hours to finish putting all the books, papers, and other things in the brown boxes I had bought from the moving company. After sealing each box firmly with tape, I wrote a few words about the contents and the place where it should go, such as *office, apartment/books,* and so on. Luckily Dartmouth was going to pay the moving expenses. I took two boxes to the kitchen because

I was sure they would be enough to hold all the plates, kitchen utensils, and odds and ends. I didn't cook much, but I had accumulated a considerable quantity of spices to make dishes that I was trying to perfect; there was no point in leaving the spices behind. I realized this was the seventh time I had moved in the United States and the third time I had moved from one state to another. It was also the first time I would live in a whole apartment to myself. I had lived alone in California but in a room with a bathroom that was part of a complex housing the workers on an almond farm. I wondered what all this meant. Was I taking stock of the transformations and migrations I had gone through? The telephone rang before I could find a convincing answer. I didn't go to the bedroom. I just left it ringing till I heard the beep on the answering machine, and then Ali Hadi's voice. "Nameer. This is Ali Hadi. They say you've been away." I put down the plate I had in my hand and hurried to the bedroom, as I heard him say, "Are you back yet? When you get back give me a call." I picked up the receiver before he had finished leaving his message. I greeted him as usual: "Hi boss." "Good to hear your voice for a change. I have to talk to strangers to find out what you're up to," he replied. "No," I said, "I swear I was going to call you today." We agreed that I'd drop by that evening.

THE COLLOQUY OF THE AL-ZAWRA'

Al-Zawra' City is on the eastern bank in Baghdad. It is called zawra', "crooked," because the qibla in one of its mosques is misaligned. Al-Jawhari wrote, "And the Tigris in Baghdad is called al-Zawra'. Al-Zawra' is also a house built in al-Hirah by al-Nu'man ibn al-Mundhir."

The poet al-Nabigha mentioned zawra' in this line: "With a zawra'
in the folds of which musk is drunk aplenty," and Abu Amr said:
"A zawra' here is a drinking cup made of silver, rather like a taltala."

I don't know much about my origins. I might be from China,
India, or Persia. I don't remember how I came or was brought
here. Naked I was, as the Lord created me and as His wor-
shipers made me. But what I do remember is his face and
eyes that guarded me for many a night.

I didn't move for months, until he untied me gently and
wiped the dust and the rigors of travel off my faces. He ran
his fingers gently over every spot as if he were relieving me
from the ordeal of traveling and reassuring me that I was safe
with him. He dressed me in gazelle skin that he had procured
especially for me. He had me sleep next to his head after
wrapping me in the skin. He would disappear for hours, but
he didn't let a day pass without spending some time devoted
to me. He gazed at my body lovingly and spoke to me as if
there were no one but me in this world.

At first I didn't realize what he wanted from me. He took
the gazelle skin off me, sat down, and looked at me without
doing anything. A few days later I felt a pricking sensation
and a little pain. He did it for the first time while he was scru-
tinizing me and repeating "In the Name of God the Merciful the Compassionate." Then he said, "You are going to
preserve the most beautiful poetry that has ever been written
about this city, and you will live long after me and after what

comes after me." I felt a cold liquid running across me. Beads of sweat formed on his brow, but he did his best to make sure not a single drop fell on me. But even so one or two drops did drop from his forehead. When that happened, he reproached himself, quickly dried the sweat, and blew on the spot where the drop had fallen.

Every day he repeated what he had muttered the previous time and traced with his index finger the marks on my body before resuming his act. Sometimes he would wake up in the depths of the night, rush to see me, and pull the gazelle skin off me as if he wanted to add something he had forgotten or to retrieve something he had left in my body.

Many humans after him stared at me with eyes full of admiration and touched me gently. Of course that made me happy, but with none of them did I feel that shiver that ran through my body when his fingers caressed me and his eyes were pinned to my body. His eyes were wells full of night. His eyebrows almost met at the bridge of his massive nose, and he had a mustache like a sultan sitting upright on a throne. Although his mustache and beard were bushy, his head had only a few hairs that had survived his baldness, alone and lost like the remains of an oasis in the desert.

When there was no longer any spot on my body that his fingers hadn't passed over, he kept staring. Then he cried and said, "Death is harder for me to bear than what I am about to do." The last words he branded me with were:

"Finished, praise be to the Almighty, on the sixth of the month of Rajab."

He folded me up, then kissed me and hugged me in his bed and went to sleep crying. The next morning he covered me with a piece of cloth, put me under his arm, and took me out into the city. He walked and walked till he came to a palace and handed me over to a man with rough hands who carried me to a man he called "my master." His master, who became my master for some minutes, looked me over, praised my good qualities with a laugh, then threw me to a slave girl, saying, "Read to us, Mayya." Then my new master asked, "Is it the only one?"

"Yes, master."

"And if we sent troops to your house, they wouldn't find another copy?"

"No, master."

He threw him a bag of coins and told him to leave. His descendants passed me on and then the descendants of those who killed them. I was passed from hand to hand. I was placed with others like me in dark vaults. Most of them were taken captive and burned or thrown in the river. That's what I heard. But I survived, though I wish I had died. Years went by and I was still asleep in the dark. When someone's eyes fall on my body or their lips move as they read me, I remember only his eyes and I long for him. Years passed when no one touched me. Then along came one of those foreigners carrying a device that took pictures of my neighbors but not of me. Is that because I'm a gray-haired old lady or because I have a wrinkled face? I thought I had been completely forgotten. The years passed without any sound or disturbance until the day came when the earth trembled as though it were about to bring forth its burdens. It was wintertime but I felt my skin drying out from the heat. Was it the sun? They had long worried about the effect the sun might have on me. From afar my ears picked up the crackle of fire as it consumed my neighbors and rushed toward me. Tongues of fire lapped my edges and I cringed in fear. Before shedding a tear I gasped a one thousand–year gasp and saw myself rising up as a cloud of smoke in the sky over Baghdad.

I had heard much about him, even before I moved from California to Cambridge four years earlier. When I arrived, as soon as people heard I was from Iraq and interested in Arabic literature, many of them, Arabs and Americans, kept saying I had to meet him and visit his famous library. On my way there I realized he would be the friend I missed most when I left. I used to meet him about once a month, but our meetings would be long. He was my father's age but his mind was still lively. He had an encyclopedic knowledge of Arabic literature and was passionate about culture and music. He had completed a doctorate in engineering decades ago, but he was mad about Arabic literature. He studied it and completed another doctorate, writing a dissertation on al-Shidyaq. He taught Arabic at Harvard for many years and had assumed he would stay there, but his contract wasn't renewed because of departmental conflicts. Someone had plotted against him. He moved on to teach at the University of Massachusetts. I thought I was a veteran because I had spent a whole decade in the U.S., but he had come at the end of the 1950s, so he was a real old-timer. When I visited and talked with him, I felt I was visiting Iraq. The conversation always led us back to Iraq, its sufferings, its pleasures, and its songs. We delighted in the Baghdadi dialect and the expressions that we missed. He loved collecting books, manuscripts, and old pictures. After his divorce, which might have been caused by his obsession with books, his house was transformed into a vast library with more than twenty thousand books. It was in effect a guesthouse open to any Arab in the city who was interested in culture and literature. He hosted a monthly soiree there, with readings from Arabic novels, and I attended several times. Although he was in his sixties, his spirit was still youthful, and he remained on the far left politically, as he had been as a student activist in the radical 1960s. You would see him in all the demonstrations, seminars, and other gatherings in the city. He refused to let us call him "doctor" and preferred that we call him just Ali Hadi. But I liked to call him "professor" or "sir."

He was as cheerful as usual when he opened the door. We hugged and kissed each other on the cheek. "Ah, here comes the returnee," he said with a smile; "it's good to see you safe."

"Returnee to Iraq or to America?" I asked.

"As you like," he said with a laugh. "Sit down while I get you a cup of tea."

"I'll come with you," I said.

We walked to the kitchen and he asked the first question: "So tell me, what took you to Baghdad? And without any warning? Why didn't you tell me? I didn't call you because I thought you were busy finishing your dissertation."

"Some artists making a documentary got in touch with me from San Francisco. Nice people. They were looking for someone to go with them who knew the city and could translate. So I went."

"Okay, and what did you make of the situation?"

"Chaos and confusion. It's all fucked up."

"Of course. It was expected."

I noticed there was a picture hanging on the kitchen wall that hadn't been there in the past, with a river and some Ottoman writing in it. I stood in front of it and asked him about it. Picking up the teapot and putting it next to the teacups and the sugar bowl on the tray, he said, "Yes, it's new. It's a picture of the Tigris flooding in Baghdad in the fifteenth century. It's a laser-printed color copy, not an original. The original is in the British Library. I asked one of my students to bring it for me." I tried to help him carry the tea tray but he refused.

We headed to the large study and sat on chairs at the table where he read and wrote. He put the tray on an arabesque-style side table.

I told him about the visit, about my conflicted and odd feelings, about how pale and shabby Baghdad was, and the chaos and the negligence and the sight of soldiers in helmets and barbed wire and tanks in Abu Nuwas Street. He was shaking his head and saying "alas" whenever I stopped to drink from my teacup. He had hated Saddam and the Ba'thists for decades, but he was opposed to the invasion. We had gone together to the massive demonstrations in Boston before the war. We had watched the news in his study throughout the invasion. We watched stunned at the moment when the statue came down in Firdaws Square, and we remarked how strange were the feelings in play at that moment. Both of us had dreamed of the fall of the regime, but not through military occupation.

"The Americans are jerks and they're going to destroy the country. But I couldn't go. I wouldn't be able to take it."

"When was the last time you went?" I asked.

"I went in 1985 after my mother died. So how are your relatives there?"

"They're fine. None of them have been hurt."

"You must write something about your visit."

"I'm trying to but I haven't been able to. My mind isn't clear. But I do have some news for you."

"Good news?"

"I landed a job."

"Congratulations. Where?"

"At Dartmouth."

"That's great. But it's rather isolated. I visited the place once, long ago. There was nothing there but the college and three streets and just a few stores."

"Now it's several times bigger. Now there are *five and half* streets."

We laughed. "But what can I do? I want to pay off my debts," I added.

"No, that's good. What kind of courses will you teach? Language or literature?"

"Three quarters language and a quarter literature," I said.

"Excellent. Besides, the best place to finish your dissertation is somewhere isolated, with no social life and nothing to distract you."

"And no one at all!"

"Why? Where's your girlfriend?"

"She has a one-year grant in Bolivia to do some fieldwork."

"So you'll be 'playing with your tail'?"

"I'm not sure I'll even have time to play with any body parts. Mine or other people's."

"I think you will."

We laughed.

"You can spend your time with Abu Nuwas in the cold. When are you going?"

"Tomorrow morning they're coming to take my stuff and then I'll go."

"Good luck. You deserve it. But don't cut yourself off and forget us. Come and visit every now and then."

"For sure," I said.

I gave him the yellow envelope in which I'd put his present. "What's this?" he asked. "A present for you. Something simple," I said. I hadn't sealed the envelope so he opened it and took out the two booklets I had bought for him—*An Introduction to Iraqi Folklore* by Abdilhamid al-Alwachi and Nouri al-Rawi (Baghdad, 1962) and *On Mudhayyal Popular Poetry* by Hashim Mohammed al-Rajab (Baghdad, 1964). When he saw how old they were, he put one of them gently on the table and leafed through it. "I've never seen them before. A very nice gift. Where did you find them?"

"I went to al-Mutanabbi Street on my last day and found an excellent collection of books with someone there." I was about to tell him about Wadood and his project and the first chapter of the manuscript I had brought with me from Baghdad, but I didn't do so. I don't know why. Usually I told him everything. I thought about this later. Maybe I wanted to keep Wadood strictly for myself. Ali Hadi had already yawned several times and he looked sleepy. When I looked at the clock on the wall above the bookshelves it was after midnight. I had to wake up early, clean my room, throw some bags in the trash, wash my clothes, and put them in the suitcase before the movers arrived.

We said goodbye. He told me I could sleep at his place when I visited the city. He repeated his advice to me: "Finish your dissertation so you can relax a bit."

Veterinary Science, French Without a Teacher, Hamlet translated by Jabra Ibrahim Jabra, *The Collected Works of al-Rusafi*. An old copy of the third volume of *The Collected Works of al-Jawahiri* caught my attention. It had *Al-Rabita Printing and Publishing Company, 1953* on the cover in small print. I bent down to pick it up off the ground. The light green cover was torn at one corner and the pages were yellowed. I turned the pages carefully. His poem "Whatever You Want" was the first in the collection. *Whatever you want, do it/A chance not to be missed/A chance for you to rule/To bring*

people down or raise them on high. The poem was from 1952, but as
if it were written about what is happening today.

He was in his late thirties, of medium height, with black hair
and a light beard peppered with a few gray hairs. He was wearing a
beige shirt, faded jeans, and flipflops, sitting on the pavement on a
white plastic chair and reading al-Zaman newspaper. I guessed he
was the stall owner and I asked him the price of the book. He put
the newspaper down in his lap, gave me a strange look from his
honey-colored eyes, and asked me to show him the cover. I did so.
"Forty thousand," he said. "Okay, I'll take it," I said.

I didn't want to haggle about the price because the book was
worth much more. I carried on looking through the books and
found selections from Imru al-Qays published in Beirut in 1947.
I didn't ask the price. I added the book to al-Jawahiri. I noticed that
he was throwing lengthy glances at me as he browsed through the
newspaper. In a tone that had hostile undertones, he suddenly said,
"You're clearly one of those who've come from abroad. When did
you leave?"

"In 1993," I said.

"Welcome back," he said sarcastically, adding, "So where do
you live?"

"In America."

"Wow, lucky you," he said, shaking his head in scorn.

"Look, I haven't come to govern you and I'm not being paid by
anyone. I came with a group to make a documentary film about the
situation and the people. No more and no less."

My sharp response took him by surprise and he backed off.

"Sorry, that's not what I meant. But you know we've been seeing some strange characters."

He showed me what he was reading in the newspaper, saying, "Like these people. Half of them lived abroad for twenty or thirty years and after all that now they come to rule over us."

"I'm with you, my friend, but I have nothing to do with them."

"So that means you're a film director?"

"No, I'm an academic, but I've come as a translator."

"So which satellite channel is your group from?"

"No, not a satellite channel. They're independent."

"I'm honored. And what's your good name?"

"Nameer."

"Doctor Nameer."

"Not yet."

"Welcome, Mr. Nameer. I'm Wadood, and if you'd like to see, in the warehouse I have plenty of poetry collections and the rest of the series of al-Jawahiri's works."

"Thanks, I'd be delighted. Where's the warehouse? Is it far?"

"No, it's here, across the street."

He rose from his chair and asked his neighbor to watch his books till he came back, then he beckoned me to follow him. We crossed the street and he put his hand in his pants pocket and took out a bunch of keys. We stood in front of an old wooden door. He opened it and went into a dark entrance that led to a staircase. I thought we were going to go up the stairs, but he headed right and stood in front of another wooden door painted green. There was a padlock, too, that he unlocked before putting another key in the keyhole of the door and opening it. He went inside, pulled up a white plastic chair like the one he had been sitting on in the street, and invited me to come in and sit down. He pulled a cord hanging from a lamp in the ceiling, but the light didn't come on. He pulled it again and said, "There you are, there's no electricity." "No problem," I said.

The place was dark, and the only glimmer of light came through a window to the right that was covered by a curtain that seemed to have once been dark blue but was now faded by the sun. He drew the curtain back and the fierce Baghdad sun flooded in, lighting up specks of dust that were floating upward. The walls were covered in shelves crammed with books all the way to the ceiling, with piles of newspapers lying here and there on the floor. There was a small bed with a simple mattress and some crumpled sheets in the right-hand corner of the room. Next to it stood a small table with a small radio and the remains of a candle on a plate. To the left of the bed stood a closet of medium height with newspapers piled on top of it, and next to that a half-open door that led to what looked like a bathroom.

Wadood interrupted my inspection of the room to say that he sometimes slept here when it was dangerous and hard to get home after sunset. He moved some newspapers and books from a chair, put them on the floor, and stood on them to reach the top shelves.

"This is all al-Jawahiri and Iraqi poetry here," he said. "I have piles of it."

After brushing the dust off them he passed me a set of books that seemed to be the rest of al-Jawahiri's complete works. I went to take them. "Do you like al-Bayyati?" he asked.

"What do you have of his?"

"I have *Smashed Jugs*."

I told him I loved poetry but I was also looking for rare books, and first or early editions.

"These here are all old or first editions," he said. He passed me *Poem K* by Tawfiq Sayigh, the collected works of Abdulamir al-Husayri, and some other books. I noticed that one of the lower shelves was full of files arranged quite carefully, with papers and newspaper clippings protruding from the edges. There was a collection of medium-sized notebooks interleaved with pieces of paper of various sizes. I was curious and I asked him about them.

"Those are private papers. A sort of project," he said.

"On what?"

"A documentation project."

"Research?"

"No, a different kind of text. Not traditional."

"Meaning what?"

"Meaning everything. History, but circular history."

He pulled out one of the files and started leafing through the contents: notes in his own handwriting on small pieces and slips of paper. Cuttings from newspapers.

"This is the project of a lifetime, an archive of the losses from war and destruction. But not soldiers or equipment. The losses that are never mentioned or seen. Not just people. Animals and plants and inanimate things and anything that can be destroyed. Minute by minute. This is the file for the first minute."

"You mean this last war?"

"Exactly."

"And what are the sources you rely on?"

I noticed a sparkle in his eyes as he spoke about his project.

"Everything. News. Oral history. Personal observation. Imagination."

"But that's a massive project that calls for a whole institution."

"Oh man, you think we still have institutions here? I can do it myself."

"And what's the title?"

"*Fihris.*"

"*Fihrist?*"

"No, *Fihris*, a catalog of every minute, of everything that died in that minute."

"That's a wonderful idea. So have you published any of it?"

"No. I'm not interested in being published," he said rather irritably.

"Why not? It's an outstanding idea. So that parts of it can be translated into English. I'd be willing to translate it."

"Do you work as a translator?

"I translate poetry and prose into English."

"We'll see."

Suddenly he didn't seem to want to discuss the subject. "Sorry but I have to get back to the books and earn my daily bread."

"Yes, of course."

He put all the books in a large bag and I gave him the money. I wrote my new address in New Hampshire and my email address and asked him to send me a message if he needed any help and if he changed his mind about being published or translated. He looked at the piece of paper, folded it up, and put it in his shirt pocket, saying,

"Thanks a lot." "Where are you staying?" he asked me. "At the Waha Hotel in Karrada," I said. We shook hands and I resumed my stroll.

THE COLLOQUY OF THE KASHAN

The vast majority of Kashans are born in the city of Kashan, of course. But the Kashan I'm talking about here is a Baghdad Kashan in body and in spirit. She was born in the women's prison in Baghdad in the late 1940s. Her birth wasn't difficult but it was slow. For months her mother knelt in front of her every morning with the patience of someone who has taken a vow of endless prayer. With tired hands she gradually coaxed her into this world. She didn't have a midwife to help her, nor a nurse or a doctor. For months she stopped only for a short rest at noon, when she would go off to have a simple meal, then come back and work on the body of her daughter until the guard told her to stop, a little after sunset. Then she would touch the face of her daughter affectionately as if she were saying goodnight, before she and the other women working in the room went back to their cells. Some of the mothers would sing softly or quarrel with one another when the guard wasn't around. But this mother worked in stony silence most of the time. A smile rarely found its way to her face. In the first few weeks Kashan was very small and couldn't see or understand anything. She couldn't make out the features of her mother's face until the features of her own face emerged. Her features

were no different from those of thousands of Kashans, because they were all heirs to a limited number of designs, with
variations that had been in circulation since the sixteenth
century. Her mother's mouth was as small as a cherry, and her
eyes were deep blue under bushy eyebrows. Her complexion
was the color of wheat, and her black hair was hidden under
a turquoise headscarf that framed her sad face. On her right
cheek a knife had left a deep scar—the same knife that she
had picked up off the ground after the attack and planted in
the chest of the man who had tormented her for years. That
silenced him forever. But she paid a high price for his silence,
and she wasn't free for long, less than four hours.

The old Iranian foreman who, along with his colleagues,
had been brought from Iran to supervise the training of the
women, and who had himself chosen her after giving her a
test, would wander around every day inspecting the progress
of the work, stand in front of each Kashan and watch or make
observations. She was delighted when he praised her several
times, muttering in Persian, "Bah bah, very good," and "Very
nice, madam." After a few months Kashan had grown in stat-
ure until she was almost the height of her mother, who no
longer sat cross-legged or bent over, but sat on a chair. Pride
began to fill her heart when she saw the intricate patterns
and the fringes of her firstborn Kashan coming toward com-
pletion and the colored lines converging. The lines met, di-
verged, and skirted the geometrical shapes arranged regularly

within the rectangular frame. When the last knot of Kashan was in place, her mother stood up, amazed at what her hands had made. She ran her hands over the surface of the carpet, kissed it at several spots, and smelled it as her mother had smelled her when she kissed her, because she knew that she would never see her again.

The next day two men folded it up, tied it in several places with cord, picked it up, and put it in a storeroom in the prison until other ones were ready. They stuck a pin in it to hold in place a piece of paper with "Kashan/1/1949" written on it. The next day the mother started work on another Kashan that she would also have to abandon as soon as it was finished.

The new Kashan lay slumped in the darkness of the storeroom for a month while they put others like it nearby. When there were ten of them, men loaded them into a van that took them to a carpet store in the Danyal market. It spent two months there until it won the admiration of a woman who, along with her husband, was looking for something to decorate their new home. The merchant lied about Kashan's provenance; he didn't say it was born in Baghdad but insisted it was imported from Iran. The woman added two other ones and our Kashan ended up in the reception room, where it stayed for many years without moving, except at the start of every summer, when the carpet beaters came and picked it up with the other ones to beat the dust out of them. Then they rolled them up, tied them up with pieces of cloth to put them behind the furniture or in another room to wait for the weather to turn cold again. But the first time the carpet beaters came, it was frightened and thought they were getting rid of it and it would languish in darkness for eternity. But it got used to this in subsequent years and began to enjoy its long slumber. It slept and dreamed of the sheep that had given it their fleeces. It saw the sheep grazing on distant foothills corralled by a shepherd under a balmy sky and a sun blocked from time to time by clouds driven gently by the wind. Kashan also dreamed of its mother's face and eyes.

The lady of the house would later decide to move Kashan to the living room. Her four children would play on it and imagine that the lines that ran across the design were streets for their tiny cars. They would see the arches and the small circles as traffic circles where the cars could turn and passersby could sit. They would drop crumbs of food and spill drops of tea mixed with milk and other drinks on its surface. Even drops of blood sometimes. The lady would get angry and tell them off whenever they did that. They would lie on Kashan, put cushions under their heads so that they could be close to the television when they were watching cartoons or a long film. They would grow up and get married, move to new houses and have their own children. But they would still visit the family home with their children on special occasions and holidays.

Some of its colors would fade and slight wrinkles would appear on its surface, but Kashan would retain its splendor. From time to time the lady of the house, who lived into her seventies, would remember the day she bought it. As they sat alone together in front of the television, she would ask her husband if he too remembered. A war would come and then another, and as usual she would worry about her children and her grandchildren and ask them to gather in the big family home to allay her fears for them on the first night of war. Some of her grandchildren slept on the bedding she asked them to put on Kashan, and then Kashan suffocated, not from the weight of the children sleeping on top, because they were lighter than birds, but from the rubble when the house collapsed on them and silenced them forever. Kashan imagined it could see its mother's face, weeping for it and for the children.

There wasn't enough space for me in the movers' truck with the driver and the two men who were helping him. So I took the bus from South Station in Boston to Dartmouth. After the bus driver collected our tickets, he gave out small bottles of water, bags of nuts, and headphones to the passengers. Then he took his seat and, as soon as the bus moved, took the microphone and told us with enthusiasm that the trip included a movie we could watch on the small screens that were hanging down at intervals of every five rows. Those who wanted to watch should use the headphones, which they should hand in at the end of the journey. I was surprised that although he repeated this performance several times a day, he did not appear to be bored and managed to maintain his enthusiasm, or pretend to. I couldn't remember the movie I had seen the first time I had taken the bus to Dartmouth to give a talk on Abu Nuwas and to interview for the job. It was a silly commercial movie and I had been busy going over my talk and cutting it back so that it wouldn't be longer than forty-five minutes, as they had asked. It was a small bus company with only one line, and its budget rarely allowed it to buy the rights to show new or high-quality movies. On the way back after the interview the movie was *All the Pretty Horses.* I watched it intermittently because I was tired, but Penélope Cruz's voice and her distinctive accent in English intrigued me and woke me up from my sporadic sleep.

Half an hour out of Boston the landscape gradually started to change. The farther north we went the greener it became. There were the lovely farms and little lakes that make New Hampshire one of the most beautiful states in summer and fall. But the winter was long and cold there, as a British professor who taught Chinese in the department whispered in my ear. "You'll have to be ready for the coldest winter you've ever seen. I've been here for seven years and I still haven't got used to it." I asked him what drove the European settlers to come to the far reaches of the cold north in the seventeenth century. And how did they endure the winter? Or rather, why didn't they move somewhere warmer after their first winter? He told me that the man who founded the college was a Protestant cleric who wanted to train Native Americans to become missionaries. But the number of Native Americans willing to embrace the white man's faith was very small at that time, so the college instead attracted the children of the rich and influential. I liked this grumpy British man because he was candid with me, and he was one of the most enthusiastic and liveliest people at the lecture. He spoke about the positive aspects of his work there and what the college had to offer, but he didn't hesitate to be critical. The others, on the other hand, didn't mention anything negative. "There's no social life except for students," he said. "Married people socialize with other married people and their families." "What about you?" I asked him at the time. "Are you married?" "No," he said, "but my partner works in New York and we spend most weekends together there." When he said "partner," I thought he could be gay. "What about you?" he asked. "My girlfriend's abroad," I said. I asked him about the students. He said they were very smart. The vast majority of them came from good private schools, and even those who came on scholarships were good students. Then he added, "But they're conservative. Before I taught here I naïvely thought that most young people were bound to have leftist inclinations, and then affluence and the pressures of bourgeois life gradually induce them to abandon their noble objectives and their dreams of changing the world, so they compromise and become conservative. But many of my students are eighteen years old and they're right-wing conservatives, like their fathers and grandfathers before them. Since you teach things related to the Middle East and the chaos there, you'll have to be careful."

The bus stopped in front of the Hanover Inn, the only hotel, a small one owned by the college. I had spent the night in the same hotel and we had had dinner there after my lecture and the interviews. It was on one side of the aptly named Green at the center of the college—a vast lawn surrounded by venerable elm trees and the old buildings that formed the nucleus of the college in the early years, before other buildings were added, most notably the red-brick Baker Library with its tall white tower.

I asked a woman who was getting off the bus where the housing office might be and she showed me the way. I signed some documents and was given the key to the apartment I had chosen from their website after looking at the pictures. I walked to the building and opened the apartment door. It was small, smaller than in the pictures, but it would do. There was one window in the living room and one in the bedroom, looking out onto the parking lot. I had asked the movers to get in touch with me when they were half an hour away. I called them to check and they said there was heavy traffic on Route 89 because of an accident, and they would arrive within forty-five minutes.

I closed the door and went along the main street to the White Horse café and was pleased to find that it was close to my apartment. I remembered the old saying "As long as there's coffee and tobacco, nothing else matters," although I don't smoke and in my case it should be "As long as there's coffee and chocolate, nothing else matters." I was addicted to chocolate and other sweet things. When I had visited the town for the interview two months earlier, I had stopped at the White Horse and drunk a double espresso to be ready for the lecture. I remembered that the selection of cakes and pastries that they had was as good as one would find in a big city. When I asked the British man that evening, he said the café owner hired a woman who used to work in a fancy restaurant in New York and who had escaped the city for the quiet of the countryside.

I was hungry, even hungrier when I saw the pastries carefully arranged behind the glass. I ordered a croissant with a *Yirgacheffe* coffee, which was the coffee of the day, according to the sign on the wall. The woman who took my order wrote a number on a piece of paper and stuck it into a metal holder that she asked me to put on my table. I looked at the newspapers that were on sale, the *New York Times* and the *Boston Globe*, and decided not to buy one. Why should I bother reading depressing news so early in the day? My decision took me by surprise because it was unusual. I sat in the corner studying the place and watching the other customers. A few minutes later one of the waitresses brought me my order with a smile. The croissant was perfectly flaky. I ate it slowly to savor it. I put a little milk in the coffee cup and drank half of it. Then I decided to go for a short walk to discover the town. I put the rest of the coffee in a paper cup and took it with me.

No one dies in traffic accidents here. There are few cars, they drive slowly, and the drivers stop patiently to let pedestrians cross. Everything is calmer and slower here. I remembered what the British man said about his blood pressure falling after he moved here from Chicago to be closer to his lover in New York. After less than fifteen minutes I reached the end of the main street, where there was a small gas station, and after that the street turned into a country road leading to Lebanon, the next town. The European settlers had stamped names from the Bible on the towns since this was their promised land, or names that evoked their European origins, prefixed with the word *New*.

I crossed to the other side and retraced my steps. There were three small restaurants, one of them Chinese, a small cinema, a bookshop, and a post office, as well as clothes shops, one of them a Gap, of course. I was about to turn right and head to the small museum and the college's art department, but someone from the moving company called me and said they were fifteen minutes away.

Unloading the boxes, the chair, the table, and the mattress didn't take more than half an hour. I asked them to put the boxes in the corner of the living room. I promised myself I would sort out the apartment and buy some nice furniture later, but I was busy preparing for my classes and completing my dissertation. Most of the boxes stayed parked where they were until the spring, except for two boxes of books and articles related to the dissertation, which I took to the office in my bag in stages day by day. I opened only three of the other boxes and took out some basics for the kitchen and bathroom, some pillows and sheets and blankets. I liked the apartment empty. It looked poetic.

My office was on the second floor in Bartlett Hall, which housed the Department of Asian and Middle Eastern Languages and Literatures, the longest name for any department in the university. Anything that wasn't European had been crammed into the department, in a red-brick building built in the nineteenth century. It had been renovated of course, but it retained its splendor. The ceilings and doors were very high. My office was enormous, and the window looked out over a side street and a towering elm tree with leaves that changed color several times in my first fall.

77.

THE COLLOQUY OF THE CHRIST'S THORN TREE, OR ZIZIPHUS SPINA-CHRISTI

Ziziphus, that's my name, or let's say one of my names. After all, names change depending on who is speaking and in what language. You may well wonder: how can I know this when I'm just a tree that hasn't moved an inch since I was a seed? Did you not know that trees have colloquies, like birds and people? We talk to each other just like you do. If you listen you can hear the wind carrying what our branches say to each other. Even our roots in the ground call out until they hear an answer from the trunk of a nearby tree, or a tree far off.

I can't remember a time when I wasn't here, on this spot. But I wasn't alone: this was a crowded orchard and I was surrounded by other trees—young oranges, blood oranges, and palm trees. Then one day I heard a wail in the distance, a scream from roots being pulled up and branches being broken. Humans came with those machines of theirs. I thought my fate was sealed. They uprooted all the trees in the orchard but they left me and several palm trees. One of the trees heard me crying at sunset, after the people had gone. "Don't worry, Ziziphus," it whispered, "they won't uproot the likes of you." I was young then and I didn't know much about the affairs of trees or humans. "Why not?" I asked in a quiet, frightened voice. "Their holy books say good things about us and the likes of you," said the tree. "They're frightened something bad might happen to them if they dig up a ziziphus tree, so hold back your tears, little one." I didn't believe the old palm tree at the time. I thought it was senile, and they would come back in the morning to slaughter me and feed my limbs to an oven or a brazier. But the old tree was right.

Once they had dug up the bodies of the other trees and cleared them away, they started to measure the place and survey it, leaving markers on the ground. Then they dug it as I watched. They brought piles of bricks and sand and cement and started to work like ants. They built a towering house that completely blocked my view of the old palm tree. Although I couldn't see it, I could hear it talking to another palm tree farther off. It asked me how I was from time to time. When the house was finished they brought a gardener to plant flower seeds and saplings around a rectangle that they planted with grass. Humans are odd. They pull trees up by the roots and then come back to plant similar ones in their stead. The young orange, mulberry, and fig trees grew taller, but I was the tallest and the oldest. Children born in the house grew up and started playing beneath me in the garden. When I was bearing fruit, from my third year on, they asked their father to shake me so that they could enjoy the fruit. They rubbed my bark and were surprised to see gum oozing from my trunk. In my shade they read and played. They defended me when other kids came and threw stones at my branches because they wanted to bring down my fruit. When they grew up they began to shake me themselves so I would feed them, and they would thank me, and I would reward them. I had a delightful life and was the princess of the garden. The bees fed on the nectar of my flowers and sometimes birds nested in my branches. The other trees envied me my status and my height. Maybe it was envy or fate that almost killed me. They and the termites that invaded the walls of the house and the furniture. The queen, whose orders the other termites follow, had moved into a spot behind the house. But the expert they brought misled them into thinking that the queen's chamber was under my trunk, and he advised them to kill me. I was panic-stricken when I heard what he said to the house owner. I remembered that all the trees in the garden had been massacred when I was a child, before there was a house. A few days later, when the owner of the house asked the gardener to get rid of me, he flatly refused. "That would be quite wrong," he said. Because I'm the tree that's in heaven. "At the lote tree of the far boundary, where the Garden of Refuge lies, where the lote tree is covered with what covers it, the Prophet, may God bless him, used to wash his hands with its leaves." In my fear I shouted out, "The termite queen isn't underneath me. She's over there in the garden of the neighbors' house!" but of course they couldn't hear me. The gardener, who I knew loved me, dug in his heels. He said he wouldn't look after the garden any longer. He warned the owner of the house one last time, saying disaster would strike the house and the people in it if they did me any harm. The owner of the house said disaster had already struck the house, long ago. The army of termites had devoured the furniture and the books and had damaged the walls, and they had to be wiped out. The gardener shook his head and walked to his bicycle, which he had parked close to the garden gate. He opened the gate intoning, "Those of the right hand—what of those of the right hand. They are among lote trees without thorns and among acacia in clusters." He got on his bike and cast a sad look at me from the street as if he were saying goodbye, then rode off. The owner of the house disappeared and came back an hour later with a vicious ax in his hand. Blows rained down on my trunk. They tore at my bark and cut into my bast, but I held out. I was crying in pain and the mulberry and oranges trees were weeping in sadness and fear. "Sir, there's no queen under my trunk," I implored. But he didn't hear. After hundreds of blows, he tired and stopped, left the ax next to my trunk, and went into the house. I spent that night groaning in pain and sadness as my neighbors consoled me. The next day he came back with a massive saw with a long tail that he attached to a spot in the wall. When he activated it, it emitted a terrifying, constant roar. He brought it close to the spot where my trunk was damaged and I felt hundreds of sharp teeth stripping away my bark and cutting into my heart. The colors around me faded and the world turned black. I heard the gardenia, the myrtle, and the pomegranate: they were all crying with me, and for me. My trunk snapped and my upper half collapsed. My branches fell to the ground. I could no longer see anything. I was shouting but I couldn't hear my own voice or what I was saying. No other tree heard me, and my branches were no longer mine.

All that remained was the wounded half of my trunk and my shredded heart. This wasn't the end of it. He came back later and injected my heart and what was left of my insides with some foul-smelling liquid. He flooded the ground around me with it until my roots suffocated. I could hear them dragging my branches, breaking them and carrying them off. I thought I was about to die, but I didn't die. I was blind and mute, without branches or fruit. But a spirit part of me was still here. The horrible liquid evaporated and the rains washed it away. The years passed. Once when their son graduated from university, they tied a sheep to my trunk with a rope, to what was left of me. The sheep was frightened, as if it knew its fate. I envied it, saying to myself, "You'll be slaughtered and die, whereas I was killed years ago and yet I cannot die."

Then a day came when I heard the sky splitting open and volcanic ash raining down. It was as if the bottom of hell had burst. A flame found its way into the remains of my heart and started a fire inside me. I was frightened but I saw it as a good sign. It may be painful but now my long drawn-out death, which had started years earlier, would finally come about.

I thought my soul would fly off to heaven, content and satisfied to be close to our big sister, the lote tree of the far boundary. But I'm still here hovering around my memory, and I feel as if my trunk is still here.

I was expecting an email from Wadood as he had promised in the letter he had sent with the manuscript, so that I could send him a message to express my enthusiasm and say how much I admired his project. I had prepared a draft of my message. But I didn't receive anything from him. In the first week of classes I passed by the office of the department secretary to pick up my mail. Among the internal university communications (information about pension plans, and mortgages for those who wanted to buy houses) and the offers from credit card companies (they had long turned down my applications, but the situation had now changed and they had found out that I had a job), I noticed a brown envelope with foreign stamps and writing in Arabic. I turned the envelope over and was delighted to read the name of the sender: Wadood Abdulkarim. I had given him the college address. I opened the envelope impatiently. But the letter was surprisingly disappointing:

Dear Mr. al-Baghdadi,

Greetings.

I hope you arrived safely and are well. First, I'd like to make sure that you received the envelope that I left for you at the hotel. I'm very sorry but I now realize that I was much too hasty. Two days after meeting you I sat down and went over the draft of the first chapter of Fihris and realized it was still merely a draft. I started erasing things and changing and re-writing some passages. That means that the draft that you have should have stayed with me. It's a bird whose wings are not fully formed yet. So I request that you return the manuscript to me as soon as possible to the following address:

Wadood Abdulkarim c/o Mr. Yasir Alaa,

Adnan's Bookshop,

Al-Mutanabbi Street,

Baghdad, Iraq

Please don't translate any part of it or publish it anywhere or tell anyone about the idea. Please understand my position and respect my wishes. I appreciate your interest and I apolo-gize for any inconvenience.

Yours sincerely,

Wadood

I took the letter to my office and read it three times without under-standing his decision. I had to go teach my class and I was still con-fused. That afternoon I went to the apartment and brought the en-velope and Wadood's manuscript to the department. I scanned it carefully in the copy room and sent it to my email address in PDF format. I also printed a copy and put the hard copy in a file marked "Wadood's Fihris." I decided to copy it by hand into the notebook I had taken to Baghdad and that I had filled with silence, blank space and the word *Baghdad*. Didn't Wadood, who himself lived in the street with the Xerox shops, know how easy it is to copy anything? I sat in my office thinking about the letter I was going to write him.

I called my cousin, who had given me a lift to the hotel and who had given me his phone number. I chatted with him and asked about the situation in Baghdad. Then I asked him whether he could make inquiries for me about "someone I met in Baghdad," as I put it. "What, are you going to get engaged? And you want to know what her reputation is like?" he said. I laughed and told him it was nothing to do with a woman, but rather a man I had met briefly while visiting al-Mutanabbi Street and that he had sent me a letter. "No problem, but why? What's the story, I mean?" he said. I didn't tell him the whole truth. "It's really nothing. There's a translation project we might do and I want to know more about him before I decide to work with him," I said.

He called me three days later and said that his detective work on my behalf revealed that Wadood had been selling books in al-Mutanabbi Street since the 1990s. "He lives alone in a room and doesn't have any family. He's very smart and a voracious reader. He's weird but he's not crazy. They threw him in prison in the mid-nineties and tortured him, on the grounds that he was selling banned books. No one knows what his story is. He lives with books and has no family. He says he's written twenty books but he's never published anything. They told me not to get involved with Wadood, because he's a mess. He's damaged."

The phrase "he's damaged" kept ringing in my head. I didn't comment. I thanked him for his efforts. When he insisted on knowing why I was inquiring after Wadood, I said I was looking for someone I could rely on to buy books regularly and send them to the college library. This wasn't a lie. The college library was poor as far as Arabic literature was concerned, and the head of the department had obtained a promise from the dean's office that some funds would be allocated to buying books.

> Dear Wadood,
>
> Greetings,
>
> Forgive me the delay in writing this letter. I was expecting a message from you by email, as we agreed, so that I can communicate with you. I was really delighted with the two valuable gifts you left at the hotel for me before I left. The collected works of al-Karkhi, whose works I love, will enable me to delve deeper into his poetry. It's now the most valuable thing in my fledgling library, so I am very grateful. But the most valuable gift was your wonderful Catalog, which I started to read in the desert on the way to Amman. I didn't stop till I'd finished, and I ended up hungry for more. I have reread it several times since then and I thought seriously about translating it into English. I was intrigued by the unusual idea of the project, and the language in it was also fluent and poetic. I am really fortunate that you allowed me to wander around in this magical world. Thus what you said in your second letter seems like a massive loss for me personally and for every reader. Now you're asking me to send back the valuable gift with which you enticed me when you lent me a part of it. Of course as the author you have a right to do so, but allow me to disagree with you. It is no doubt rare to feel completely satisfied with any work, especially in the case of writers, especially those who treasure and appreciate the meaning and value of writing, and you are clearly one of those. Faulkner says that a work never lives up to the ideal-

istic dream with which the writer started. But I believe you are doing yourself and your text an injustice if you withhold it from others. The prologue might need some rearrangement of the sequence of its tumultuous ideas and some trimming here and there. But when it comes to the body of the text, I think you are too hard on it and on yourself.

I won't take up much of your time. Please find enclosed the work you entrusted to me, which was the most precious thing I took with me when I left Baghdad. But please reconsider your decision, and I repeat that I am interested in translating the text, or at least parts of it, into English. You should think seriously about publishing it in Arabic first. Whatever you do, please stay in touch and let's be friends at least. Can you send me a telephone number or an email address? There's another project I have in mind and I would like to hear what you think of it. That project would be writing a novel about you.

> With affection and admiration,
> Your friend
> Nameer al-Baghdadi

Roy sent me an email asking after me and saying that their Egyptian-American friend, who had volunteered to translate the tapes, was having trouble translating some of the material because he didn't understand colloquial Iraqi. He said he realized I was busy teaching so he was asking me to recommend someone I trusted who could produce an accurate translation within three weeks or a month. I wrote saying I was willing to do it myself. He was delighted and sent me a link with a password for downloading the film, which wasn't yet in its final form. They had chosen three hours out of the thirty hours we had filmed in Baghdad, with the intention of cutting it back to just an hour and a half. He sent me the text of the interviews that had been translated, with the problematic sentences, or those where the translator was unsure of the meaning, marked in red for me to check or translate.

I sat down in my office in front of the big computer screen and watched the whole three hours. How would the poor Egyptian have known how to translate *sondat* (rubber tubes), *hwaaya* (very), *qashaamir* (idiots), *fannak* (I dare you), and other words that were used? I translated all the segments and the missing phrases and corrected some mistakes. He had thought that *bustuna* ("they hit us") meant the same as the equivalent word in Egyptian colloquial ("they gave us a good time"). I was saddened that some amazing and extraordinary interviews had disappeared from the edited version. I wasn't the director or the producer and I didn't know to what extent they would accept a critical opinion, though Roy had said in his letter that he was interested in my opinion as an Iraqi. Most of the material that had been cut had been about the cruelty of Saddam and the violence of the regime. It was the same old problem we faced with many of the leftists who were opposed to the war in America. They devoted all their efforts to criticizing the policy and actions of their own government, which was their right and their duty. But they turned a blind eye to the crimes of tyrants. They ignored all those crimes whenever the opportunity arose. Roy wasn't one of those, but I remember that when we were on the way from Amman to Baghdad he had said, "Our film is not about Saddam and the dictatorship but about the occupation. Everyone knows that Saddam was an evil monster. There should be films about Saddam's dictatorship, but our film is about the occupation." I argued with him that day, saying that the two were linked, but his priorities were clear.

The three hours brought back to life all the faces and scenes, all the phrases and even the smells that had been half-asleep in my head. I had shut them out for weeks because I was busy with the things around me and moving somewhere new. But they had only shut their eyes, taking a siesta or a nap, before waking up, stretching, standing up, and resuming their life in me, taking me back to Baghdad.

In the nights after I watched the documentary, my head became a screen, with a collage of scenes that Roy hadn't chosen and others that had retained their place in the final version. The tanks crouched on the pavement in Abu Nuwas Street. The American soldier who came up to us when he saw us filming the statue of Abu Nuwas and asked us who he was. The woman in her fifties who wept and said, "I'll forgive the Americans for bombing us but I'll never forgive them for the embargo years." The former prisoner we met in al-Andalus Square who, smoking with trembling fingers, told us about the torture he had endured. Then he asked us to stop filming and said, "I can't go on." The librarian at the Faculty of Arts at Baghdad University, walking between the burned books. The president of the writers' union, who said, "It wasn't our battle and we let America fight the tyrant." The kids who polished shoes outside the Sheraton Hotel. The taxi driver who was convinced that Iraq would become like Hong Kong. Other scenes of events that did not take place and that I hadn't seen in the first place. Dozens of tired, browbeaten faces, with wrinkles that grew deeper and crisscrossed like barbed wire. The people behind the faces were silent. Their lips never moved. But I heard growlings and mutterings that seemed to be coming from their eyes.

THE COLLOQUY OF THE STAMP ALBUM

He didn't like stamp collecting. He hadn't shown any particular interest in stamps before that day in 1980. He heard the bell ring and when he looked out of the living room window he saw Wisam standing at the outer gate. He went out to meet him and they exchanged greetings from a distance. Before he reached the front gate to open it, Wisam had taken what looked like a big book covered in green cloth from the paper bag he was carrying. As soon as Qays opened the metal gate, Wisam handed him the book and, in a voice tinged with a certain sadness, said, "This is my stamp album. Keep it for yourself. Look after it."

Qays didn't understand why Wisam was giving him the stamp album at that particular moment. He smiled with pleasure at the gift, opened the album and turned the thick pages. He was struck by the colors and designs of the stamps arranged in rows under a strip of transparent plastic that covered their bottom halves and protected them. Some were

Iraqi stamps, old ones and new ones, and others were from
Arab and foreign countries. Most of them had round postmarks showing where their journeys had started or ended.
Others had no postmarks because they had never officially
traveled.

"My god, that's so nice. But why? Don't you want it?"

"We're leaving tomorrow and I can't take it with me."

"Why are you leaving?"

"The government's going to deport us."

"Where to?"

"I don't know. Maybe Iran."

"Why?"

"They say it's about taba'iyya."

"What does that mean—taba'iyya?"

"It means we have Iranian origins," Wisam said with
derision.

"Are you really Iranians?"

"No, but my grandfather had an Iranian passport."

Qays didn't understand what exactly taba'iyya meant
and at the time he couldn't grasp how Wisam could become
a foreigner overnight. He felt sad because Wisam's departure
meant they wouldn't walk to school together and he would
have to come home alone after school. Before Qays could
find something to say, Wisam added, "The stamps are sold
in bookshops. You can buy them. If you can get hold of envelopes with stamps on, just put them in hot steam for a few

minutes until the glue softens, and then you can get them off the envelope without them tearing."

Qays didn't pay much attention to the details and rituals of stamp collecting. "So you're leaving?" he asked Wisam again. "And when are you coming back?"

"I don't know. No one knows."

Qays noticed the fear mixed with sadness in his friend's eyes when Wisam came up to give him a farewell hug. "Look after the stamps," Wisam added. Wisam was taller, so Qays's head only reached Wisam's chest. Wisam put a hand on Qays's head. They held each other for some seconds. Qays felt a desire to cry but he didn't cry.

Everything happened suddenly. Qays stood standing at the gate watching his friend walk away. When Wisam reached the end of the street, he headed right and turned his head toward Qays. He stopped for a few seconds and waved from afar. Qays moved the stamp album to his left hand and waved his right hand vigorously. He didn't realize he would never see him again. He went back into the house and took the bag to his room without telling anyone that Wisam had given it to him. He put the album on the top shelf of his little bookcase, next to the issues of *Majallati* and *al-Mizmar* that he kept.

This was Qays's first year at Baghdad College, while Wisam was in the fourth year there. The three years that separated them meant Wisam treated Qays as his younger brother. But what first brought them together was a request from Qays's mother, who on the first day of the school year took her son to the place where the school bus stopped to pick up children and take them to the school, which was far away in Suleikh. Qays's mother said hello to Wisam and thought she had seen him before in the streets in the neighborhood.

"Isn't your house on the right in the street where the bakery is, my dear?" she asked.

"Yes, Ma'am."

"So that's why I thought I'd seen you before. What's your name?"

"Wisam."

"Wisam, my dear. Please look out for Qays on the way back because his father and I will be at work. Walk together. Think of him as your younger brother, because I'm worried about him with all the cars."

"No problem, Ma'am."

"Thank you, my boy."

Qays's mother kissed her son on the cheek, which made him embarrassed, and told him to stay with Wisam. She was more anxious about how Qays would get home safely than her husband, who was waiting in the car, because it was she who had insisted on enrolling Qays in far-off Baghdad College, which took only gifted children. Her husband would have preferred that he go to a local school.

Wisam didn't say anything to Qays that day, just smiled

slightly. When the bus came, Wisam sat in the back seats with his "big" friends he knew from past years. Qays chose an empty place next to the window in the middle of the bus. They didn't see each other during the breaks that day. It was a big school: four buildings and large open spaces. But they met again and stood side by side after the bus dropped them off in the afternoon in the same place where it had picked them up in the morning.

The trip back to their area took half an hour on foot. They had to cross the street to the other side and walk past the Khawarnaq bar with its tinted windows. In front of the bar there was a bus stop where they could in theory take a bus to another bus stop five minutes from their houses, but it came only "on special occasions, once a year," as Wisam put it. Even when it happened to come by just seconds after they got off the school bus, it was packed with passengers and was just crawling along. It looked like an old ship that was about to sink, trying to jettison its cargo. After crossing the main street they took a side street and went past the "oxygen factory." The name caught Qays's attention when he noticed it for the first time on a sign on the outer gate. He imagined there was an enormous lung inside the factory, breathing in carbon dioxide, the opposite of human beings, and blowing oxygen out into enormous balloons as if it were at an endless birthday party. He knew that birthday balloons were filled with some gas other than oxygen, but he liked the idea. But the image didn't make so much sense when he saw a large wooden cube like a small chamber on top of the factory building, and on top of that a pipe from which water poured into the heart of the factory. Then he saw the long cylinders of oxygen stacked up in the factory garage. Sometimes he would watch the workers loading the cylinders onto small trucks that were waiting, each with its back half inside the factory and the front part on the pavement. The balloons he imagined flew far away at high speed. After the oxygen factory they headed left and walked along Canal Street. They passed by some vast old warehouses with high sandy-colored walls. This was the dangerous part that Wisam's mother worried about because the gap between the warehouse wall and the roadway where cars and large trucks went by was relatively narrow here. From the first day Wisam made sure that he kept to the left, with Qays between him and the wall. After about fifty yards the gap, which couldn't be called a pavement because it was a mixture of soil, gravel, and sand, widened out at the point where the warehouse wall ended and a row of houses began, set twenty yards back from the public street.

On the first walk back there was an awkward silence, at least at the beginning. Qays broke the silence by asking Wisam which soccer team he supported. He had once seen him playing soccer on the empty piece of land close to the house, which the local boys used as a soccer pitch.

"Tayaran, and you?"

Qays wasn't crazy about soccer and didn't know much about it, but his father liked Talaba, so he automatically said, "Talaba." Wisam quickly said, "Talaba are losers." He found a small stone and started kicking it around as if it were a ball he was going to aim into the Talaba goal. "Come on, let's get this stone home with us," Wisam said, and they started kicking it back and forth between them. They often repeated the game in the following months. One of them might get over-enthusiastic and misaim the stone, and when it strayed onto the roadway they would have to look for an alternative. Sometimes an empty tin can they found on the roadway would replace the small stone. Qays's house was farther away, so the first time Wisam insisted on accompanying him all the way to the door of Qays's house.

"Do you have a key?" he asked.

"No, but my granny's in and she'll open the door for me."

Wisam stood by the door and waited till he saw Qays's grandmother open the door for him. He waved goodbye and set off back.

In the morning Qays's parents drove him to the bus stop to stand with five other schoolchildren who lived in nearby areas. Wisam didn't speak to him much in the presence of the others, but he was still friendly. On several occasions he helped him get a falafel sandwich from the store. The boys would run to the store as soon as the bell rang for the long recess after the fifth lesson. They would jostle to get sandwiches, and it was a battle that the biggest and tallest usually won. Qays was watching the struggle in front of the falafel window but had given up all hope of getting his hands on one of those delicious sandwiches, in which the pieces of falafel came with sliced tomato and pickled mango. When Wisam saw him, he understood the problem. "Give me the money and I'll buy you one," he said.

On the Saturday morning after saying goodbye, Wisam wasn't standing with the others to wait for the bus. Qays walked home alone that day. When he walked past Wisam's family's house, he saw Wisam's father's car, a white Peugeot 504, parked in the garage with the metal gate closed. He stopped outside the gate hesitantly, then overcame his timidity and pressed the small round electric bell press with the red light. No one came out. He pressed it again and held it down with his index finger for longer, but the result was no different. The curtains were drawn closed. He walked on home, with the word taba'iyya spinning in his head. He hadn't received a satisfactory answer two days earlier when he asked his parents what it meant. His father hadn't said anything. He just kept watching *A Week of Sport* on television as if he hadn't heard the question. His mother's response was "Why do you ask?" and he told her about Wisam being deported. She put her right hand on her cheek and said, "No. Poor people, may God help them. He looked like a nice lad."

He put the question to his father again another time: "Father, what does taba'iyya mean?"

"It means they have foreign origins."

"And why are they deporting them?"

"They might have had some links with Iran."

His mother interrupted: "So everyone whose grandfather had an Iranian passport is now a spy? What's all that about?"

"What would you know about it? There really are Iranians and anyway, don't talk like that in front of the boy, and let me watch television," said his father.

She didn't argue back, but she later explained to Qays that in the old days people used to get Ottoman or Iranian passports and they were not necessarily foreigners. She was rather sad about the deportation of Wisam, but she was more concerned about her son coming home alone. Qays convinced her that he knew the way well and he promised to be careful and keep away from the traffic.

He always slowed his pace as he approached Wisam's house. He looked in case he saw any sign that they had come back. Two weeks later he noticed that the car had disappeared. A week later he saw a young man standing outside the gate smoking. Qays went up to him and said, "Is Wisam at home?" "Who's Wisam?" the man answered in surprise.

"Wisam. This is their house."

"This isn't a house, kid. This is the headquarters of the party branch."

Qays didn't say anything but went off home. His father wasn't very interested when Qays told him that Wisam's house was now the headquarters of a Ba'th party branch. He didn't offer him any convincing explanation, just made do with his favorite expression: "You don't need to think about such things." His mother didn't put her hand on her cheek this time. But she shook her head and said, "Shame. God alone knows where they've taken them." From the things that adults said, Qays later gathered snippets of information about the "taba'iyya" people being dumped on the border with Iran and that no one knew whether they were in refugee camps or whether the Iranians had let them in. But then the war started and the rapid sequence of events overshadowed the "taba'iyya" question by raising more immediate questions.

Wisam disappeared like an unanswered letter, leaving his stamps in Baghdad. But Qays didn't forget his friend. He took the stamp album out of his bookcase whenever he missed Wisam. He would look at the stamps and run his fingers over them as if they were windows through which he would find a trace of his friend. But they were strange windows, crowded with people, stones, animals, and landscapes. Qays imagined that they were looking out at him, but they didn't say anything and they didn't give anything away other than the value of the stamp or the occasion for issuing it and sometimes the year.

Abraham Lincoln (five cents), Helen Keller (unclear),

Queen Elizabeth (? pence), Charles de Gaulle (?), King Faisal I, with a beard and glasses (½ anna), the Arch at Ctesiphon (three annas), an old plane flying (four fils), King Faisal II (75 fils), the minaret at the Nouri mosque, a lute, scout troops (1967), girl guides (two fils), revolutionary leader Abd al-Karim Qasim lighting the eternal flame for the Unknown Soldier (16 fils), The Lion of Babylon (eight fils), stamps promoting savings accounts for schoolchildren (unclear), Maarouf al-Rusafi (1960), the anniversary of the 1920 uprising (a man holding a club) (June 1965), brown fish (1969), carp, butterfish (?), a butterfly (Lebanon), sandgrouse (15 fils), the first anniversary of the blessed 14th of Ramadan revolution (50 fils), Valiant Iraqi Army Day (January 6, 1968), International Day of Solidarity with the Palestinian People, the Iraqi Ground Station (10 fils), the sixth national day of the United Arab Emirates, 1977, the Literacy Campaign (20 fils), Fujeirah (five dirhams), the Arab Cup (unclear), Gamal Abdel Nasser (unclear), Arab Unity (unclear).

It occurred to him to buy stamps to add to Wisam's album. When he went to the post office in New Baghdad, Saddam Hussein's face was on the stamps that the woman behind the counter offered him. He was confused and afraid to ask if there were any stamps that didn't have the president's head on them. He bought two stamps but didn't put them in the album. He knew Saddam Hussein was the reason why Wisam was gone, so how could he put his face in one of those windows? He decided not to put any more stamps, new or old, in the album, but to leave it as it was.

The album stayed in the little bookcase. Issues of the magazines *Majallati* and *al-Mizmar* leaned against it. Next to them stood a set of the Egyptian series *The Five Adventurers*. A year later they were joined by the Agatha Christie novels that Qays had started to read when he was sitting in the bus or at home after finishing his homework. The library gradually expanded and started to take in more serious books that Qays bought from time to time, such as Gorky's *The Mother*, *War and Peace*, *A Tale of Two Cities*, *Les Misérables*, *The Black Tulip*, and the novels of Naguib Mahfouz, Abdulrahman Munif, and Ghada al-Samman. After he began studying at the civil engineering faculty of the University of Technology in 1986, engineering books and composition books started to take their place on the wooden shelves that his father had bought him. When he had graduated and done his military service in the Military Works department in A'zamiyya, he worked as a lecturer in the University of Technology and completed his master's degree. He married one of his colleagues and they lived in an apartment they rented in Haifa Street. He took the album with his books to the new apartment. As they were arranging the apartment his wife opened the album and asked him why he hadn't told her that stamp collecting was his hobby. So he told her the story of Wisam.

During the embargo years, Qays was forced to sell his

whole library in al-Mutanabbi Street to cover the expenses
of the household and the three children. His salary, his wife's
salary, and his income from the private lessons he had started
to give, all taken together, were not enough. But he kept the
album, although he knew that the old stamps would fetch
a considerable amount of money. It stayed in the bookcase,
which, now that it no longer held his books, was filled with
old newspapers and his students' research papers and dissertations.

The album was there until the moment a missile broke
through the windowpane. The apartment was empty because
they were all in the underground shelter. The fire began with
the old carpet and then reached the lower shelves of the
bookcase. The flames consumed the newspapers, including
news stories, editorials, fiery poems about the coming victory,
and pictures of Saddam Hussein meeting military leaders.
Then the flames climbed to the other shelves and consumed
plans for hypothetical buildings in graduation projects,
housing complexes that ran on solar energy, and architectural
dreams. Then it took hold of the album with its green cover
that had faded through more than two decades of exposure to
sunlight and dust. The tongues of flame soon tinged it, turning it from golden to dark brown and then settling on black.
All the kings and presidents who still looked out of the windows of the stamps were burned up. The buildings and birds
were also burned. When the neighbors and the Egyptian ele-

vator operator managed to put out the fire, the whole apartment was charred and black.

I was always saving newspaper or magazine clippings, folding them up or putting them in books associated with them. I once tried to pull them all together and sort them into a folder when I was trying to organize my papers and my life, as would happen once every year or two. But I never finished the task because I realized I was using these side projects as an excuse to procrastinate and avoid working on my dissertation. When I came back from Baghdad after meeting Wadood, saving clippings became a daily ritual. I seemed to have contracted by contagion his obsession with archives. At Dartmouth I would buy the *New York Times* in the morning from the White Horse café and browse through it as I drank my coffee and ate my breakfast: a bagel with cream cheese. I would cut out any articles about the war that caught my attention or that I thought were important. I set aside for them a folder that I put in my desk drawer along with other folders, and I wrote "Collateral Damage" on it. The term had been in circulation for a while, but its use increased after the invasion. I was especially interested in pictures, and I posted some of them on the board above my desk. I bought a small pair of scissors to make sure I didn't tear any part of the picture, as had happened several times when I tore them out by hand.

Rebecca reproached me when I told her what I was doing. She asked me as usual what I'd been doing that morning and I told her. "Frankly I don't understand," she said. "If you were writing a re-

search paper on the war, for example, that would be a different matter. But you have to finish your dissertation and focus on that. You
don't have much time if we add the teaching. Why do you want to
surround yourself with pictures of war carnage and dead people? I
know it's your home country and you feel sad. That's understand-
able and normal. I feel sad and guilty too. I know your sadness is
much deeper. But all the things you're doing won't help anyone
or change anything at all. Feeling guilty or sad won't change anything. In fact it will harm you psychologically. You tell me you can't
sleep? Of course. How could you sleep normally? I've told you several times you should go to a psychiatrist. You have PTSD. You're
obsessed with that man you met in Baghdad, and it's not healthy."

"It doesn't have anything to do with changing anything. I want
to write a novel about Iraq," I said. "You can write plenty of novels,
but after you finish your dissertation and settle down in your job,"
she said. I was going to tell her that she didn't understand me, but
I didn't say anything. I was tired of the constant arguments, which
drained me psychologically. Her reaction saddened me, regardless
of her intentions, and I didn't like her tone. I realized that we had
really started to part ways and that the geographical distance between us had started to translate into emotional distance too. She
was more practical and rational than me. She would finish everything on time, ahead of time in fact, unlike me. I would put things
off and break my own and other people's deadlines. She's going to
make a successful and prominent academic. She knew how to play
the game too. After that conversation I decided that the relationship had to end officially and that it was I who would have to deliver

the coup de grâce. She expected me to visit her in Bolivia, where she was doing fieldwork on the effects of globalization on the indigenous population and on the strategies they adopted to resist it. At first I was enthusiastic about the visit, since I had never been to South America. But that was before my visit to Baghdad and before our relationship deteriorated. Now it couldn't wait till the visit, which was due in three months' time.

"Listen, we should take some time to think about our relationship," I said.

"Think about what? If you want to end the relationship, why don't you say so without evasion?"

"Do you think things are going as they should?"

"No, but it's not a question of thinking. It's a question of changing the way we treat each other."

"And how can we change that when we're in two separate continents?"

"What do you want then?"

"I don't know . . . Perhaps I want to be alone."

My own answer took me by surprise, and then I added, "Yes, maybe it would be best to be alone."

"I can't believe you want to end the relationship this way, on the phone. You could have waited and told me face to face. Okay, enjoy your loneliness and your sorrows. You're pathetic, Nameer." She hung up. I tried to call her back but she didn't pick up. I can't deny that I felt relieved.

࿊

THE COLLOQUY OF ABU JINNIYYA

I have a pedigree from the stable of Khaylat al-Ajuz, originally
from Shammar. My forefathers accompanied princes and
kings on their raids and their trips. Poets sang their praises.
Anyone who saw me now would never imagine that I was
once pampered and cherished. The likes of those people who
now despise me used to keep me clean and comfortable in
a spacious stall that I had all to myself. But I lost everything,
even my name, Abu Jinniyya, which they gave me when I was
born because of the blaze on my forehead. Adham Abu Jinniyya was my full name. I've lost my original name, because
the person in whose hands I ended up called me I'jouzi.
Old and lazy, he called me, and he still repeats it. He doesn't
understand and he will never understand that I object to his
rough treatment of me. I'm taking a stand. I try to draw his
attention to the wound in my neck and to the metal stud
on the iron ring that I can barely lift. But he knows only the
language of the whip. Even the others who toil here like me
make fun of me when I boast of the life I used to live. They
don't believe that I used to eat carrots and beetroot and even
apples. Why would they believe it when all they know is the
dry rubbish they're happy to eat? They don't believe I used
to dash around the racetrack, leaving the others far behind
me, blinded by the dust that my hooves kicked up. I carried

a lightweight jockey and the crowds called my name, rooting for me and cheering me on when I reached the finishing line. They festooned me with garlands of flowers around my neck instead of this rusty collar. They patted me on the back and stroked my cheek as I whinnied. They led me back to my stall and took off my saddle and bridle. They bathed me, combed my hair and left me to rest. They tired me out in training before the races sometimes, but they treated me like a prince. I never had any suspicion that I would have to give up this comfortable way of life. But in one race another horse kicked me in the hamstring and I stumbled and fell, throwing the jockey off my back. It was the first race ever in which I didn't finish first. The pain in my hamstring kept bothering me and neither medicine nor physiotherapy did any good. That made me a loser. Other horses took my place. I stayed in my stall for a while, but then they took me to market and sold me off cheap to this man who keeps shouting at me. He pulled me after him through the streets between all the cars and the people to the place where he had parked his cart. He put this metal collar around my neck, fitted the bridle, the halter, two pieces of wood and ropes. From that day on I've been pulling his cart, which he loads with everything that's heavy. The hunger and thirst are killing me. No one looks after me and people don't clean me. I whisk the flies and mosquitoes away with my tail. But many spots itch. I freshen up when the sky weeps and washes me, but it doesn't rain much. At the end of every day I pull him and his cart to his house, and he ties me to a tree in the outer courtyard after he's freed me from the yoke of the cart. The children often pester me and the stray dogs bark at me too. Last night it thundered as it's never thundered before. The stars were ablaze and I thought they were falling on me. But it didn't rain at all.

In March 2004 I read a story in the *New York Times* about the process of washing the dead in Iraq. The journalist spoke to Raad Abboud, a thirty-three-year-old man who had been washing corpses since he was thirteen. He remembered the bodies that used to come in the 1980s, when the regime was executing its victims. Raad thought the situation would improve after 2003, but what happened was quite the opposite. He started work at seven o'clock in the morning and didn't finish until five in the afternoon. He felt a responsibility toward the dead, but the news always made him depressed because he knew that the bodies would soon be piling up in front of him. He was traumatized and had recently decided that he would be the last corpse washer in his family. "I won't let my son inherit this profession. It has destroyed me," he said.

I wiped away a tear and reread it right away. I was struck by the details and rituals of washing the bodies, and I kept thinking about Raad and the horrors he faced every morning. When I got to the office I cut out the article and put it in a new folder. I researched the subject on the Internet. I thought of writing a novel about Raad Abboud and people like him. Then I felt guilty, as if I were betraying Wadood and the novel I'd been dreaming of writing about him. I went to the university library and took out several books on Islamic law that described the intricate procedures for washing the dead. I copied out the relevant parts and added them to the folder, in addition to an interview with a corpse washer I found online. I imagined the narrator in the novel as coming from a family that had practiced this trade for generations. He would be from the al-Kazimiyya district of Baghdad, not from Najaf like Raad. But he would have had artistic inclinations since he was a child and would refuse to become a corpse washer. This would cause conflict with his father. Many of the details began to take shape, and I thought about it so often that everything about it seemed real to me. I began to see the washhouse and hear the characters speaking. But I had to put all this on paper. And I didn't write anything. I often tried but I didn't succeed, so the folder stayed as it was.

I'm surrounded and under surveillance, like a bird in a prison cell. I don't have a sky. What to do now? No family and no homeland. In prison. And my crime is that I know and I want to know. You might think I'm raving mad and I wouldn't blame you for thinking so, because no one else believes me. Most of the people I've revealed my secret to, by telling them about my ordeal, and they are very few, have thought I'm demented. Instead of trying to understand my ordeal, they offered me their pity, which I hate. They can't see what I see and they haven't lived what I've lived. They can't imagine the

torment I've been through. They may not realize that there
are cameras everywhere, and the patrols are on the lookout
too. They don't realize that we're in a gigantic prison and all
our movements and thoughts are monitored and carefully
recorded. Even this message that I'm writing to you now, I'm
sure they'll read every word of it. They'll examine what it
might mean and submit a report on it even before it reaches
you. They tell me I'm no longer in prison and that I'm rant-
ing. There are no bars and no guards. But they can't see and
they don't understand that I'm suffocating. I suffocate, but
never die. There's no way out of all this. The only way out is
death. But I know that there's nothing after death, no "after"
other than nothingness. Otherwise I would have killed myself
years ago in order to move on to another existence that is less
tormented than this. Nothing but nothingness. Yes. There's
no hell other than the hell we're living now. I believe what
Calvino says about hell. Besides, to die would be to proclaim
that they have triumphed over me. I may never triumph over
them, but I will not declare defeat. I will never admit defeat
whatever the price. I'll die standing by my ideas. You'll no
doubt wonder why I'm writing to you. I don't know. I have
no hope that you'll understand or that you'll fully accept my
view of things as they really are. What's it to you in the first
place? Was it your mistake that you met me? Maybe you're
just, forgive me for using the word, a pretext. A pretext to con-
verse. I may be addressing myself through you. I could have

been you and you could have been me, but for the absurdity of history and of fates. But I go back to Calvino and what he wrote in "Invisible Cities." I've memorized the passage: "The inferno of the living is not something that will be; if there is one, it is what is already here, the inferno where we live every day, that we form by being together. There are two ways to escape suffering it. The first is easy for many: accept the inferno and become such a part of it that you can no longer see it. The second is risky and demands constant vigilance and apprehension: seek and learn to recognize who and what, in the midst of the inferno, are not inferno, then make them endure, give them space." And I, sir, bet once again, and maybe for the last time, that you are not part of the inferno.

"Winter will be very harsh and it's impossible to go around on foot in this town. I advise you to buy a car," the department chair said. I liked the design of the Honda Element, so I bought a black one. The salesman gave me a temporary registration certificate, and to switch it to my name I had to obtain a New Hampshire driver's license. Since I already had a Massachusetts driver's license, I thought this would be easy. But the bureaucrat in the DMV, a woman in her early fifties with thick glasses and gray hair tied up in a style way out of fashion, told me that the new law required me to provide them with a copy of my birth certificate. I laughed and said, "I don't have a copy of my birth certificate."

"Why not? Where is it?"

"In Baghdad."

"Why?"

"Because I was born there."

"Can't you call them up and ask them to send it to you?"

"Madam, have you read the news recently or watched television?" I said. "There are manuscripts hundreds of years old that have been burned and lost, as well as antiquities and archives. Who's going to look for my birth certificate after all that?"

"I'm sorry but that's the law. I can't complete the process without a birth certificate."

"What's the point of this? I was living in Massachusetts and I was issued a driver's license there without any problem at all."

"Well, sir, an Arab like you tried to slip across the border from Canada two years ago so that he could go and blow up the Los Angeles airport."

"And do you think the terrorists would keep repeating the same plan even after it failed?"

"I don't know, sir. That's not my job."

I called the legal office at the college to help me with the problem and the person there promised to try. But he later told me that the authorities were very strict about this. "I know it's nonsense, but it's out of my hands," he said. A month later, the temporary registration expired and the police started to stop me whenever they noticed that the expiry date had passed. Although I explained the problem, and although they were sometimes sympathetic, they would still give me a ticket and I had to pay a fine every time. The unpaid fines piled up until they amounted to more than six hundred dollars.

One day I went out to find that the police had put a massive metal clamp on the front wheel on the right-hand side. I found a pink warning slip under the windshield wiper, telling me to pay all the fines or appear in court within a month of receiving the warning.

I went to court to explain the complications in the case. The cases that came up before mine were theft and serious assault cases. My turn followed that of a young man accused of stabbing his colleague at work after an argument. When I explained my problem to the judge, he rebuked the prosecutor and told him, "Do I have to waste my time on things like this?" Then he turned to me and said, "You're a university professor. Solve the problem. Sell the car." He ordered me to pay half of the fines.

In the end I sold the car at a loss to the same dealer who had sold it to me. I bought some heavy snow boots instead. On days when it was snowing heavily, I would wade through the snow on my way to the office, cursing Osama bin Laden, George Bush, and the Algerian who had tried to slip across the border.

"We must convince the living that the dead cannot sing."

I can hear the goldfinch singing. I open my eyes and I see myself under a tree laden with fruit that I cannot name. The goldfinch has landed on one of the branches. It stops singing. It turns its head and looks at me as if it knows me. When I reach out to touch it, it flies away and the branch shakes.

I notice the green fruit. They look like lemons but they're not lemons. When I take hold of them they dissolve and turn into drops of water. My hand gets wet and the tree disappears.

My apartment in Hanover remained without a television. Watching the news on American channels made me both depressed and angry. It seemed like a waste of the valuable time that I needed to finish my dissertation. I couldn't get Arabic satellite channels because for aesthetic reasons the college didn't allow satellite dishes on the roofs of the buildings it owned. Without a satellite dish one couldn't get the Arabic package. After reading so many criticisms by Iraqis of the coverage by the Arabic channels, I realized it was probably better for my sanity. But I would cheat nevertheless and break my promises to myself. After buying dinner in the students' cafeteria, I would go on some evenings to the classroom where I taught in the morning, which was close to my office and which was equipped with a large screen for showing educational films during lectures. I watched television there on the big screen. I put out the light and watched the American news in the dark. After that I watched Dave Chappelle. At 11:30 p.m. every night the janitor would come on his daily round to lock up the rooms. The first time he saw me he was rough: "What are you doing here? The building's closed. You have to leave." "I'm a professor and I teach in this room and I have a key," I said. He asked me to show him my ID card and I did. He kept opening the door every night and was about to say something, but then he would say, "Ah, you of course" and would go away.

At the beginning of fall I received a letter from Kate, one of the students in the first-year Arabic class that I taught, saying she was setting up a group called "Students Against the War" and asking me if I would be willing to be the advisory faculty and help the group if and when needed. I was surprised she hadn't spoken to me face to face, and then I realized that she was quite shy. I agreed and asked her for more information. She replied that they were planning to arrange some events to raise awareness of the negative effects of the war, and they would also try to organize a series of lectures. I wrote back encouraging her and expressing my enthusiasm for the idea. I said it would help to stimulate dialogue about the war on campus and among the students. In the two weeks after our email exchange I saw an advertisement in big letters posted on the walls, on the notice boards in the university buildings, and in the library, saying, "Are you angry about the war? Let's do something then." In smaller letters it invited students to attend the first organizational meeting. I wasn't able to attend it personally because the time conflicted with the monthly department meeting. The next day I was returning homework to students at the end of class and I asked Kate about the meeting. She smiled awkwardly and said, "Unfortunately not many people came, only seven, but they were enthusiastic. I'm hoping the movement will get more members in the future." I tried not to show my disappointment. "The important thing is it's a start," I said. "Please let me know if I can be of help."

Seven students out of six thousand. Really pathetic. But why am I surprised? Most of these students were from rich families, and many of them were right-wing conservatives. The war and its costs were far from their worlds and concerns. Even if it had mattered to them, they believed in the logic of the war.

I liked the idea of the group's first event: they were going to plant white roses symbolizing the victims of the war in the main square, stand in front of them in silence early in the morning, and then leave them there for a whole day. That way the students would see them from the half hour before they went to the first class at eight o'clock in the morning till sunset. I woke up earlier than usual and went to the place where they were going to stage the event, according to the email they had sent me. I found the members of the group, including Kate, standing in silence in front of the roses that had been planted close to one of the giant elm trees. They were carrying placards saying, "Stop the War Now," "No to War," and "Yes to Peace." Some of the other students slowed their pace to take a look at the strange spectacle. But the overwhelming majority kept on walking to their classes and just threw a quick, indifferent glance, while others laughed. I counted the flowers and there were thirty-seven. I tried to think why this number in particular, but I couldn't think of a logical explanation. At ten to eight, one of Kate's colleagues gathered the placards and thanked the participants, who broke up to go off to their various classes. I went up to her and asked her about the number of roses. "They represent the number of American soldiers killed in Iraq so far: three hundred and seventy, one rose for every ten." Before I could ask her about the Iraqis, she added spontaneously, "Unfortunately, we don't know exactly how many Iraqis have died. And in the group we decided it would be better politically to focus at first on our own troop casualties and bring up the civilians later."

I'm in a train station but it doesn't look like Baghdad Central
Station or any other station anywhere else. I'm standing alone
on the platform and there's a train about to leave. A booming
voice announces the last call for the train, but it doesn't say
which direction the train is headed in or what the final desti-
nation is. I don't understand what's happening. I look at the
train windows and I can see my family and friends waving to
me from the windows and gesturing at me to hurry up. I walk
to the nearest door to board the train. A man standing by the
door in a blue suit and a hat says, "This train is going to the
future. Where's your ticket?" I look for a ticket in my pockets
but I can't find one. He says he can't let me board and I can't
buy a ticket on the train. I have to go to the ticket office on
the ground floor. I look around to find the ticket office and I
see another train on the other side. I can see my family and
friends waving from the windows and gesturing to me to
hurry up. I head toward them and see the same man. "This
train is going to the past," he says. "Where's your ticket?" He
repeats what he said a few seconds earlier: "You can't board
the train without a ticket."

At the beginning of 2005 a journalist working with the *Valley News*
contacted me and said she was writing a feature story on what Iraqis
resident in the area thought about the parliamentary elections

taking place in Iraq. I was hesitant at first. I asked her whether there were enough Iraqis in the area. I knew about the eccentric Iraqi academic who had left Iraq in 1983 and had been teaching in the history department for years. I had met him only once since my arrival, and my attempts to approach him had failed. I had written him an email suggesting we have coffee together. We agreed on a time and place, but later he sent me an apology saying he was ill. After that I heard that he was a loner and didn't really have any friends. He lived far from campus and came in to teach only two days a week. "Yes, there are three of you," the journalist said. "There's a student from Iraq who came on a Fulbright scholarship this semester. Don't you know him?"

"No, I don't," I said.

I agreed and I answered her questions, which were naïve as usual. She was surprised when I told her that I wasn't going to take part in the elections. "Why not? There are polling stations in New York and Washington. Don't you want to exercise a democratic right that people have died for?" she said.

"I don't believe in the legitimacy of elections held under military occupation. I also can't take part in elections when I'm living on another continent and hundreds of thousands of Iraqis are denied the right to vote," I said.

"Who are the people denied the right to vote?" she asked.

"The people in Falluja, for example," I replied.

After the article was published, a reader wrote a comment on the newspaper's website agreeing with me. But the other ten or so comments condemned what I had said or described me as ungrateful. The funniest of them was from a retiree who described himself as a veteran: "It may be a sign of the moral degeneracy in our country that Mr. al-Baghdadi is allowed to teach in our universities, to systematically brainwash young people and to receive a salary nonetheless."

"Melt all your sorrows and mold them into a spear and look for a strong arm to aim it at your heart."

I missed Cambridge so I visited Ali Hadi for two days. We stayed up late drinking and chatting. Once again I was worried that we spent too much time lamenting the state of the world, while the victims had to go on living. The gods of sleep were not kind to me that night, and reading a novel by Sebald didn't help either. Ali Hadi had a television in his guest bedroom. I turned it on in the hope that it would make my eyelids droop and save me from insomnia. Switching between channels was like rummaging through trash. I looked for the right mix of noise and light to bore me and send me to sleep. At two in the morning I settled on PBS. It was *Antiques Roadshow*, in which the presenter speaks to people who have brought antiques to be valued and sold. Old clocks. Pieces of furniture. Pictures. The camera came across an ordinary-looking woman in her late fifties standing proudly next to the object she was displaying.

"What do you have there, madam?"

"It's a handmade Native American cradle. Real leather."

"Wow, that's really beautiful. And where did you get that from?"

"It belonged to my grandfather, who was a soldier. I inherited it from my father."

"And how much is it worth?"

"I've been told it could fetch $46,000."

"Wow, congratulations."

"Thank you."

It was the cradle I wanted to know more about, but the presenter moved away and the camera followed him. I turned the television off and let the darkness invade the room again . . . and the ghosts. In the darkness I tried to touch the cradle before the last child was removed from it and before the cradle was placed in the domain of "civilization," where it would become a "cultural document." Its former domain was now inhabited by ghosts. The ghost of Walter Benjamin hovered in the room, saying, "I told you, there is no document of civilization which is not at the same time a document of barbarism."

You want to write a novel about me?

My heart leaped when I read this sentence in your letter, which I was very pleased to receive. I won't hide from you the fact that I felt a certain pride, because I have long thought that my life—the parts that are past and those that are yet to come—would make an excellent novel, and even a stunning movie. But I also realize that millions of people in this world are convinced that their lives are epic tales waiting for someone to write them down. Then I had an attack of depression and that frightened off the pride, which flew away like a bird. Feeling proud apparently doesn't suit me; it challenges the dominance that melancholia has established inside me. How could pride dare to build its nest alongside my melancholia? Of course I don't mean that the idea in itself is the cause of my depression. Not at all. I believe, and this is neither an exaggeration nor a rhetorical conceit, that people are books (and vice versa). We are manuscripts and rough drafts of books. But in order to be completed and to be read, we have to die. Only then will we become known. Because things become known through being complete. It's the same with people. You can only do a full autopsy on a body after death. Then you can examine all the tissues, layers, and cavities. The "archaeology of the human" can start only when the human is a corpse. So you might have to wait till the time is right, till I descend to the underworld to wander there like my ancestors, and with them too, but without coming back as I always come back. Then you can write your novel and you'll have absolute freedom to use my real name. But there's another problem, my friend. We are all books. Yes. But we also have different histories, different genres of writing, and different types of paper and ink, different covers, fonts, and font sizes. Now I'm writing like a scribe. Anyway, we are books, and I'm a book a part of which has been lost forever. This is what I imagine, but I also feel that it's a tangible fact. Someone has torn up many of my pages or stolen them or hidden them or burned them. . . . If I knew what was written on those pieces of paper, it would be only a minor problem. But I don't know. For years I've been looking for myself in myself, but I haven't come across it yet. On the contrary, I've been stumbling around and falling apart. There are empty spaces and vast blanks in my head. I can't get inside my hand and write down on it what there was, or what I think there was. Do you remember, my friend, those olden days when there were only two television channels and the transmission stopped an hour or so after midnight? It ended with the national anthem and after that what we called "the freckles" appeared—those flickering gray and white spots, all of them practicing how to pronounce the sound of the letter *sheen*. There are spaces in my memory and even in my life where the transmission cuts out. Sometimes even the gray and white spots disappear as well. And the shshshsh sound disappears and blackness takes over—no sounds and no colors.

❧⚘❧

An assistant professor in the political sciences department invited me to attend his class on American policy to talk about Iraq and the war. He told me that another Iraqi would also be present so that we could take part in a debate. It was a big hall with about seventy students spread around the tiered seating. In his email he told me he wanted me to speak for a quarter of an hour before answering students' questions. I tried to speak objectively about the contradictions in the war rhetoric and the strategic objectives of the war, avoiding any delusional references to democracy. I went over the effects that economic sanctions had had on Iraqi society, and I referred to the escalating violence and the need to end the occupation as quickly as possible and hand Iraq over to the United Nations. He thanked me and said he was surprised to hear what I said about the United Nations, which he didn't think inspired great confidence, and he asked us to go back to that point later. The other guest was Rahim, the Iraqi student who had won a Fulbright scholarship to study at Dartmouth. He had knocked on my office door one day and introduced himself. He said he had heard there was an Iraqi professor and he would like to meet me. We chatted a while and I asked him how he had won the scholarship. He said he had been working as a translator with the U.S. Army and the officer in charge had written him a letter of recommendation. When it was his turn he spoke about how his family had suffered under Saddam Hussein's regime, which had executed one of his brothers. He said he had come from Iraq two months earlier and he was surprised by what I had said, but he understood it because I had been far away from Iraq. He said that Iraqis had been dreaming of freedom for thirty years, that America had helped them obtain it and that he appreciated the sacrifices of the American troops and thanked the American people. The students applauded him warmly. He looked at me and smiled, elated by his triumph.

Destruction also has a tablet preserved, somewhere in the netherworld. On it are written the names of everything that will be obliterated and everyone who will die. Every night I see myself flying and I read what's written and I come back to write it down in my catalog.

༚ঞ৯

I went into the classroom early as usual and put the cup of coffee I had bought on the table and my bag on the chair. I took out the textbook and the folder of corrected homework and put them on the table. I looked for the CD that came with the Arabic language book to put it in the CD player. It contained a dialogue designed to train the students to use the expressions in the lesson, in which Maha, an American of Egyptian origin, appears and speaks about her life using practical and useful sentences such as *My name is . . .*, *My father works as . . .*, *My mother works as . . .*, *I'm of . . . origin*, *I live in . . .* In came Cindy, one of the students, who also comes early. Apparently she went to the gym straight after class because she always came in her gym clothes. She sat at the front as usual after wishing me a *good morning*. As always, I reminded her to use Arabic as much as possible, especially as we had learned to say *sabah al-khayr.* She apologized and greeted me in Arabic. I put the CD in the right place so that we could start practicing the conversation after a short dictation test I insisted on to reinforce their writing skills and consolidate the new vocabulary they had learned. The students started to drift in and I gave them their corrected assignments. Tim came up to me—a student with very short blond hair, a flat nose, and freckles on his cheeks. I was pleased to hear him say in Arabic that he had a question, an expression that was in the book with other useful expressions such as the Arabic equivalents of "How do you say X?" and "What does X mean?" which I had asked them to always use, though they could then ask the same questions in English because they were still in the first year and didn't have the vocabulary.

He took me by surprise with a strange question: "Sir, when are we going to learn imperatives?"

"Not yet," I replied in English. "We're still at the early stages of the present tense and then we have the past and then the imperative. Why?"

"There are some imperatives I want to learn how to say in Arabic."

"For example?"

"Kneel down. Stop. Put your hands up. Move back."

I was amazed at his request, and Cindy raised her eyebrows.

"Why do you need them?" I asked.

"After I graduate this spring I'm going to join the army and go to Iraq or Afghanistan, and these phrases will be essential. I have a scholarship from the DOD."

I didn't know what to say.

"We're not in the Pentagon here," I finally said. "The book we use is for civilians and to introduce students to Arab culture."

"Okay, sir. Could you write those phrases for me on a piece of paper?"

"No."

"Okay, thanks."

I was very angry. I left the class and went to wash my face in the bathroom and get my breath back. I had been growing bored with teaching Arabic even before he made this extraordinary request, but at that moment I decided I had to do whatever it took to find a job at another university, where I would teach only literature and could avoid these situations.

Did I tell you that I can hear things speaking? Yes, I can hear what they say. They know me and sometimes they call me by name and beg me to listen. Sometimes they talk like people, slowly and with a logic that's easy to understand. But they can also groan and snarl and scream. I can hear their screams with painful clarity, and I don't understand them. No, that's not true. I understand them well because I know they're suffering the same things that I'm suffering, and in many cases they can't say what's troubling them. They scream with all the strength, all the misery, anger, and despair they have. What do I do when I hear their constant screams? In the beginning I would block my ears with my hands, but that didn't silence the screaming. It just made it sound a little distant. Then I felt pangs of guilt and I accused myself of narcissism. The least I could do is feel solidarity with things and scream them. Yes, scream them. That's the right expression and you haven't misread it. Maybe it's me who coined it. I've certainly never read it anywhere before. So I decided not to ignore the screaming of the things. It's not enough to open your heart wide. The heart isn't enough. I opened my ears. And whenever anything, or any creature, shouted at me, I would try to calm it down. Sometimes I succeeded, and often I failed. I would add my screams to the screams of the thing. I would scream at it and it would scream at me until I collapsed from fatigue. I've grown used to this, and now it's normal as far as I'm concerned. But human beings, the vast majority of whom are heartless or have deaf hearts that can't hear what I hear, run far away from me when I take part in a screaming session. If any of them do come close to me, then they do so in order to force me to stop! They think it's an illness and that the medical profession can cure it. But I know it's a rare talent. Once I dreamed that everyone endowed with this talent gathered on the stage in a theater, as if they were in an orchestra. They wore smart black clothes and sat in chairs in regular rows. When I came in they all stood up, and the audience stood up and clapped warmly. I bowed to the audience, then I turned and clapped for the orchestra and motioned to them to sit down. They didn't have any instruments or any scores in front of them. Their throats would do. All I had was the baton that I picked up to give them the signal to start. So they started. Their screams rose to the heights. They flew across the open dome of the theater to the sky, where the deaf ears of the gods are. What happens after that in the dream? Whenever one of the people screaming falls down, two men come and drag his body into the wings and a new screamer soon takes his place. Then I too collapse from exhaustion and wake up.

So which things talk to me, you might ask. All of them. A solitary piece of paper cut out of a book flying down the street. A loose pebble hurt by passersby when they tread on it. A frightened cloud escaping its fate. A head of lettuce trembling at the sight of a knife. A brick massacred by a builder with a sledgehammer. A sad statue drenched in the urine of passersby. A tree branch with its back broken. A word in a dictionary that no one uses any longer. A drop of water clinging to the mouth of the tap before it falls, and so on.

Animals also talk to me, of course. A hungry fly. A stray cat. An old donkey that's tired of being enslaved. A goldfinch that sings to me from its cage.

Dead people, not the living. The dead call out to me. I once read a sentence Paul Klee wrote: "I live just as well with the dead as with the unborn."

The library at Dartmouth closed its doors at 11 p.m., but there was another old building that was almost separate and that stayed open around the clock. I spent many hours there working on my dissertation. I didn't work in my office because there I would waste time checking news websites again and again. The library was half-empty most of the time, except for a handful of students who stayed late working on papers or studying for an exam the next day. The heating in the building was an old-fashioned steam system that didn't work very well. I often had to wear a coat indoors. On those snowy nights Abu Nuwas seemed very distant and alien. I felt tired and sleepy, of course, so I resorted to coffee. One night I went out to buy a cup of coffee from the gas station, a fifteen-minute walk away. I forgot to wear gloves and it was extremely cold. I couldn't put my right hand in my coat pocket, as I had done with the left hand, because it was holding the coffee cup. On the way back I began to feel a tingling in the fingers that were exposed to the cold air. When I got back to the library I had lost all sensation in my fingertips and I was worried I might have frostbite. I put them as close to the radiator as I could and rubbed them for more than half an hour before they came back to life.

Six months after I finished checking the translation for the documentary, Roy invited me to the first official screening of the film in Boston. It was being shown as part of a festival for alternative documentaries. I asked him for an extra ticket for Ali Hadi. I assumed that I would be staying at his place to attend the event and that he would also want to see the film. The theater was full and the reaction of the audience was very positive. That was no surprise as the area was well known for being liberal and for opposing the war. Roy asked me whether I wanted to stand with him and Laura to answer questions from the audience after the film, but I thanked him and declined. I was pleased that he began his talk by thanking me. "The translator who accompanied us to Baghdad is present with us today," he added. He asked me to stand up, and he led the audience in applause. Most of the questions and comments were about U.S. policy and the situation in Iraq, and not about the film itself. Many people criticized the mainstream media, their version of the war, and the failure to portray Iraqis as human beings. "What can we do now?" some of them asked. Ali Hadi praised the film and whispered in my ear that I had been very harsh in my criticism of its shortcomings and that it was much better than he had expected. He put up his hand to speak and praised the directors and the team for "bringing the voices of Iraqis to this continent and reminding us of their humanity." I introduced him to Roy and Laura at the end of the evening.

"Memory does this: lets the things appear small, compresses them. Land of the sailor."

Wednesday lunch was the most important social event for the college faculty. It was the day when the Hanover Inn offered its buffet lunch. The food wasn't bad, especially the desserts. Sometimes I would go with a few of my colleagues from the department. The conversation would be boring, about bureaucratic issues in the department and the trials and tribulations of teaching. When I was late for the start of lunch, I would have to sit at one of the other tables and meet other professors. Some of them were pleasant and welcoming and tried to chat. Some of them were silent or would continue with their conversations even after someone new had joined their table. When friends asked about social life after I had been at the college for a few weeks, I would say, "The overwhelming majority of those who live here are either seventeen years younger than me or seventeen years older."

I did meet one woman who was in my age range and wasn't married (most of the faculty were settled, with children, beautiful houses, and dogs). She was a German woman who was an assistant professor in the film department. Tall, elegant, blond with green eyes. I was sitting alone at a table having a salad and reading the newspaper when she came up holding her tray and asked if she could sit down. I folded up the newspaper and we started talking. Like me she had been appointed that semester. She had taught in Florida for two years and before that had studied in London. We competed to find fault with the little village where we had to live: the cold, the paucity of social life, and our longing for big cities with their restaurants. "But let's be fair. The cinema program is excellent, and it's the only breathing space we have," she said. I agreed and told her that I often went. "Yes, I've seen you there several times," she said. "We should go together from now on." We went to see the new Lars von Trier film *Dogville* and then to a nearby bar to talk about the film. She said it didn't rise to the level of his previous works, but she admired my enthusiasm. We ended up in her apartment and we slept together that night. I felt that the sex was rather mechanical and lacked something. But maybe both of us decided not to waste this opportunity. I couldn't sleep so I got dressed at 3 a.m. and walked back to my apartment. Two days later she sent me an email suggesting we have lunch, but I made the excuse that I was busy grading exams. She didn't try again.

I see what you can't see and I hear what you don't hear.

A friend sent me a message drawing my attention to an ad for a job as assistant professor specializing in non-European literature at New York University. The wording was strange and I guessed they were casting a wide net in order to get as many applications as possible. I decided to try since I had nothing to lose. If worst came to worst, I'd get a trip to New York for the interview and I'd spend two nights there. I sent my CV with a cover letter and copies of two articles of mine that had been published. Two weeks later my phone rang and it was the head of the search committee, who wanted to set a time for a phone interview with the members of the committee. I did the interview a week later and the questions were not difficult. Then an email arrived, telling me I was being invited to visit the university and give a talk.

After sleeping just two hours, I gave a talk about obscene literature and the importance of Abu Nuwas in Arabic culture, which raised many questions. I was exhausted by meetings with faculty and students that had lasted the whole day. I decided that I wouldn't get the job. This was my policy to protect myself from disappointment. So some of my answers at the end of my interview with the dean of the school and her assistant were strange and somewhat flippant.

She asked me if there was anything I would miss in New Hampshire if they offered me the job. I was surprised by her question but I answered honestly: "The color of the sky." The color was different— deeper and clearer. "And who will come with you from there if you get the job?" she added. I remembered I had read in some article that such questions were illegal. She had no right to ask about my private life, because that might have an effect on the appointment decision. But maybe she was asking to find out how large an apartment I would need. I had heard they had many applications for the apartments owned by the university. For some reason I answered, "Three wives and eleven children."

But she didn't smile, and nor did the assistant sitting beside her. I realized that my joke had fallen horribly flat, so I quickly added, "Sorry, I was joking. I live alone."

She still didn't laugh but just smiled tensely. "Do you have any cats or dogs?" she then asked.

"No," I said, "but I love cats, especially Persian cats, and if it would improve my chances of getting the job I'd be happy to get one."

This time she laughed and the assistant smiled.

"I'll tell you honestly," I added. "I grew up in Baghdad, which is a big city, and although I like nature and tranquility, I love cities, and New York is the city of cities. I know I'd be happy here." The last sentence was an exaggeration overlaid with much optimism and hope.

But I had lied. What I would miss was rambling in the woods near the college, or what was left of them, which I discovered only a year and a half after I arrived. My British colleague had advised me to explore the woods and the riverbank, but I was too busy and put it off. At the end of spring in the second year I walked northward to the last of the college buildings, and beyond I found a road that passed along a small lake called Occom Pond and then split in two directions—one leading to the nearby golf course that belonged to a country club for the rich people living nearby and the other leading to the woods. I felt a peace of mind I hadn't previously known when I walked under the tall elm trees. I could hear the roar of the Connecticut River, which runs parallel to the path and marks the border between New Hampshire and Vermont to the north and the west. I became more inquisitive about the origins of names when I lived in New Hampshire. I learned that Connecticut means "upon the long river," and it transpired that Occom was a Mohican man who lived in the late eighteenth century, converted to Christianity, and became a missionary. He was the first Native American to have a book published in English. Several times I heard woodpeckers tapping their messages on the bark of trees. But the most beautiful sight was that of the small family of deer that I once saw and that reminded me of Wadood's manuscript and of the gazelle and the prey. The mother doe was standing between two deer, and behind them stood a stag with big antlers. The doe moved her right ear, which was edged in white. I stopped moving as soon as I saw them. I wondered what they were doing here. And then I realized that they were no doubt asking the same question. The mother flicked her white tail, and then the family ran off into the woods.

A week after the interview the dean in New York called me to offer me the job and negotiate the salary with me.

Two days after I arrived in New York and arranged the apartment, my sister Wafa called me from Greece to congratulate me on the new job. I reminded her of a conversation we had had about a quarter of a century earlier back at home in Baghdad. I may have been eleven years old at the time. We were drinking tea and eating cookies. "When I grow up I want to live in Paris or New York," I told her.

"These are dreams and delusions. You have to be realistic," she replied.

"I never said any such thing!" she said on the phone.

"Oh yes you did. I remember it very well," I replied.

"Oof, Nameer. Why do you keep rummaging in the past? Even if I did say that, it was because I wanted to protect you from disappointment."

"It doesn't matter. I forgive you. But if your young son has any dreams, encourage him and don't bludgeon him on the head with talk about being realistic."

"No problem," she said; "so now that you have a doctorate you're going to teach us how to bring up our children? Anyway, are you going to invite us to come and visit you, or not?"

"You're welcome anytime, come along. But the apartment's not that big. I mean, you'll have to sleep on the floor."

But she still hasn't visited me.

"Each stone he finds, each flower he picks, and each butterfly he catches is already the start of a collection, and every single thing he owns makes up one great collection . . . Only in such a way does a man who is being hanged become aware of the reality of rope and wood."

THE COLLOQUY OF THE WALL

I've been around as long as this house. They put me here, little by little, until my body was complete. They gave me a good coating and then painted my face. I saw them doing the same thing to the three others that stand with me here, to my right and my left and in front of me, and to the fourth one, which rests on our heads. I called out to them so often in the first years and tried to speak to them. Then I gave up when I realized I was speaking to myself. They seem to have been born dead and I'm the only one alive here. Whole days have gone by with me envying them their blindness, their deafness, and their muteness. How I wish the tedium that surrounds me would draw a sword and kill my ability to see and hear everything, because I'm tired of this burden. And I'm tired of the emptiness, loneliness, and waiting.

His mother is the only person who hasn't tired of waiting. Even his father stopped coming here two years ago. He came back twice after their son disappeared but I haven't seen him for a while now. His mother, on the other hand, doesn't stay away for more than a few days or weeks. Then she turns up again, opens the door opposite me, and turns the light on. Then she comes to the window on my left and draws back the curtains so that the sunlight can come in and spread some warmth. She opens the windows and the room can breathe a little. She walks around, inspecting things and tidying up as if her son were about to come back. Sometimes she whispers to herself, "It could do with a cleaning." So she brings a broom and sweeps up the dust that has accumulated, that's waiting on the ground. It's as if, with the dust, she's sweeping away any doubt over whether the son will return. Then she brings a bucket full of water and a piece of cloth. She starts wiping the dust off the small table, the wardrobe, and the windows. And off the mirror that his father hung on my forehead many years ago. She comes up to it, wipes it carefully, then sets it straight. I look into the blackness of her tired eyes waiting behind her big glasses, but she can't see me. She has grown old and her hair is turning gray. The years have taken their usual toll on her forehead, hands, and the corners of her eyes. But all these years have not succeeded in stripping her of her faith that he will return.

I would hear her come in at night from time to time and sleep alone in his bed. I could hear his father calling her, but she wouldn't reply. Or she would say, "I'm here sleeping. Let me be" and I could hear her crying. I remember how she used to sleep with him in the bed when he was still a child. She would sing to him. How she suffered weaning him. He resisted the nipple on the bottle with incessant crying. He pushed it away angrily with his hands. Sometimes she was forced to compromise and give him her own nipple to keep him quiet.

Although I didn't suckle him or hug him or kiss him, I did at least keep watch over him all those years. My eyes observed him asleep and awake. When he played and when he studied. They stayed up late with him and watched over him at night when everyone was asleep. My eyes watched him grow up. And like his mother, I would say goodbye to him when he stood in front of the mirror before going out.

When he began to wear khaki, he started to stay away often, but he would come back once a month. The last time I saw him was before that devastating winter that almost broke my back. Since then his mother and I have been waiting.

His mother was afraid of dying only because she knew it meant she wouldn't be home when her son came home. And now even the house is no longer . . . a house, and I too am no longer a wall.

∾⊙⊚⊙∾

I had to take an early flight back from Saint Paul, Minnesota, to New York after giving a lecture at the University of Minnesota. There was one store selling breakfast and coffee at the airport, and the line was very long. The civilians in the line were a minority. The rest were soldiers who seemed to be on their way to the fronts in Iraq or Afghanistan. Apparently this was their first deployment and they had just finished their training. I know what troops coming back from the front look like. They are tired and wasted, like broken machines. I had seen the maps of death and destruction in Iraq on the faces of those coming back from the fronts during the war with Iran.

Most of these were white men from poor backgrounds, with some blacks and Latinos. I realize that most of them were also victims of the massive machine of inequality, exploitation, and discrimination administered by the new Rome. Some of them still showed traces of innocence in their faces. But they would soon master the roles they had to perform. One of them was holding the metal rail with his right hand as he waited in line. He was moving his index finger backward and forward as if he were pulling a trigger. Had he started shooting Iraqis already?

I go back to the past and sleep on the path on which time marches, in order to make it stop and change direction.

Wadood's catalog introduced me to the most beautiful woman I've ever met. I was sitting on the eastern side of Washington Square Park at midday one Thursday. I was waiting for the jazz trio that plays there three times a week. I loved to listen to them, especially the excellent trumpeter. My notebook with the catalog was in my bag. I took it out to leaf through it, reread the Colloquy of the Christ's Thorn Tree and then one of Wadood's letters to me. Her voice interrupted me: "Excuse me. Is that script Persian?"

When I looked up and turned toward the voice to my right, I saw her face. I already knew her. She had short black hair. Her eyes were brown and her lips full. She was wearing a black leather jacket and a green blouse with very large collars. She was eating a salad from a plastic container on her lap. She had long nails painted in different colors and designs.

"No, it's Arabic," I said.

"It's very beautiful."

"Thank you."

I had thought that the days when books or newspapers in Arabic elicited complimentary comments from strangers were long gone, never to return. An air hostess on a plane had once said, "What pretty shapes the letters have. I wish I could learn it."

But all that changed after 9/11. The looks of curiosity mixed with admiration changed into ones of apprehension and suspicion. Like many Arabs, I unconsciously started to avoid carrying Arabic books with me when I traveled by plane, and took only books in English instead. New York might be an exception, of course.

"Is it your language?" she asked.

It was a simple question, but at that moment it acquired a certain depth that I hadn't previously thought of. Was it my language? We're used to saying "my mother tongue" or "my first language," but "my language"? Mine? I didn't want to sound more academic than necessary. Although I had doubts that any language, as I imagined it in its entirety, could be the property of any one individual, I said, "Yes." Then I remembered where I had seen her face before. "You work at the coffee shop on Bleecker Street, don't you?" I said with a smile.

"Yes. My name's Mariah."

"Mariah. Your name has a nice meaning in Arabic. I'm Nameer."

"I know. Someone once told me that, but my family didn't know that. I'm Mariah, like Mariah Carey. And what does your name mean?"

"Fresh water."

"Nice."

"Your name's nicer."

She laughed, looked at her watch and added, "Sorry. I have to go back to work. Lunch break's over. Sorry."

She wiped her mouth with a paper tissue and then put it in the transparent plastic container beside her. She put a green lid on it and put it in her bag. She smiled and said, "I enjoyed the chat, Nameer. See you."

"Me too."

I watched her walk away toward the street. Did she really mean it when she said, "See you"?

The moment has white walls and its ceiling is a screen on which we can see the lives and memory of the moment. Every moment was other moments before, but moments seldom remember their previous lives. There's a door in the middle of each wall. I open one of them and see another moment: a device and a sign over it with the words: "To go down and move to another history. Destruction is what will bring us all together. The moment is a wound."

"I'll ask you a question. Do the dead sing?"

The night takes up two thirds of the picture and the darkness takes up the upper half of the girl's gaping mouth, which looks like a cave from which the tongue is trying to escape on the back of a scream. But it will fail of course, because it's small like her and tongues never manage to escape. We can't hear anything because the pic-

ture is deaf and mute: it can't hear anything or make a sound. All
the picture can do—it's not blind—is see how the light and shade
are distributed and where the blocks, the bodies, and the colors are
located. The edge of the circle of light touches the girl's nose and
lights up half of her face, showing the right side with red tears running down from her right eye. Her eyes are half-closed and they are
outside the main circle of light. The ends of her brown hair are invisible against the night. She's wearing a gray dress that's too big for
her (maybe it belonged to her elder sister?). It reaches her feet and
is embroidered with red flowers. The floor in front of her is gray. It
might be concrete or asphalt that looks pale because of the strong
light. At the heart of the strongest circle of light there are red spots.
To the left there's a dust-colored army boot treading on the edge of
the circle of light. The front part of the boot is inside the circle and
the rest is outside, but we can see his other foot and his khaki cam-
ouflage jacket. We can see his body up to his thighs, but we can't see
what's above that because it's completely out of the picture. We can
clearly see the barrel of his machine gun and, above it, the source
of the strong light.

I took three ice cubes out of the plastic ice tray to add to the glass
of cold water she had asked for. I didn't have any alcohol. When
I came out of the kitchen carrying the glass of water I found her
transfixed in front of the pictures and clippings that I had hung up
on the wall. I had brought them from Hanover when I came and
had since added many more. She turned when she heard my footsteps approaching. She wiped her eyes with a sweep, then took the

glass of water, thanking me. I asked if she'd been crying. "Maybe" — her favorite, and endearing, answer. It was often the mask that her "yes" or "no" put on. I found this "maybe" genial from the start and saw it as a distinctive aspect of her personality. Then she quickly said, "No, just a speck of dust in my eye." I asked her to sit down, pointing to the sofa. Then I told her I had to use the bathroom. I went into my room, which led to the bathroom. I urinated, and then I decided to soap my face because a greasy layer had gathered on my pores as usual. I dried my face and looked in the mirror before going back. She was sitting on the chair at the table, with her back to the wall where the pictures and clippings were. The glass of water, half-empty, was in her right hand as she looked out of the window at two tall buildings.

"It's a small apartment, but the beautiful view makes up for it," she said.

"Thanks."

"So this is how professors at your university live?" she asked.

"They come in different classes. Those who have lots of books or a family and children live in bigger apartments."

She laughed. "So you'll have to hurry up," she added.

"Hurry up having books published or having children?"

She laughed again. "It's up to you. Which is easier?"

"I don't know, but I'll try my luck with one book at least, or else I'll lose my job."

"Do all these pictures on the wall have something to do with your book?"

"Yes, they do, but not with the academic book. With another project."

"What's that?"

"I don't know exactly."

"If you don't like to talk about your book I won't ask again."

"No, believe me, I don't know exactly. I'm still collecting material and trying to find my way. Seriously, I don't know."

"Does it have anything to do with the man you met in Baghdad that you told me about?"

"Yes, in a way. I wanted to write a book about him and his project. But I've been too busy finishing my academic book for the past two years. Anyway, he refused to let me write about him and he asked me to postpone the project."

"Does he have to agree?"

"No, but I wanted to use his real name and details of his life."

"Hmmm. And have you finished your academic book?"

"I still have one chapter that will take me two or three months."

"Excellent."

"And what about you?"

"What about me? I'm not a writer."

"Are you a musician?"

"No, I'm a listener. I studied history and decided to take a year or two to think about my next step."

THE COLLOQUY OF THE OUD

I don't have a name. My father gave numbers to my brothers who were born after me. But I don't have a number, because I was the first. I have no father other than my father. And I

have more than one mother. One in India and another in
the mountains of Kurdistan. I know how I was born. Not because I observed my own birth, but because I observed all my
brothers being born, one after another, the way I was born. All
of them were copies of me, with slight differences, because
we were born in the same spot and were made by the same
hand. Our frames are the same, but some of my brothers have
ribs made of beech or sandalwood, or a mixture of the two.
The ribs of some others are made of mahogany or walnut.
My ribs are made of Indian rosewood, as my father always repeated whenever he referred to me.

I saw my father making my brothers. Many times I saw
him laying out the ribs and putting them in place one after
the other. He took the first rib and put it over a gentle flame.
He bent it and arched it carefully. Then he laid it in the
middle of the mold, which looked like the belly of a pregnant
woman. He fixed the two ends with two pieces of spruce at
the front and the back so that they were attached to the mold.
Then he repeated the process with the other ribs, which lined
up to the right and the left and were stuck to their neighbors
with glue. Then the back was complete and he left it to dry
and stick together.

Then he took a sheet of spruce for the soundboard. He
cut it, sanded it, and fixed the large and smaller rosette sound-
holes in place and inscribed his name—Omar al-Mufti—on
it decoratively. Then he attached the bridge that holds the

ends of the strings. Then he put the soundboard onto the back, sanded its edges, and stuck them together. After that he added the neck, the head, and the pegbox, and installed the fret that the strings pass across. Then he came to the strings, which he tied and pulled tight, and then he tuned it.

This is the first moment of my life that I remember. When I felt his fingers strumming my strings when he had finished me. He was alone in this shop of his. He played me for two hours. Then he kissed me as if I were his loved one, parked me on the chair, and sat looking at me as he drank his tea, as he often did. He seemed proud of his handiwork. He spoke to me as if I were human, saying, "I'm not going to sell you. You bring me beginner's luck and I see you as a good omen, so you'll stay with me."

I've watched him breathing life into my brothers all these years. With a mixture of joy and sadness. Every brother would leave sooner or later. Musicians would come and point to my brothers and my father would hand them to them. They would play them and bargain over the price and another brother would leave without me seeing him again. And I would be left alone with my father.

But he hasn't been here for three days now.

I had enough coffee to last two weeks, but I deliberately went to the Puerto Rico Importing Company store three days after meeting Mariah in the park. When I went in, the young white woman I usually see there was grinding coffee for a customer. I guessed that Mariah might be in the storeroom inside getting something. I walked between the rows of large sacks containing types of coffee from remote and exotic places. From Indonesia and the Philippines to Tanzania, Burundi, Jamaica, and Brazil. There were delicious varieties flavored with hazelnut, chocolate and vanilla, or orange, with various degrees of roasting. I had tried many of them. Sometimes I was attracted just by the name. Once I bought a coffee only because it was called Fragrance of Heaven. I had read that it came from forests at very high elevations above sea level. I usually buy half a pound of each kind. Sometimes I'm seduced by the story of the coffee and the changes it has undergone. Like Monsoon Malabar, which in British colonial times was shipped to Europe from the Malabar coast in southwest India in wooden sailing ships on a long journey around the Cape of Good Hope. The coffee matured from the effect of the moisture and the tropical sea breezes over months and acquired a special texture and taste. After the Suez Canal opened, the voyage was shorter and the coffee lost its flavor. But coffee companies have devised a new way of curing the coffee and storing it until the tropical monsoon winds arrive and then exposing it to the moist monsoon breezes by storing the beans in ventilated warehouses. I breathe deep its aroma when I grind it in my kitchen and think back to stories of its journeys.

I didn't know or like coffee before I left Iraq. We used to drink tea, which I still like. But I stopped drinking it after I left home. I didn't approve of teabags, and for some reason I wasn't inclined to make a whole pot of tea for one person. For me tea was still a family drink to be drunk with family or with friends in a public place, while coffee was a drink for individuals and sustenance for late nights and solitude. Taste and aroma are important to me, and I started looking for high-quality varieties of coffee. My years in California helped me develop my taste. I heard the young white woman say goodbye to the customer. She came up to me and asked whether I needed any help. I told her I wasn't looking for anything in particular. Then I added, "Is Mariah here?" "No, she doesn't work on Saturdays," she replied. Disappointed, I looked at all the various mugs and cups and espresso machines on display in a corner of the store. I'd have to wait till the beginning of the next week. I thanked the woman and left. I went to Café Dante nearby to read a book about the life of Walter Benjamin and the archive he collected.

In a dream two days ago I again thought I was a bulbul, but the cage I was in was someone else's bones, maybe yours. A voice in the distance was saying, "Fly away. The sky's nearby." I could hear my heart beating like a giant drum. But in order to fly away I had to rip your lungs and kill you. I stayed, hesitant and uncertain what to do.

"Your apartment is a mass grave!" she said, looking at the wall again.

"Does that mean I'm dead?"

"No, you're alive. But it's like you're guarding the dead."

"You know that I really like cemeteries?"

"Why?"

"I don't know. I like the symmetry of the gravestones and the green grass. The names and the dates inscribed on the stones. I feel at peace there. When I was in Boston I visited one of the most beautiful cemeteries in the country at Mount Auburn. You have to visit it one day."

"I'm beginning to worry that you might be a vampire."

I laughed out loud.

"I am a creature of the night. I like to kiss necks and bite them gently or sometimes not so gently, but I'm not a vampire."

She laughed flirtatiously.

I saw myself living in a faraway country, where everything was clean and tidy. A quiet life without wars, sects, or religions. Immigrants and refugees had all the rights and freedoms that humans could dream of. Even animals were respected and had rights. Science and technology were so developed that human beings could travel to the future or to the past, to visit or to stay, provided of course that they were adults and in good health and didn't have a criminal record. Even as I dreamed I knew I was dreaming, because I had lied on the application form. I wrote that I had never been in prison and that I didn't have any health problems. I signed the form without hesitation. I also knew I was dreaming because I was speaking their language fluently. Even the blond civil servant, who reminded me of an actress I had once seen in a sad Swedish film, whose character died at the end of it, said, "You have completely mastered our language. How did you get rid of your accent?" I laughed of course and said, "Thanks for the compliment. It's thanks to your schools." They carried out many rigorous tests with modern devices in a clean hospital where classical music was playing everywhere, and the nurses smiled with maternal tenderness. I was worried I might fail the medical tests, but I passed. They would let me travel only in one direction, into either the future or the past. On their website there was a message saying that the Ministry of Time was currently studying the possibility of allowing citizens in the future to travel in both directions. I wasn't interested in the future, of course.

I think that people are divided into two types: those who escape from the past and those who escape to the past.

Is life also an unwritten novel in which dozens of major and minor characters live? (Wadood says we are books or manuscripts.) When I saw one particular man for the hundredth time perhaps, it occurred to me that life is a novel of phenomenal size that can neither end nor be written in full. I don't know his name and I might never know it. I see him almost every day, sometimes more than once in the same day, but I have never spoken to him. Although I want to know his story, I don't want to disturb him. The only time I said anything to him was some months ago in the Wendy's on Broadway

close to the university. I was on my way back from one of my long
roams and I had to take a piss and couldn't wait till I got back to my
apartment. I went into the restaurant and headed for the bathroom.
I saw him there approaching the door of the men's bathroom from
the other side, with a thick paper cup in his hand. We reached the
door at almost the same moment. Maybe he beat me by a fraction
of a second. The indicator under the door handle showed red so
we stood waiting our turns. He leaned against the wall and began
shaking the empty cup and looking inside it, as if he were checking
that a die that no one else could see was there. Then he rolled out
the invisible die from the cup to the floor, and then he repeated
the process. He avoided looking straight at me or at anyone else.
In fact, he seemed to be looking into the distance. *Avoid* is not the
right word here. I don't think he was interested in anyone else anyway. I never saw him trying to speak to anyone or ask for anything,
as most homeless people do. Except for coffee and water, and even
those he obtained from the nearby cafés without speaking. He was
wearing what he usually wore at that time of year: a khaki shirt half-
open at the chest and sleeves that reached to his elbows. He had
loose, longish trousers of the same color. The hems were frayed and
blackened from being stepped on. He was wearing black rubber
sandals that showed his socks, which were black most of the time.
He carried a small gray bag made of rough cloth. He was very tall,
like an old spear, and his hair was braided in the Rastafarian style,
held together by a large black woolen hat that reminded me of Bob
Marley's hat. So for a long time I thought he was of Jamaican origin. His eyes were brown and full of a serene and mellow sadness.
His nose was prominent over a thick mustache and beard. He didn't

take much care of his appearance. But three or four times I had seen him cross-legged on the ground near the heating grate on Greene Street, holding a small round mirror and a pair of tweezers, with which he was plucking some of the excess hairs on his cheek.

I heard the sound of water in the basin, then the whine of the hand dryer, and then the sound of the door being unlocked. The indicator turned from red to green. The door opened and a blond young man rushed out wearing a Miami Heat basketball shirt, apologizing for taking so long. "After you," I said to the other man who was waiting. But with the hand holding the cup and without looking at me, he signed that I should go before him. "After you, please. You were here before me," I said. He shook his head and waved me in again. When I came out he was still standing there. I thanked him and smiled, but he didn't say anything as he made his way inside. I would have asked him his name, but I was certain he wouldn't answer.

He always walked alone. He had nothing to do with the gatherings of homeless people who sit on the benches close to the library or sometimes on the side opposite the Think Coffee shop. He didn't squat or sleep in front of the soup kitchen on Mercer Street. He didn't stand in line to take one of the meals offered to the poor and the homeless inside. On cold winter days he wrapped up in a dark green blanket and slept on the sidewalk on Greene Street on the big ventilation grating that blows up warm air. He walked at a leisurely pace, speaking to himself quietly in a low voice, always in Spanish and not English. He sometimes got excited in his arguments with himself or with the demons he was fighting. He would raise his right hand to emphasize some point he was making, but that hadn't happened often in the past year since I started watching him. I never saw him shout or quarrel with anyone.

Once I was having a coffee with a colleague in the Pane e Cioccolato café at the intersection of Waverly Place and Mercer Street, and we saw him walking toward Broadway along the pavement outside the café. "There's that elitist homeless man," I said out loud.

"Why do you say that?" asked my colleague, who was from Puerto Rico.

"Because he never talks to anyone. He doesn't mix with the other homeless people."

"Yes of course, because he's still at war somewhere far away."

"What do you mean?"

"I'm sure he fought in Panama during the American invasion. I hear him mumbling in Spanish. He says things about Panama. I was standing behind him in line to buy coffee from the Delion deli once, and I heard him talking as if the battle was still raging. Haven't you seen the dog tag around his neck? It has his army number and rank."

"What was his rank? Did you speak with him?"

"I said hi to him and spoke to him in Spanish. I asked him if he needed any help."

"And what did he say?"

"Fuck off!"

I laughed and he smiled. "In Spanish or in English?"

"In Spanish. There's one phrase he often repeats."

"What's that?"

"Estoy aquí."
"And what does that mean?"
"I'm here."

I'm here.
We're here.

"Memory is not an instrument for exploring the past but its theater. It is the medium of past experience, as the ground is the medium in which dead cities lie interred. He who seeks to approach his own buried past must conduct himself like a man digging. . . . Above all, he must not be afraid to return again and again to the same matter, to scatter it as one scatters earth, to turn it over and over as one turns over soil."

I don't remember a time when I didn't write. Ever since I learned to write letters and words I've been writing incessantly. Even before that I often used to scribble. All children scribble, but my grandmother, who died before I was eight, used to say she had never seen a child who scribbled as much as I did. She even called me Scribblekins. How I loved forming the words on the lines in my school exercise books. I'd finish all my homework as soon as I got home from school, even before having lunch. The exercise books weren't enough. I would write on any scrap of paper I found anywhere. The walls were also like wonderful pieces of paper that enticed me to write. I'd fill them as far as I could standing up, then bring a chair to climb onto and fill the spots I couldn't reach otherwise. The consequences were dire. My father scolded me and punished me several times because I'd covered the walls at home with sentences written in pencil. A vicious slap brought an end to my "wall phase." My cheek was red for hours. My sister was frightened and cried, although she didn't write on the walls like I did. My father broke the pencil in my hand and gave me a warning: "I'll break your hand like I broke your pencil if you scribble again. Understood?" Then he warned my mother, who came running to protect me from his anger: "I don't want to see a single word on the walls ever again. Do you understand? It looks like your son will turn out to be an 'arzahalchy." As usual my mother tried to calm him down. She wiped away my tears that day, kissed me, and whispered, "Come on, never mind. Tomorrow I'll take you to the Saray market and buy you notebooks and pencils. Write as much as you like, my love, but not on the wall, my son, please." "What's an 'arzahalchy?" I asked her. "Someone who sits outside the courts and writes out legal documents for people," she said.

Two days later two men came and painted all the walls a slightly yellowish white. All my words disappeared under a sticky layer with a smell that hung around the house for a week, as if to keep me away.

My mother fulfilled her promise to me, took me to the Saray market and bought me a dozen notebooks, a bunch of pencils, pencil sharpeners, and scented colored erasers. As we were about to leave the market, I heard a bird singing. I looked for the source of the sound and found it was coming from a cage hanging outside one of the shops. I went up to the cage and saw a bird that looked as if it was wearing a multicolored dress at a costume party. Its face was mottled red, black, and white. The top of its head was black, its breast feathers were white with a sandy-colored edging. Its wings were a mixture of yellow and black. It seemed happy that I was interested in it. The shopkeeper noticed I was standing in front of the cage. "What is it, sir?" I asked him. "That's a goldfinch, my boy," he said. Its voice enchanted me, and I insisted that my mother buy me one. "They have them at the Ghazil market if you want one," the shopkeeper said. I noticed that my mother was hesitant, and I pretended I was about to cry. "Please, mom, please," I said.

"Okay, my dear, okay."

We walked to the Ghazil market, which was full of cats and dogs and all kinds of birds, all of them waiting in cages. My mother asked about goldfinches and we found a man who sold them inside the market. My mother negotiated with the salesman over the price of a bird and cage while I busied myself inspecting my new friend. I heard her asking him what it would eat and how to look after it. I wanted to carry the little cage myself but I wasn't strong enough, so my mother carried it. She stopped a taxi to take us home. She put the cage between herself and me on the back seat. We hung it up in the corridor between the kitchen and the sitting room, close to the big window. We would take the cage out and put it on the veranda in the afternoons. When my father came home that day, he heard the goldfinch singing before he saw it. He liked the sound but he shook his head and said to my mother, "You're going to spoil the boy. That's not good."

I started sitting near the cage to do my homework, and I read and filled my notebooks with stories as the goldfinch sang. My sister Wafa was envious because I told her the goldfinch was mine and mine alone.

I wrote down everything. The names of people, cities, and countries and all the new words I learned every day. The words of songs and poems. Useful and useless phrases, which were the most beautiful. Everything that happened to me and around me at school, in the street, and at home. Even things that hadn't happened and could never happen, and things that should happen. Now I know that I was writing for the sake of writing, and maybe to eliminate the divide between the real and the imaginary, or to leave it open. When I was ten, I started a weekly magazine that I wrote out by hand. I handed out the seven copies to the children in our street during the summer vacation.

I wanted everyone to read what I wrote. I would give it

to my mother, who read it and smiled. "Well done, clever boy," she said. My father would sometimes be pleased, but he found it strange that I could write such nonsense. But this desire gradually diminished when I was in secondary school. I don't know why. Maybe because I began to appreciate the importance of literature and of writing as an act. Apart from contributing to the bulletins that were put up on the school walls and writing in composition classes, I no longer showed other people anything I was writing. I started to keep my notebooks to myself. As time passed I developed a powerful aversion to the idea of writing itself. I started to be frightened by the blankness of the paper and to worry that what I wrote would be unworthy. I tore up my notebooks and threw the overwhelming majority of them into the trash. I no longer thought I would necessarily be a writer. In the first lecture in the first year of university the lecturer who taught us literary criticism asked us, "Which of you write? Poetry or prose?" I was surprised at the hands that went up. There were more than thirty students in our section and half of them wrote? I didn't put my hand up that day and I didn't say anything. I was following everything that was published in the newspapers and the literary magazines and I read voraciously, but I didn't try to have anything published. I don't regret that I didn't have a single piece of writing published throughout those years, or even up to now.

My correspondence with Wadood was interrupted for about a year and a half. But I thought about him from time to time and went back to his catalog and browsed through it. I was busy teaching and finishing my dissertation, since my contract with Dartmouth College stipulated that I had to complete it within a year and a half. It gave me no great pleasure when I submitted my dissertation, defended it, and was awarded the doctorate after all those years. The title didn't interest me in the first place. I don't deny I felt that a heavy weight had been lifted off my shoulders. But I also felt empty and sad. Ali Hadi, who held a dinner in his house to celebrate my graduation, said it was a natural feeling, similar to postpartum depression. "Whenever you finish a major project that has lasted years and on which you have worked so hard, you're going to feel that way. There's no escaping it," he said.

Four months after I moved to my new job at New York University I found a large envelope in my mailbox at the university. I knew from the address that it was from the department where I used to teach at Dartmouth College. When I opened it, I found a letter from the secretary saying that a large number of personal letters from Iraq had been piling up at my college address in the past few weeks. He enclosed them all and asked me to inform my friends of my change of address. I knew from the handwriting on the envelopes that they were all from Wadood. Naturally I was surprised. I opened the envelopes and read the contents one after another as I sat in my office. But surprisingly, they were not in fact letters, and most of them didn't include any greetings or remarks addressed to me or any signature, and they were undated. In some of the texts Wadood narrated beautifully a sequence of events that had happened to him, sometimes with an internal rhythm. I was delighted as I read them, and I thought that perhaps he had accepted my request and now wanted to help me write the novel about him, although he had been evasive when I broached the subject with him. But most of the other texts were fragments of poetry and musings written on scraps of paper. Four of them were incomprehensible ramblings. I put the envelopes in a box that I set aside for Wadood's envelopes and added the writings to the notebook, to be with the catalog. I was unsure how to reply. Two days later I wrote to him to say I had received and read his writings, which had arrived late because I had moved to another city. I asked him not to hesitate to send me more of his writings and in the future to send what he wrote to my address in New York.

This is my memory with all its treasures, and with all the destruction in it, laid out before you. Take what you want.

Little by little I started going into the building through the service entrance at the back and using the service elevator to reach my office on the fifth floor. This elevator was used less than the main ones, which were crowded with students and faculty. But I realized that I had started to prefer it for other reasons, such as avoiding meaningless courtesies and annoying conversations. Once, for example, two weeks before spring break, a colleague got into the ele-

vator and asked me, "Are you going back to Baghdad for the break?"
Her question stunned me. The news reports for the previous few
weeks had been saturated with images of corpses and explosions,
and a civil war was raging. She knew I was from Baghdad because
she was on the search committee that approved my hiring, but apparently she had forgotten that I had left Iraq in 1993. In silence I
cursed the gods and the universe and said calmly, "No, I'm staying
in New York. I have things I have to finish." "Ah, work never ends. I
know how it is. Try to enjoy the break anyway." "You too," I replied.
This conversation persuaded me to abandon the main elevator. The
service elevator was empty most of the time. Sometimes the jani-
tors and maintenance workers used it, and most of those were mi-
norities. We smiled and exchanged greetings without feigning any
fake interest in each other. Sometimes, especially at night, I would
find myself alongside transparent trash bags full of the paper that
was gathered from the trash bins, and I thought of the ink and all
the words that would be buried in the landfills.

In a dream he again thought he was in a cage made of human
bones. He thought he was a bird. Then he discovered he was
a heart and in order to fly he would have to rip a lung and kill
the owner of the cage. He was hesitant and unsure what to do.

I sneak into Wadood's catalog and hide my dismembered body
parts and my ramblings in the folds of his first minute. I extend it.

You think a moment is but a small speck, but it encapsulates an entire world.

As usual I arrived a quarter of an hour early. Ever since I had moved to New York, and especially to the Village, everything was close to my apartment and I could walk there in a quarter of an hour— my office, the university library, the café, the restaurants, the jazz club, the park, the market, the university health center, and even the funeral parlor were all no more than ten minutes' walk away. Only the cemetery was a little far, outside the city, because the city was crowded with living people. I stood in front of the building entrance on Lafayette Street. The facade was made of red stone and it was built about seventy years ago (the date was carved on a stone above the entrance), but it looked as if it had been recently renovated. I looked for the name of the doctor, Sarah Friedman, on the brass plate with buzzers. I found the name and pressed the button next to it. Her voice said "Yes" through the speaker. I gave my name and heard the buzz that let me in. I had booked the appointment online through the health insurance website. I had read some reviews whose authors had praised the doctor and the way she treated her patients. I took the elevator to the fourth floor and pressed another button to the right of the office door and heard a buzz that was less jarring than the buzz at the front door. I opened the door and went into a large windowless waiting room with plush leather chairs in the middle and soft lighting. The wooden floor creaked audibly when you walked across it. I sat down on one of the chairs and checked out the magazines that were on a table. I chose an issue of the *New Yorker* and looked at the cartoons. There wasn't enough time to read a whole article. There were four doors to four offices, all of them shut. I didn't know which of them I was headed for. Two minutes later the door on the far left opened and I saw a young man come out of the office, followed by a bald man in his mid-fifties who said, "See you next week." I went back to the cartoons after exchanging a quick glance with the young man, who looked like one of those people who work on Wall Street. He was wearing a smart gray suit and a red necktie and carrying a small leather briefcase. He hurried out.

A while later another door opened on the right, and a woman in her twenties with long hair came out. She was wearing a black skirt and black boots that went up to just below her knees. I had the impression that she was drying tears with a handkerchief. Another woman I couldn't make out because of the sunlight streaming through a large window in the office came to the doorway and said goodbye to her. The young woman walked to the main door without a glance back. "Mr. Baghdadi?" said the woman in the office. I put the magazine back on the table and made my way into her office. She shut the door behind me and gestured to me to sit down to the left on a leather sofa big enough for two. She sat opposite on a chair of the same kind, with a low wooden table between us. On the table there was a square wooden bowl holding dried flowers around a large white candle. I had a quick exploratory look around her office while she sat down. The walls were a calm off-white. The room had a high ceiling, as in old buildings. There was a framed print of one of Miró's paintings on the wall opposite me. Her certificates were framed in dark wood. To the left was a large window that welcomed the sun and under it a small bookcase with files and psychology books. She put a laptop on her lap and asked me for a health insurance card, which I handed to her. She entered the information into the laptop. She was in her early forties. Her hair was light brown and shoulder-length. Her eyes were green and her complexion was fair and clear. Her fingernails were long but not painted and she had no rings. She was wearing a black V-necked blouse, a silver necklace, and a green skirt that showed the upper parts of her thighs when she sat down. She's attractive, I said to myself as she entered the information, and if I get bored during the session I can at least enjoy the view. Her breasts were still pert, with no signs of aging, I thought to myself as she reached out to give me my card back. Then I remembered those deceptive push-up bras and how widespread they are these days. She put the laptop on a small side table on her right and retrieved a large notepad. She opened it and picked up the black pen that was inside it.

"Okay, how can I help you, Mr. Baghdadi? Why are you here?"

"Because my girlfriend told me I should try therapy."

"Aha, that isn't a good start—coming here because of someone else. You have to be convinced that you need treatment."

After a moment's silence, I said, "If I wasn't partially convinced, I wouldn't have come."

"Why do you think your girlfriend urged you to start therapy?"

"She says I'm severely depressed and that I have posttraumatic stress disorder."

"Do you agree with her? What do you think?"

"Millions of people are depressed. That's the price we pay for living in this world."

"You didn't answer my question. Are you depressed?"

"Yes, I've definitely been depressed for many years, but I don't want to take any pills."

"Therapy doesn't necessarily mean pills. Talking can help."

"I talk to myself all the time. Anyway, I'm tired of talking. I talk a lot in lectures to students and that's enough."

"But talking here, with me in particular, is different."

"We'll see."

"Here you can say everything and anything without any consequences and without any censorship."

"What about self-censorship?"

"You'll overcome that gradually. Do you think your depression has grown worse recently?"

"Maybe."

"How?"

"I feel drained emotionally and existentially, and 'nothing pleases me,' as a poet I like very much once said. This isn't new but it's intensified recently."

"Can you say more?"

"I carry out my basic tasks as required in my work. I teach and I grade students' papers and I attend boring meetings. But I don't interact with people, or I avoid that as much as possible, except with my girlfriend, of course. I neglect lots of things. I don't open my mailbox and I let letters and bills pile up for no reason. With emails

I answer only urgent ones. I take the service elevator to avoid silly conversations with my colleagues in the main elevator. I prefer to be alone, and all I do when I'm alone is binge watch films and follow the news, of course, unfortunately. But I've stopped reading books, even novels. I read the newspapers, of course, and sometimes poetry. I've been trying to write a novel for years, but I haven't written more than a few stupid pages. I have terrible insomnia. I fulfill my responsibilities when it's related to others, but I neglect everything that's related to me personally."

"Believe it or not, and I don't mean to belittle your sufferings in any way, but your situation is not extreme."

"I know. That's why I was hesitant to come in the first place. Because these are trivial bourgeois problems that happen to many people. There are famines and wars and . . ."

She interrupted me: "No, they're not trivial. The suffering is real and applies to everyone regardless of what's happening in the rest of the world. But the most important thing is that you don't try to play my role or usurp it. Let me decide and judge. Can you take off your university professor's hat when you're here?"

"I'll try."

She asked me whether my relationship with my family was healthy. I told her I hadn't spoken to my father for more than a decade, that my mother was dead, and that I spoke to my younger brother and my sister on the phone once every month or two. She said we ought to focus on my relationship with my father in the next session.

"I'm sorry but our time is running out and I have another patient in five minutes. We can continue, but I want to know

whether you'll make a commitment to come once a week. I'd prefer that you come on the same day and time every week. It's important that it becomes a fundamental part of your life."

THE COLLOQUY OF THE POW

Hasan al-Aseer, or Hasan the prisoner of war, whose real
name was Hasan Jasim al-Lahhaf, was born in the Khan
Lawand district in the al-Fadil area of Baghdad in 1892. He
worked with his father and his brothers sewing quilts. He
is said to have had a fine voice since he was young. He fell
in love with the kind of music known as *maqam*. Credit
for discovering his talent should go to the famous maqam
singer Ahmad al-Zaidan, who was visiting Hasan's father's
shop to buy a quilt in 1903. He heard the boy singing and
was stunned by his melodious and powerful voice. He asked
whether he would like to learn the elements of maqam, and
the boy was delighted. But his father dismissed the idea and
scolded him when he brought up the subject later. Hasan
began to frequent the Majid Karkar coffeehouse in al-Fadil,
which was owned by Zaidan and was a meeting place for
maqam performers. He would sit cross-legged outside the
coffeehouse to listen to them. One day his father was passing
by and saw him there. He was angry and beat the boy and told
him to go back home. His father's punishments and threats to
throw him out in the street failed to deter him from visiting

the coffeehouse. Zaidan's heart went out to him when he saw him crying one day, and he asked what the matter was. When he heard about the boy's problems with his father, he offered to find him a job and persuaded the tea maker to take him as an assistant in the coffeehouse. Hasan's father was angry at first and threw him out of the house, and Hasan slept a few days in the coffee shop. But his mother managed to persuade his father to let him come back home, on condition that Hasan give them his earnings to make up for no longer working with his father.

During those years working in the coffee shop, Hasan took in the various modes of maqam music and learned the principles behind the system. He learned from Zaidan, Reuben ibn Rajwan, and Salih Abu Damiri. Zaidan took an interest in him because he sensed that he had exceptional talent. He began to take him along to his concerts and encouraged him to perform. Hasan al-Aseer sang maqam for the first time in a concert in 1912, when Zaidan was ill and asked him to take his place. He proved himself, and after that his name rose to prominence among maqam aficionados to such an extent that he rivaled Rashid al-Qundarchi and surpassed his master.

After the First World War broke out and the Ottomans joined the Germans, a general mobilization was declared. Al-Aseer tried to escape the war and hid in an orchard in al-Silaykh. But the authorities detained three of his brothers and told his family that they wouldn't release them until he gave himself up. He handed himself in and was taken off with others to fight the Russians. The train took them to Samarra, and from there they walked for many weeks until they reached the front, in the Caucasus Mountains. He saw most of those who fought alongside him die of cold and hunger. He didn't die himself, but he lost his sight as a result of an injury. The Russians captured him, and he stayed in Russia for five years before coming back to Baghdad. His father had died while he was in captivity, and his brothers had inherited the quilting business. The maqam people welcomed him back from captivity and invited him to sing. His voice was as fine as ever and had in fact acquired a huskiness that made it richer. But he had not come back alone. It was clear that the war and its ghosts had come with him and were still pursuing him. He drank too much when he sang, and he would shout and swear and have fights with imaginary people, then cry like a child. The invitations dried up and most of his friends shunned him, apart from a joza player called Salih Shameel. Hasan shut himself up in a room at home and cut himself off from the world. In 1925 Butrus and Gabriel Baida, the owners of the Baidaphon company, started recording Iraqi singers on gramophone records and marketing them under the Ghazal label. Their agent in Baghdad heard about al-Aseer's voice, but some people warned him that the man was an alcoholic and prone to frequent tantrums. Salih Shameel played in a troupe that accompanied maqam singers. He lied to the agent and assured him that al-Aseer hadn't drunk arak for two years and that he would do a recording without creating any problems, and the agent agreed. Then Salih had to persuade al-Aseer, who was in the depths of depression, to do the recording. At first he refused, especially as one of the conditions was that he should stop drinking for a week. Salih kept pressing him and played on his envy by mentioning the names of all the other people who had done recordings. Then al-Aseer warmed to the idea of a record of his voice that would survive even after his bones had turned to dust. He gave up arak temporarily and began to practice, to restore the suppleness of his voice. Salih went with him to the room that had been turned into a recording studio and he did three hours of recordings for them. When he had finished, the recording technician told him the choice would be up to the Baida brothers in Beirut, who wouldn't press records for all the songs. The pressing process was done in a factory in Berlin.

Come give me wine to drink and tell me that it's wine,
Don't give it to me in secret if it can be done in public.
It would be fraud if you were to see me sober,
But when I'm roaring drunk, then it's all for the best!
God now sees us as the worst gang,
Without pride we dragged debauchery by the tail.
Many's the lady publican I've roused from sleep,
After Gemini has set and the Vulture Star has risen.

If you complain of love, you're not one of us.
You bring antipathy and revulsion, you churl.
Arise from sleep and drive away our cares.
How pretty he is when he walks with a swinging gait.
Arise, the birds are up and singing
Shall the doves sing better than us?
You claim to follow the doctrine of pleasure and then
    complain,
Where is your call for pleasure, you churl?
We did not fall in love with you for your attributes, but
We are people who fall in love once we look.
Like a dove you grew tame at night
You became like a gazelle shying away from us.
Whenever the bottle went round our heads spun,
The ignorant reckon we've gone mad.

> (played in *rast* mode)
> Tabla—Shaul Haroun Zangi
> Joza—Salih Shameel
> Qanoun—Azouri Haroun
> Hasan Effendi al-Aseer—Baidaphon Records

Five months later the Baidaphon record reached Hasan
through Salih. He was quite delighted. Hasan felt it and
smelled it and then asked Salih to describe it to him and
read out what was written on it. Salih told him about the
yellow paper sleeve and described to him the gramophone

player and "Baidaphon Records" written in large letters and
under it the words "Beirut, Cairo, Berlin, Butrus and Gabra
Baida." Hasan wasn't interested in that of course, but Salih
was testing his patience. Salih wound up in a dramatic voice:
"Hasan Effendi al-Aseer, 'If You Complain of Pleasure,' a rast
maqam."

"And the other records?" Hasan asked.

"The others are with them."

Hasan was saddened and disappointed, but Salih
cheered him up, saying, "Come on, man, you should be
cheerful. They'll hear you in Cairo and Beirut and Aleppo,
and they sell in Basra too."

He didn't own a gramophone player, so he would put
the record on his lap and sing to it as he drank alone at home.
When Salih bought a gramophone player, he invited Hasan
to his house to listen to himself singing. He had expected to
feel happier than he actually did. That day they listened to
Rashid al-Qundarchi and Muhammad al-Qubbanchi, and
Hasan asked Salih, "Honestly, aren't I better than all of them?
Except that I went blind and had a rough time in captivity."
"If only you'd sober up and stop drinking arak, for God's
sake," Salih replied.

But Hasan didn't give up arak and he died in 1932, hugging a tiny bottle of it, before he was even forty years old. He
never married, and all he left behind him was that recording,
which was the only evidence that he ever passed through this

earth. There were two copies of his songs—one in the Baida-phon office in Berlin and the other in Beirut. Allied bombing in the Second World War destroyed the company's office in Berlin, and the civil war in Lebanon took care of destroying the Beirut archive. The surviving record in Baghdad remained in Hasan's room with his clothes and some other things. When his nephew and his fiancée moved into the room, they put his stuff in a small chest, which they placed in the court-yard. A few months later a junk dealer called at the house and bought the whole box. He sold the clothes to the secondhand clothes dealer, and persuaded the owner of the coffee shop to buy the record. So Hasan's lamentations echoed through the coffee shop when his luck was in—that is, whenever the owner, who insisted on choosing the songs himself, was in the mood to hear him. Then new technologies arrived and forced the earlier ones into retirement. Al-Aseer's lamentations and his gramophone record then disappeared into a box that lan-guished in a storeroom for many years, awaiting the fire that would consume it one fine spring day in the year 2003.

I told the therapist about my mother and how I was the first to dis-cover, by chance, that cancer had spread through her body. I was getting dressed and preparing to go out one evening when I heard her screaming. I rushed to her room and found her shaking violently in bed with her hands in the air. She was frothing large amounts of saliva from her open mouth and her eyes were closed. "Mama, mama, what's wrong with you?" I shouted. I grabbed her rigid arms for some seconds, shook her and tried to hug her. I wiped the saliva off with my shirt sleeve and called on her to wake up from what I thought was a nightmare. Twenty seconds later she opened her eyes and was surprised to find herself in my arms. She said she had gone to bed because she had had a chronic headache that had grown worse in recent weeks, and then she couldn't remember what had happened. Maybe she had had a nightmare. She kissed me on the cheek and apologized, then got up and went to the bathroom to wash her face. I insisted she go to the doctor because her trembling was very unusual. As usual my father played down the importance of the incident. "It's because of the tea you keep drinking," he said. I went to the doctor with her. After some tests the doctor advised an MRI as soon as possible. We went to the hospital and she made me laugh when they laid her on the gurneylike platform that goes into the scanner and stays there about an hour while they take a magnetic image. "What's this?" she said, "It looks like a coffin. So they're training us for death." Two days later the doctor's assistant called and asked us to make an appointment. The doctor asked to speak to me alone first since it was my name written on the form. I could see the fear in my mother's eyes. I realized that this was an exceptional situation. The doctor told me that the cancer had spread through her body and reached her brain. I was stunned because she had had a mastectomy two years earlier and all the subsequent tests had shown that there weren't any malignant cells left. But he said that this does happen, unfortunately. Even when one is in remission from breast cancer, some of the cancer cells lie low and migrate toward other parts of the body. I asked him about the possibilities of treatment, and he said she would have to go into the hospital. He would prescribe radiotherapy and give her some medicines, but the chances of recovery were slight—ten percent. He asked me whether I thought she was ready to hear the news, and I told him she was a strong woman who had lived through much in her life. I went out and asked her to come in. We sat down in front of him and he repeated what he had told me, adding some other details. I had to translate everything for her. "I won't lie to you, madam. The condition is very serious, but the human body is strong, and it can resist and recover." Her eyes teared up and she took a handkerchief out of her handbag to wipe the tears away, but she thanked him and then said to herself and to me, "It's the will of God, and God is merciful." My father's reaction was strange. I read some fear on his face when we told him, but I couldn't detect any real sadness. He kissed her on the forehead and said, "We'll have to tell your family," as if she had already died. After that he started criticizing her for using too many chemicals for cleaning things, as if that had anything to do with it. Her condition deteriorated with surprising rapidity. It was as if the cancer cells, once they had been discovered, no longer tried to hide behind other cells and tissues. During the radiotherapy and after some other tests, it became clear that the cancer had spread to her lungs as well.

My work tutoring Arabic privately as a freelancer allowed me to have a flexible schedule and I had saved up a considerable amount of money, so I stopped teaching temporarily in order to be with her all the time.

My father would come to the hospital after ten in the evening, after he'd finished work managing the gas station. On the first days he would kiss her on the forehead after coming in, but he later made do with just putting his hand on her head. Then he would sit down to watch the television suspended from the ceiling in the left-hand corner of the room. He wouldn't say much, other than his routine questions, or else he would say to me, "Go and have a rest at home if you like."

My sister Wafa wanted to come to join us from Greece, where she had been living since 1989 with her Greek husband, who had been working in the Greek embassy in Baghdad. But the process of obtaining a visa took two months, and when Wafa arrived my mother was almost unconscious because of the morphine they were giving her in her final days. Wafa burst into tears when she stood next to the bed for the first time and saw how frail Mother's body had become and that the cancer cells had spread even into the skin on her face. "That's not Mama," she said, but Mother smiled when she woke up and saw Wafa, then joined her in crying. Half an hour later she said, "Enough, I don't want any crying or weeping. Save the crying for the funeral. I have quite enough to worry about." Wafa started to sleep near her in the hospital and rest at home during the day, while I took her place until six o'clock every afternoon. I had long ridiculed those who say that the dying sense the approach of death. Hours before she died, between two periods of unconsciousness, Mother asked to see my younger brother. "I want to kiss Naseer," she said. I called him on the phone in the room and asked him to come. "Why? What's up?" he asked. "Mama wants to see you. She asked after you," I said. Naseer took the bus and arrived half an hour later. He looked worried, as if he knew too. He had been visiting her only once a week and he was disturbed and emotionally withdrawn, keeping his distance from the situation, and I didn't blame him for that. When he arrived she was asleep and none of us woke her up. We sat down in silence and he squatted on the floor, leaning against the wall with Walkman earphones on his ears. Three quarters of an hour later we heard her say softly, "Where's Naseer?" He jumped up and went over to her. "Come and kiss me, my love. I want to smell you before God takes me back into His care." Her lips were now as pale as thin paper. Wafa sobbed when she saw her embrace Naseer and kiss him. He cried too. Five minutes later the morphine took hold of her again. I took Naseer home and while we were in the car he asked me what we were going to do. "What can we do? We'll wait," I replied. The telephone woke me at five in the morning. Wafa was crying at the other end. "Mama's gone," she said.

We buried her in the Muslim cemetery in Virginia. On the third day of the period of condolences, the number of men paying their respects declined. In the afternoon there was no one but me, my father, and Naseer, who had taken a siesta. I went out for a walk for a while, and when I came back home two of our neighbors' sons were playing soccer in the parking lot. I stopped to watch them and one of them kicked the ball toward me and I kicked it back. They invited me to join the game. I tucked the ends of my trousers into my socks and played with them for half an hour or more, then went back home. My father was looking out of the window of the sitting room but he didn't say anything.

My sister went back to Greece. A month after my mother died my brother Naseer told me that he came home early from school one day and found Father leaving the house with a woman and he suspected she was his lover because it had happened several times. When I asked him how he knew she was Father's lover, he said he had found a packet of condoms in Father's room and he had smelt the woman's perfume in the room and on the bedsheets. I hugged him, ruffled his hair, and tried to console him. "So you're Sherlock Holmes, are you?" I said. I later felt convinced that she was indeed his lover because the pattern was repeated. She was an Indian woman, much younger, who worked in a shop next door to the gas station that he managed. I confronted him. "Do you have no shame? It hasn't even been two months," I shouted. "Don't be so rude. How can you speak to me like that? It's you who should be apologizing to me," he replied angrily. "I apologize? For what?" "Because you played soccer during the condolences." "You're comparing that with this?" "What's 'this'?" "Your Indian whore." "Get the hell out of here and don't come to this house again," he shouted angrily.

THE COLLOQUY OF THE FETUS

It can't see anything, although its eyes are fully formed and it can open them. But they're shut. It can't see anything. But it's dreaming. And it dreams a lot because it spends most of its time sleeping. Its dreams aren't dreams in the traditional sense. In other words, they don't consist of events and they can't be narrated sequentially or even nonsequentially. They are phantasms of pleasures in their raw state. They can't easily be described because they are in a liquid state and haven't yet assumed fixed form. There is of course some pain in dreaming, and in the waking state as well.

It can't see, but it can hear everything. Music has a positive effect on its mood and can speed up or slow down the rate at which its little heart beats. The sound of its mother and of her breathing has the same effect as either music or noise, depending on the mother's mood. Its heart is almost a miniature copy of the mother's heart. They play to the same rhythm. Even in the absence of any external sounds or influences it can hear what sounds like the roar of the sea. It can hear its mother's pulse, too. Her breathing in and breathing out. It'll miss that roar when it's born. But it might try to express it and what went with it in the language it acquires in its early years. The language that will be the only, or maybe the clearest, way to convey everything. There are, however, feelings and desires that language cannot accommodate, that it fails to convey, and that the lips and other organs will handle. But much will remain buried and will come to the surface only in dreams and nightmares.

That's if it had been born!

But it wasn't and won't be born.

Lauren, an MA student whom I was tutoring, noticed that I was worried, and I told her that I needed temporary accommodation.

She said that the woman she lived with was going away for a month and I could stay in her apartment. I lived with Lauren and stayed on in her apartment even after the other woman came back. That was because our relationship had developed. I had told her that I wanted to leave Virginia, but I didn't have any firm plans. When the semester ended she suggested I drive to California with her in her car, and I agreed. I felt sad and a little guilty saying goodbye to my younger brother because I would be leaving him alone with my father. We went to California in Lauren's car, a red Jeep Wrangler, and reached San Francisco in three days. This sense of guilt pursued me. But I couldn't take him with me and I couldn't support him.

THE COLLOQUY OF THE TAPE

A rectangular plastic object, dark brown in color but transparent enough to reveal the two small rollers at the lower corners, and the other small pieces that a thin tape sometimes passes over or between. The tape is brown, too, and it runs around two reels that look like eyes staring into the eyes of anyone who's looking at them. One of these eyes sometimes grows larger, as if it's swelling, as the tape wraps around it, while its twin sister shrinks, growing smaller and smaller. If it wasn't for the pieces of paper stuck on both the A and B sides of the rectangle and the inscription on the bottom part of both sides, "SONY, CHF 60," it would look very much like the face of a little robot.

The tape itself carries a recording mostly of two voices,

with a third that joins them at the end. The first is a man who was in his early thirties when the tape was recorded, and the second is a child who was still finding his feet on the rungs of the ladder of language. When the jaws of a little (or big) recorder open and it is fed a rectangle and the right button is pressed, a little tooth moves at the bottom of the jaw, covered in a piece of sponge. It presses on the thin copper-colored piece under the mouth of the rectangle and this reads the sound on the tape that is forced to pass under it. When the tape goes through it repeats those voices from the past as it heard them the first time—the time that the tape still remembers.

The man set up the red recorder he had bought that afternoon from the central market on a small wooden table that he placed in front of the only sofa in the sitting room. He drew the yellow curtain aside to let the rays of the afternoon sun filter through from the window. The boy was sitting close to his father, swinging his bare feet. His legs were so short that they hung in the air over the edge of the sofa, and the boy hit the sofa leg with the heel of his right foot. The child asked his father about the new device: "What's that, father?"

"A tape recorder."

He asks him what he is doing and why he has asked him to sit next to him. The father asks him to be patient and promises him something that will make him happy.

There's a rattling noise and the sound of someone breathing close to the microphone. In the background the laughs of the child and his voice saying, "Come on, dad."

The man: "Be patient a little, my son. Look, it's recording now. See this red light? Come on, come a little closer . . . See this here . . . Come on, speak."

The boy: "Speak."

The man: "Well, speak, so that your voice comes out later."

The boy: "Where?"

The man: "Here. See this microphone here? It'll hear your voice and record it on the tape."

The boy: "Really?"

The man: "Yes, really."

The boy: "What shall I say?"

The man: "As you like. Say who you are. What's your name?"

The boy: "I'm Somy."

The man: "Somy. Bravo. But what's your full name?"

The boy: "Ah okay, Husam."

The man: "Husam, bravo to the hero. And what's dad's name? Who am I?"

The boy: "Dad. You're Nazim."

The man: "Bravo, clever boy. And mom?"

The boy: "Aysar."

The man: "Clever boy. Okay, you know the song ku-kukhti?"

The boy: "Kukukhti

> Where's my sister?

> In Hilla."

Silence.

The man: "And what does she eat?"

The boy: "And what does she eat?

> Beans.

> And what does she drink?

> God's water.

> And where does she sleep?

> On God's earth."

The man: "Excellent, bravo (he claps). Come on, give Husam a clap (they clap together). Hey, come here, where are you going? What else do you know?"

The boy: "I know . . ."

The man: "Hajanjali. Go on, say it."

The boy: "Hajanjali, bajanjali,

> I went up the mountain.

> And found a dome or two.

> 'Oh uncle, oh Hussein,' I cried.

> 'This is the sultan's tomb.'

> 'Move your foot, 'Umran.'"

The man: "Bravo. And then?"

The boy: "Then what?"

The man: "Balboul."

The boy: "Balee ya balboul, you haven't seen a bird

Pecking at the bowl.

Milk and myrtle

On Titi's grave.

You haven't seen my love.

Titi.

You haven't seen my love.

Dad, I want to hear my voice."

The man: "Just a moment, hang on a while. Sing Ghazala Ghazziluki."

The boy: "Gazelle, they spun you,

In the water they rolled you.

Sitting on the bank, sitting combing your hair.

She fell asleep."

The man: "What did he say to her? Get up, wasn't it?"

The boy: "'Get up,' he told her,

'This is your horse,

I pull it and mount,

The skiff, the skiff of the desert,

For you to cry over me,

Cry over your anklets,

Your anklets worth four hundred,

And your neighbors are thieves.'"

The boy, encouraged by his father, continued to recite:

"My bird flew out of my hand,

My bird's above the trees.

Come down, come down, birdie, eat the seeds without husks.

My bird was tinsy winsy, I reared it by hand,

When it grew up and fledged, it started pecking my cheek.

I fed it with seeds of love and gave it a tear to drink.

Everyone envied me and they took my bird from me."

After the series of rhymes, the father pressed the STOP button and the boy insisted they listen to what the father had recorded, so he pressed REWIND and when the tape was back at the start he pressed PLAY, and they sat and listened. The boy laughed when he put his ear close to the little speaker in the red recorder to listen to his own voice with a mixture of delight and amazement. When the tape reached the last section, the father stopped it. "Dad," the boy asked, "When Mom comes, can she sing too please?"

"Yes, son."

"Let me do it."

"No, son."

"Why not, dad?"

"This isn't a toy, son. Come and I'll turn the television on for you and you can watch some cartoons."

The father turned the television on and gestured to the boy to sit on his small green plastic chair in front of the television, which he did. Then he picked up the tape recorder and put it on a higher table next to the telephone. The father went to the bathroom and then to the kitchen, where he opened the fridge looking for something to eat. The boy took advantage of the opportunity, left his chair and climbed up on the sofa to reach the tape recorder. He played with the buttons and managed to press the PLAY and RECORD buttons. Then he started whispering:

"The sun came out on Aisha's grave,

Aisha the pasha's daughter.

She plays with the rattle.

The cock crowed in the orchard.

God help the sultan, our people and . . ."

Then he heard his father's footsteps approaching so he got off the sofa and went back to his chair to watch the cartoons without stopping the recording.

The voices of the characters in the cartoons continue in the background. Then we hear the sound of a plate of watermelon and cheese touching the surface of the table when the father puts it there and sits down to eat. The boy laughs from time to time and follows the cartoon. Ten minutes later, the father says, "That'll be your mother come back." They hear the door opening and closing and footsteps. "Go and give mom a kiss." "Mom, mom." "Hello, my dear, how are you?" "Ha, welcome home. How was your day?" "Lots of cases to deal with. My head hurts. I'm going to brew some tea." "That would be great." "And you?" "I'm fine. I left work early."

They chatted at length that day about work and about the trip he had promised her to Lake Habbaniya and the need to visit her relatives, who had told them off for not visiting. Usual conversation of no importance. The boy's mother didn't notice the tape recorder till the tape came to the end of the first side and made a click when it stopped. The tape did not of course record what the father then said: "Hey, you naughty boy, how did you manage that? Has that been recording all this time? That's really terrible, you little devil."

The boy's father didn't record anything on the second side, and he wrote "Husam" on the label of the tape. The idea was that after a few years they, and especially Husam, would listen to his voice as a child. Husam grew up and every two or three years he would listen, not to his own voice but to their voices, which were far away after they were killed by war in his childhood. And now it was the tape's turn to join them: the firestorm of another war would turn it into ashes and leave Husam alone with memories that no longer had a soundtrack.

෨෧ఴ෧ఎ

"Can you tell me about your background. Your name is unfamiliar. Where did you grow up?"

"I was born in Iraq. But I came here in 1993."

"Ah, that's interesting. How old were you when you left Iraq?"

"Twenty-three."

"Did you take part in the war?"

"No, the war was over when I began my military service."

"And why did you leave Iraq?"

"The situation was very bad, especially after the 1991 war. My father sold our house and we went to Jordan and we stayed there several months. One of his friends there got him a work contract and we came with him."

"Do you visit your relatives there?"

"Most of them left many years ago. I don't have many relatives left."

"When did you last visit Iraq?"

"Three years ago."

"Tell me about the visit."

"I went as a translator to make a documentary film."

"Were you happy with the visit?"

"No. After that my depression grew worse."

"Why?"

"That's the million-dollar question. Where should I begin?"

"Wherever you want."

"There's a friend I know who says there are no real beginnings or endings."

"Is that philosophy or are you trying to avoid the subject?"

"You don't seem to understand."

"Help me understand. Talk!"

I bend down by the wall of the cave and draw a picture of a window on it. I recite silently the poetry I remember, so that I don't forget it. My hands are tied with a cord, and the people with me are laughing but their laughs are in a different language. You'll laugh, Nameer. Aren't all laughs much the same? Do peoples and nations matter when it comes to laughing? Yes, this is what I see in the nightmare. I beg them to untie me and I promise to show them the sun outside the cave.

I hadn't seen him since 1987, when he disappeared from class in the second or third month of the school year and never came back. We were in the same class in the Markaziyya secondary school. We later heard that his father, who was a director general in the Ministry of Planning, had obtained special permission for him to travel to the United States to finish his education there. Years later I heard from a mutual friend that he had started studying medicine at a prestigious American university. We weren't close friends but we often played soccer together, and I remember that we hung out with the same group several times after school. After I left Iraq I didn't hear any news of him until I received an email, written in English. "Dear Nameer, I hope you are well after all these years," it said. "I heard from Ali Abdilkhaliq, who I met by chance in Abu Dhabi, that you were living in New York. I've been in Dubai for years but I'll be visiting New York (which I miss very much) for business next week and it would be a wonderful opportunity to meet after all these years (how many? seventeen or eighteen?). I'd like to invite you to dinner. My secretary will make a reservation and send you the details if you agree. I look forward to meeting. Adnan." Under his name I read the sign-off added automatically to his emails: Vice President, Middle East office, Goldman Sachs International, Dubai International Financial Center, Sheikh Zayed Road, Dubai. I searched for his name on the Internet and found he'd been working for Goldman Sachs for many years and had moved to Dubai four years ago to run their office in Dubai. I usually viewed people who worked in investments and capital with suspicion, and I told myself I was lucky I didn't have to deal with them. But I was pleased to receive his message and I didn't hesitate to accept his invitation. I told myself it would be a chance to go over memories of our time in secondary school in Baghdad and to catch up on news of colleagues with whom I had lost contact. I immediately sent him a short reply saying I was delighted and looked forward to meeting him after all these years. That same evening a message arrived from his secretary, and I told her I would prefer the Thursday evening. Then she sent another message naming the restaurant, Fig and Olive.

I didn't take the subway because the restaurant was in the Meatpacking District, a twenty-five-minute walk from my apartment. I arrived a quarter of an hour early. The restaurant seemed to be new and recently opened. The lighting was soft in the interior, the details of which were dominated by gradations of two colors: white and blue—an allusion to the "Mediterranean restaurant" theme. I was met by an attractive hostess with a very short haircut and green eyes, wearing a short black dress.

The barman welcomed me and volunteered a simple smile as he put a white napkin and a glass of water in front of me and then handed me the drinks menu. I decided to have a glass of red wine, and I looked for a variety that I knew. I was surprised to find arak on the menu. Then I remembered that the restaurant was Mediterranean and that arak was common in Greece, Turkey, and Lebanon. They had Kefraya, the Lebanese arak. I hadn't drunk arak for years, so I ordered a glass and insisted that the barman bring me cold water and ice separately so that I could mix the *payk*, as Iraqis call a shot of alcohol, myself. I wondered where the term *payk* came from. I would have to look it up. It must be from Turkish or Persian. The waiter brought my order, saying, "Here's your araak," with the stress on a lengthened second syllable. I reproached him in silence, in the voice that always popped up in my head to correct mispronounced words, especially important ones: "It's 'árag, buddy, 'árag." That's the voice that's grown hoarse after teaching Arabic to Americans for more than eight years and that I now have to silence because I will never have to teach it again. I put in twice as much water as arak, and the clear liquid turned milky, reminding me of the Iraqi term for it: lion's milk. I sniffed the smell of anise and took a sip that blew a cold breeze onto my heart. The barman brought a small bowl of green and black olives of various sizes.

"Sorry I'm a little late," he said, putting his hand on my shoulder. I turned around and we embraced and kissed. He was wearing a gray suit, a white shirt, and a red tie, and was carrying a small leather bag. He hadn't changed much, apart from the glasses he now wore and the fact that his brown hair was receding slightly on his temples. Each of us told the other that he hadn't changed much.

"Half our gang are now bald, you know," he said.

"Our turn will come," I said.

"God forbid," he replied.

Then he looked at the glass of arak and said, "What's that? You're in New York and you're drinking arak?"

"What's wrong with that?"

"So didn't you write a dissertation on Abu Nuwas?"

"How do you know that?"

"I went on the university website to check you out."

"And what's the problem? So if I write on Abu Nuwas then I can't drink arak? I like all kinds of forbidden fruits, and besides, arak is our national drink."

He laughed and said he had to go to the bathroom. When he came back the hostess with the intoxicating smile arrived and took us to a table in a corner. She gave us menus and put a drinks menu in the middle of the table. He picked it up and said, "But let's drink wine rather than arak."

"I like wine anyway," I said.

"Red or white?"

"Red."

He insisted on choosing himself, saying he had become an expert and loved to collect wines.

"I'm inviting you today," he added.

"No, no way."

"But yes. I want to celebrate. Today I signed a fantastic deal and made a pile of money, so don't bother about the price. Order whatever you like," he said with a laugh.

The last remark irritated me a little but I decided to let it pass. "Congratulations. Let's drink now and we'll figure out who'll pay later."

He asked the waiter for a bottle of Gigondas and said I would like it. He said he had been to the Rhône valley on vacation the previous year and drunk the wine in the village where it is made. I asked him if he often traveled, and he said that ninety percent of his trips were for business, and that his wife complained that he didn't spend enough time with her and the children. He was surprised that I wasn't married yet. "Still holding out? I had lots of fun, but in the end you've had enough and you have to settle down."

The waiter brought the bottle and showed it to Adnan, who looked at the label and nodded. The waiter pulled out the cork and put the bottle on the table in front of Adnan. Then he poured a little of the crimson wine into Adnan's glass. Adnan picked it up and smelled the nose of the wine as he swirled it in the glass. He tasted the wine and closed his eyes. I felt he was showing off to some extent. Even the waiter raised his eyebrows when he saw it. Adnan had another taste. "Excellent," he said, and the waiter filled our glasses. We drank a toast to "the old days," as he put it. The wine had a silky texture and I praised his taste in wine and in choosing the restaurant. He took his wallet out of his pocket and showed me a picture of his wife with their two children, Sami and Nour. She was wide-eyed with long hair, an American of Iraqi origin whom he had met at Goldman Sachs here in New York and had married five years ago. He said he loved her and had never cheated on her. He raised his right index finger as he said the last phrase, as if he were preaching. The waiter apologized for interrupting to take our order. I chose a beetroot salad with arugula, walnut, and goat's cheese, and then roast chicken with rosemary, while he ordered gazpacho and a Moroccan tagine. We gave the menus to the waiter. Adnan asked me about my girlfriend: "What's she like? Where's she from? Is she blond?"

"No, she's black."

"I've tried everything, but I've never gone out with a black woman," he said.

"The loss is yours," I said.

"So I thought you studied medicine?" I asked.

"I set out studying medicine and I finished the first stages for two years and then I switched to economics. I did a master's in economics and business management at Johns Hopkins."

"How come?"

"Why not? There are plenty of doctors."

"Yes, and plenty of economists."

"It was one of the best decisions I ever made. My family were upset at first, but now they're pleased."

"Where are they now?"

"In Amman. They left in 2000. I insisted they leave and I rented a house for them there. Where are your family?"

"In Virginia."

"When did you leave?"

"In 1993."

He talked about his education and how the first years were easy and enjoyable. He said his father sent him enough money and he was living the good life. But the situation changed after sanctions because it became impossible to transfer any money, and the Iraqi dinar was worthless anyway. "My father said, 'It's over, my boy. We can't go on. You'll have to rely on yourself.'" Adnan had to work for the first time in his life and went through some difficult years. He didn't find a job in his field after graduating. But he began to write a monthly report on the economic situation and the prospects for investment in the Middle East. He made use of email, which was in its infancy at the time, and started to send the report to hundreds of email addresses on a list he had compiled of people who worked on investment in "emerging markets," as he called them. He received messages of thanks and encouragement from a considerable number of those to whom he sent his reports, but without any offers of work. He continued to write and send out the report regularly for a year and a half before the manager of a well-known investment fund contacted him and invited him to New York. He came to New York from Baltimore, and after the meeting the man offered him a job with his team. He moved to New York and worked with him for four years, gaining experience and forming a network of relationships in the world of Wall Street. Then he received the attractive offer of a prestigious position with Goldman Sachs, so he worked there. When he did well they asked him to move to their office in Dubai. When he got around to talking about Dubai, I had reached the last piece of beetroot. I put the goat's cheese that was left on it, and there was also a piece of walnut stuck to it. That was really delicious, I said to myself, but the price, at sixteen dollars, is criminal. He poured more wine for me and for himself and said, "Now you tell us, doctor. How did fate bring you to New York?" I was reminded of the song that goes "Doctor, forget my first wound. My new wound your eyes can see."

I told him about my trip from Virginia to California without saying anything about my disagreement with my father. I said only that I wasn't willing to work with U.S. government departments or Arab embassies, so I worked as a private tutor to students learning Arabic as part of Middle East studies. "So you're one of those idealists," he said. "There's a saying. If one isn't a leftist in his twenties then he has no heart. But if he's still leftist in his thirties, then he has no brains."

"I wasn't in my twenties at the time. Now do you want to listen or do you want to philosophize?"

"Apologies, doctor. Please continue."

I told him about my trip to California with Lauren and working on the almond farm that her father owned, that I worked in the fields in the beginning and drove the machine that shook the trees and gathered the almonds, and that I then moved to the factory to oversee the hulling, shelling, and packing. I told him how much I enjoyed my years in California because I loved the peace, the isolation, and the rhythm of work. Although it was sometimes physically exhausting, it made me feel that I was part of the earth and in harmony with the seasons. I never had insomnia in those years. I slept like a log. I still miss the beauty of the almond trees when they awoke from their long slumber in the cold season between December and February, after they had recovered their breath and absorbed what they needed from the ground. I told him that bees would be brought specially to pollinate the trees and that the trees would speak in pink and white from late February to early March. Then the nuts would grow until they started to dry out at the end of July. From the middle of August to October the trees would be shaken, and ten days later the almonds would be gathered. The waiter brought the main dishes and the bottle of wine was empty, so he asked whether we wanted another. When the waiter brought it, Adnan told him to pour it without him tasting it. "Good, so what took you from almonds and California to studying for the doctorate?" he added.

"Be patient, I'm coming to that. You're going to be surprised because there's some similarity between our stories."

I told him that I spent my spare time reading and translating to improve my English and at the same time to keep up my Arabic. The works of Abu Nuwas was the only Arabic book I had taken with me, so I began to translate his poems. I sent a collection of them to an academic journal that's interested in translation and is published by the comparative literature department at Berkeley, which was an hour and a half from the farm. The academic in charge of editing the journal contacted me a month later to praise the translation and to tell me they were going to publish two of the poems. He was in charge of publishing a series of translated poetry collections at University of California Press, and he advised me to submit a proposal to publish selections from Abu Nuwas's poems with an introduction. He told me I would need to look at some scholarly references to write the introduction, and he invited me to visit him at the university, promising to help me get a visiting researcher's pass so that I could borrow books from the library. I took advantage of his generosity and set about translating more of Abu Nuwas's poems. I also wrote a long introduction on his importance and on poems in praise of wine and debauchery. I sent it to him and he liked it very much and suggested that I turn it into a project for academic study. He said that the comparative literature department gave grants and I could apply to obtain one. I had to take the Graduate Record Examination and get high scores to increase my chances. I had never thought of going into the academic world, but luck was on my side. I was awarded a scholarship on condition that I teach Arabic. So I finished my master's at Berkeley, and after that I was emboldened to apply to do a doctorate in four universities. I was accepted at Harvard with a grant. After that I taught for two years at Dartmouth, where I finished my dissertation before moving to New York University.

I asked him about our other colleagues at school and what they were doing. He said that Ali Abdilkhaliq was working as an oil engineer in the United Arab Emirates. Nash'at al-Dabbagh had become a doctor like his father, emigrated to London in the late 1990s and was doing cosmetic surgery for rich Arabs and their wives. "He's a millionaire thanks to them. He takes fat out of their asses and puts it on their faces and lips!"

"Fat from their asses, or silicone?" I said.

"It's all the same shit," he said.

But the news that took me by surprise was that Zaid al-Titinchi, who had been with us in the same class, had been an undersecretary in the Ministry of Communications for a year and a half in the government of Ayad Allawi but had lost office when the government changed. "Zaid who used to play soccer with us?" I said.

"Yes."

"I know he was a good guy and very smart but what qualifications did he have? He's the same age as us."

"He did engineering and he's bright. His father founded one of the new parties."

"Well that's the most important qualification," I said.

"He's still better than others," said Adnan.

I remembered how good Zaid was at mimicking the teachers, especially Mudhar, the fat math teacher who, whenever one of the boys made a mistake, would ask him, "Where do you live?" as if where he lived had anything to do with his ability to grasp mathematical formulas. I reminded Adnan of Mudhar and we spent a while going over shared memories from our school days. There was Fouad, the biology teacher who spoke classical Arabic peppered with strange expressions and overused the word *bughyatan* to mean "in order to." Adnan raised his glass and said, "My God, I'm so happy to see you."

"Me too."

"And for your sake I gave up the happy ending," said Adnan.

I didn't understand what he meant so I asked him. He said big corporations offered their customers a complimentary package after successful negotiations, and it usually included a massage session in the spa with a pretty young woman who would be slim and half-naked and who could make a man feel he was in paradise. When she was about to finish the massage, she would ask the customer if he wanted a "happy ending." But he had given up the happy ending that day in order to have dinner with me.

"And you usually take the happy ending?" I asked.

"Of course. Only an idiot wouldn't take it."

"But didn't you say you never cheat on your wife?"

"This doesn't count as cheating. I don't touch the girl with my hand. She does the massage and then throws in an extra. My little friend stands up and greets her and then shoots his load."

The waiter waited till we'd finished roaring with laughter and then asked if he could take away the empty plates. He took them and came back with the dessert menu. I studied it and asked for the tiramisu with Arabic coffee (the menu called it "Greek" coffee), while Adnan ordered a crème brûlée with a cappuccino.

I asked him about the deal that he had concluded with such success, and he said that besides working for Goldman Sachs, he had set up an investment company in Baghdad a year earlier and intended to open a branch in Irbil. The purpose of his visit to New York was to give a presentation to persuade a number of major investors to finance his company, which would buy and sell shares on the Iraqi stock exchange. He said most of them were hesitant and wary because the situation was unstable, but he had succeeded in persuading one big investor to enter a partnership with him.

"So there's a stock exchange in Iraq?" I asked.

"Yes, it's a small exchange, but active."

"Fine, but what's the use of investments and shares now if the infrastructure is in ruins and the basic necessities of life still haven't been fixed?"

"When there's investment, everything will follow."

"That's the same old 'trickle-down economics' story—hand everything over to the big companies and the financiers, and gradually everyone will benefit. But in the end only the elite benefit."

"So now you're an economist? That's not your business."

"It doesn't take an expert in economics. Things are clear."

"So what have you all done for Iraq?" he said angrily. "Go on, tell me. Just negativity and grumbling. When you stand up in the lecture hall at university and philosophize, is that going to give Iraqis bread to eat?"

"And who told you I benefit Iraqis or that I've ever claimed to do so?" I said.

"So you want us to leave it to the riffraff?"

"And what's the difference between thieves from the Alwiyya Club and the riffraff thieves?"

I rose from my chair, threw my napkin onto the table and

walked to the bathroom. The further away I went the angrier I felt. I was surprised I had remembered the Alwiyya Club like that, on the spur of the moment. Then I remembered the day when we decided to skip our last two classes and play hooky. Titinchi's son suggested we take a taxi and go to the Alwiyya Club. I had heard them talking about the club and about the swimming pool they went to in the summer, but I had never been inside. I thought I was going to go in with them as their guest. When we reached the club, which was next to the Sheraton Hotel, we got out of the taxi to go in. They greeted a man called Abu Emad who was standing at the gate. I don't know how the son of a bitch knew, but he asked me, "Are you the son of a member?" I was a little flustered and said "no." The other boys told him they were taking me in as a guest and they would register my name in the book. But the man said, "It's not a guest day today and only members who are over eighteen can take guests in." It was an embarrassing situation, so I said, "You go in and I'll go home, no problem."

The bathroom walls were turquoise and there was pleasant music coming from the speakers. As soon as I approached the wash basin a black man standing next to it opened the water tap, then took one of the small white towels placed next to him and then got ready to give it to me once I had finished washing my hands. As I put two dollars in the bowl in front of him, I asked him about the music. "Sorry, I don't know, sir," he replied. I came out of the bathroom and asked the hostess. "It's fado," she said. I had heard about this genre of music that originated in Portugal. I had decided not to go back to the table. I walked to the main door and went out into the street. I thought of the check but I remembered that he had invited me. Let him pay with the money he would plunder from Iraq. I regretted that we had clashed before the tiramisu I had ordered arrived. I walked back to my apartment, stopping on the way at a shop on West 3rd Street to buy a Flake chocolate bar. I remembered a line that appeared in the ads for another brand of chocolate, but it would also apply to a Flake: "Sometimes chocolate is your best friend."

THE COLLOQUY OF THE TWINS

We were neighbors in our mother's womb, and we were born as exact copies of each other. Even our mother was uncertain which of us was which. She often couldn't tell us apart. Grandmother suggested she tie a colored thread around the wrist of one twin to distinguish her from her sister, so she tied a red thread around my wrist, while leaving Hadil's wrist free. When Grandmother asked her why she'd tied it around my wrist, she replied that I was a minute and a half older than Hadil. Many years later Grandmother gave us chains made of 18-carat gold. Each of them was engraved with the owner's name to show whose it was. Mother insisted on dressing us in the same clothes, as usually happens with twins. Even the way she combed our black hair left no room for any clue that would make it possible to tell us apart. Everyone who met us was amazed at how similar our features, voices, and gestures were. We grew tired of hearing the same remarks from strangers and relatives and replying to the constant question: "Are you Asil or Hadil?" But time, or something else we don't quite know, contrived to bring out a simple difference with consequences that would gradually become more obvious. When we graduated from grade four to grade five of primary school, Father bought us a small electronic organ. At first we argued over it because each of us wanted to have it all to herself. Then Father got angry and hid it in his room. He threatened not to let either of us touch it and said he'd decided to give it to his nephew. But he later calmed down and changed his mind after Mother proposed a compromise that would satisfy everyone—that we should take turns on the organ. We did that successfully under her supervision. Once I had learned which keys played which notes, and after some fumbling, I managed to play a tune that I knew. Hadil took to the organ enthusiastically at first, but her enthusiasm and interest waned after simple attempts ended in failure. Maybe she didn't have enough patience or willpower. Or maybe her ear wasn't musical enough, unlike mine. She gave up asking for her share of playing time on the organ and left it to me. I started to spend many hours with it. Father was delighted with my talent and bought me a bigger one two years later. Naturally the family's admiration for my playing and the fact that they gathered around me in a circle on family occasions when I played the songs they requested provoked Hadil's envy, though not beyond the bounds of "normal" envy. Hadil tried to draw but she grew bored of it after a while. But she did get high grades. By chance I saw a program on television about the music and ballet school in Baghdad, and I very much liked the way the school was organized. I found out that I could fulfill my dream there, learn music, and play with an orchestra like the one I had seen on television. Mother was watching it with me, and I asked her to enroll me in the school after the sixth grade. When I brought it up with Father, he was reluctant to agree and skeptical about how useful studying music would be for my future. But Mother explained to him that the curriculum at the school included, besides the musical curriculum, all the usual subjects as in other schools, and that when I had a secondary school certificate from the music and ballet school, I could go to university and specialize in another field, so he was convinced and agreed. I passed the entrance exam, which was much easier than I expected. I chose piano, of course. The keys were much bigger than I was used to with the little electronic piano, but my fingers danced across it with an agility and a confidence that amazed the examination board, and I was accepted immediately. I enjoyed the studying, which was tiring because my working day was much longer and the school was a long way from home, so I came home exhausted. Hadil, meanwhile, made up for her envy by making fun of me and my sufferings. I did well, and in the graduation year the piano teacher, Mundhir, chose me to play in front of a delegation visiting from Germany. He asked me to play a short piece by Schubert, his Impromptu in B Flat, and I did so. I had played it dozens of times before. They clapped warmly for me when I finished. One of the three members of the delegation embraced me and took me by surprise by asking whether I would like to study in Berlin. In my confusion I just smiled, and the German woman thought I hadn't understood what she said. So she repeated the question and asked Mundhir to translate. "Asil, they want to give you a scholarship to study at the Music School in Berlin," he said. I couldn't control myself and I clapped for joy. On the way home I was worried Father might not agree to me going away alone, but I trusted in my mother to persuade him in the end. And that's what happened. I left four months later. Hadil didn't hide her jealousy from me, but she cried when I said goodbye to her.

Berlin opened doors for me, and I was supported by a woman called Rebecca Ullmann, who taught there, and who had helped set up the bursary for young musicians from the Middle East to study music. In Berlin I discovered that she was one of the best piano players in Europe. Even so, starting in Berlin wasn't easy. I had to learn German quickly and get used to Berlin's bitter cold and the lack of sunlight in winter. The teaching system was strict and the competition was fierce. But I excelled and I was chosen to play at the final concert of the first year. I went back to Baghdad in the summer to spend the vacation with my family. In the second year I started to play beyond the confines of the school when Ull-mann nominated me to take her place with the Berlin Quartet when she had to have surgery. The Berlin Quartet was my stepping stone to other opportunities. I took part in the international Bach competition that is held in Leipzig every other year and won with my playing of his Partita No. 2. The audience gave me a standing ovation that lasted three minutes. Invitations poured in for me to play in Vienna, Paris, and New York.

All this was going to happen and I would have become the most famous Arab pianist at the start of the twenty-first century. But in fact I didn't leave Baghdad. I didn't go to the music and ballet school. I played the organ for many hours and I saw the program about the music and ballet school, and I was going to apply and pass the exam. But a few months earlier, during that winter of fire, we were all in the car with my father driving fast to get to the house of my grandmother, who insisted we come because her house was safe and not close to any military installations that were likely to be bombed. The traffic lights weren't working and Father was slowing down a little at the junctions. But he didn't slow down enough at one of them. The driver who was coming at high speed from the right didn't slow down—he too was escaping to a safe place. I never played music after that and Hadil wasn't envious of me.

I don't like the taste of the coffee they sell in Starbucks, and I hate the company and its role in the demise of dozens of beautiful little cafés in New York and many other cities in the world. But I love their comfortable seats. Whenever I found Think so full that I couldn't find a place to sit (it happened about once every week or two), I would buy my coffee there and then go to the Starbucks at the corner of West 4th and Washington Square East, to look for somewhere to sit and mark my students' weekly assignments, or to read the newspapers and kill time (however often you kill it, it comes back to life the next day). Whenever I went to Starbucks, I would find him there in the same corner, even during the vacations when there are fewer students around. But the staff here were pleasant toward him, and I never saw them harassing him, maybe because he too never harassed any of the customers. He always sat in the corner under one of those pictures that often hang in branches of Starbucks, showing the streets in the neighborhood around the store as they were at the beginning of the twentieth century, in black and white. There were horse-drawn carriages and men standing on the pavement selling fruit and vegetables to passersby.

He was like a character who had escaped from a sad play in the early 1950s. He had unkempt gray hair hidden by a woolen cap that he put in the old leather bag that he parked on the ground to the right of the table after removing his papers and spreading them out. Sometimes he picked up the next table if it was empty and put it alongside his own to make space for more pieces of paper. On the first occasions that I saw him, in the fall of 2005, I guessed from afar that he was working on some research or something similar. But once en route to the bathroom I had to walk past where he was sitting, then stand and wait in a short line. I allowed myself to cast an inquisitive glance at the pieces of paper he had spread out. Some of them had only a single word written on them in large letters. I read the words *hope, pain,* and *truth.* I was going to ask him whether he knew that in Arabic the words for hope and pain were almost the same, with just the two consonants transposed—*amal* and *alam.* Some of the pages were blank, and some had a circle or just one letter. I never saw a computer or even a pen. Lost in thought, he was looking at the street through the window. His eyes were green. Clean-shaven. His complexion was a little ruddy. He was wearing a blue-and-white shirt with a small checkered pattern that reminded me of restaurant curtains I had seen somewhere, and a blue suit, without a necktie, and Newport trainers. Sometimes he would change the position and arrangement of the pieces of paper and look at them for a while before going back to the window. After that I saw him several times and I deliberately went to the bathroom so that I could sneak a look at his pieces of paper, which didn't change much. There was still plenty of blank space . . .

The last time I saw him was in the summer of 2006, and after that he disappeared.

Obvious questions that don't dream of an answer.

Is it the same moment everywhere? Or is each moment tied to its place in this universe? If the latter possibility is correct, then there is more than one time. There are billions of times that might overlap with one another but are never identical.

The barbed wire coils as if it's weaving a spider's web that is trying to hide the scene from us. Some of the coils, those closest to the lens, are not clear. But there are enough of them for others to appear as clear circles, with savage, regular teeth. In the upper right and left corners we can see more barbed wire, coiled more compactly, surrounding a space with a sandy surface. On the sand are many footprints around a seated man. His legs are stretched out in front of him and his back is vertical as though he's leaning against an invisible column. He's wearing a white dishdasha and leather sandals. His left hand is on the forehead of a young boy, no more than four years old, who has his eyes closed and is resting his head on the man's right arm. The boy's mouth is open. He has short black hair and is wearing green pajamas. The man's right hand is holding the boy's right hand, and his arm is wrapped around the upper part of the body of the boy, whose legs are stretched out at an angle. The boy has put his right foot, which is soiled with mud, over his left foot at the ankles. Two feet away from them we can see a pair of trainers, and it is clear from the size of them that they belong to the boy. The sun is fierce. The man has a black bag on his head.

I am a fish, without scales.

A window with bars running vertically and horizontally, except for the lower part where an enormous man is squatting on yellow tiles. His bottom is bare and there are signs of bruising on his left buttock. His left foot protrudes from under his right thigh and is held tight by a thick rope tied to the bars of the cell. His right hand lies on the ground, and the upper part of his body is covered by a red short-sleeved shirt. His left hand is tied to a bar in the ceiling with a thick rope. His head is bowed and he has a white blindfold splattered with blood over his eyes.

The same man with the massive body is lying on his stomach on a brown piece of ground. The white dishdasha he is wearing is rucked up to reveal his buttocks and his legs. I can see signs of injuries and bruises, and his back is stained with blood. His hands are tied together. He has a slight beard and short black hair. His neck is twisted far to the right as he tries to look upward, but the dusty-colored blindfold prevents him from seeing anything. There's an enormous gray dog that seems to be about to pounce on the man. Its front legs are on the man's bloodied back. In the background there are bars with darkness beyond, and the bars of another cell deep in the darkness.

Say that I can hear what you can't hear, and that I can see what you can't see.

I felt restive and decided to go out for a walk. While I was on my way to the elevator, my octogenarian neighbor, Mrs. Cartwright, came out of her apartment and turned toward me when she heard the sound of my footsteps. She was one of what I called "the indigenous people of the building," a tenant before the university bought the building and allocated most of the apartments to faculty and staff. The indigenous people in general were bitter toward the university. They felt they were an endangered species. "Oh, professor, I haven't seen you in a long while, but you're busy no doubt," she said.

"How are you, Mrs. Cartwright?" I asked.

"Very well, I have a new hip that I'm trying to get used to."

"Congratulations."

"There's still a lot of pain but it's better than before."

"That's excellent."

We went into the elevator and I pressed the button to take us down to the ground floor. "I met someone from your country last week. I was invited to my granddaughter's house and I met him and he reminded me of you," said Mrs. Cartwright.

"Really? What was his name?"

"Oh, sorry, I don't remember, but he was also from South Africa. He said the situation there is bad because of the violence and the crime," she replied.

Years ago I stopped correcting people who confused me with someone from some neighboring country, usually Iran, but South Africa is a very long way from Iraq. Even so, Mrs. Cartwright often had confused ideas and vague information, and I had no wish to correct her. At that moment I envied her the imprecision that allowed her to change geography and maybe history and give her neighbors new histories and identities. "Yes, levels of violence are high there, unfortunately," I said.

"Tell me, do you visit your family there? Do you go back?" she asked.

"No, I haven't been for three years," I said.

"It must be a very long and tiring journey."

"Yes, it is really tiring."

The elevator door opened and we went out together. I said goodbye to her and walked off.

A child. Me. A child sitting in the garden of our house, which is no longer a house. A gift from the sky turned it into an enormous pile of rubble. I pick up a piece of glass from a broken window. I feel the edge and it cuts me and draws a drop of blood. I feel a slight pain and watch the drop fall to the ground. The moment is a wound. I put the piece of glass on the body of time to cut it. I will cut it and draw a drop of blood. A moment. I will make it bleed to death, just as they all died.

"Here's the night owl, starting his usual ramble," Dino, the Ecuadorean doorman, said with a laugh.

"Did you know that in the country I come from owls are seen as symbols of stupidity?" I said.

He put out his hand to shake mine and smiled. "Oh sorry, my friend. That's certainly not what I meant. So what's the right metaphor for those who stay up late in your culture?"

"Star shepherds."

"Ah, beautiful. I'll call you a star shepherd, but where are the stars here? We cannot see them because of all the light pollution."

The residents and the other doormen and staff called Dino "the philosopher." Although his education ended at secondary school and he hadn't gone to university either in Ecuador or in the United States, where he had emigrated forty years earlier, he was an intellectual and a voracious reader. He would argue and debate with the faculty who lived in the building. He followed world news with interest and read the alternative and leftist media in English and Spanish. He was leftist by inclination. He was even a member of the local committee that represented doormen in the union and wore its badge on the lapel of his black uniform. He was fairer than most of the people in his home country. "My mother's Italian and she gave me my skin color," he would say with a laugh, then add: "But my father's ancestors were of Inca descent." Galeano was his favorite writer.

Dino was obsessed with a personal project to save the world from its worsening problems. He told me the details several times.

Truth be told, it was an amazing and carefully thought-out project. Dino had found cheap land on a mountain in Ecuador, close to some natural springs, and had bought it two decades ago. Recently he had bought the land around it and he intended to build an eco-hotel for tourists, relying on the fertility of the surrounding area, where he would grow quinoa and breed Indian rabbits, which he planned to export to China. It would employ the local people, whom he would take on as partners in the project.

"I've toiled for more than thirty-five years and sent four kids to college, but I want to ensure their future," he said. "On the farm I'm working to set up in Ecuador, you can see the stars clearly and gaze at them as much as you like."

"I'll definitely visit you there."

I thought about what Dino said as I walked west toward the river. Was I an owl? Or a shepherd? Maybe I was neither. I was a lonely bat, with no wings.

THE COLLOQUY OF THE EYE

His black hair is receding to the corners of his forehead, which is expanding to look like one of those surfaces that he stares at and then colors. His eyebrows are almost horizontal above his hawklike eyes, which convey all the sadness he has passed on to me. His nose is thin between his eyes, but it gets bigger farther down. His beard and mustache are always bushy, and the beard reaches the top of his cheeks. Wherever and whenever I roam in my earliest memories, his face is there. It even seems to me that I was conceived in his eyes and born from the marriage of his eyes and his hands. At first I thought I was his only child, but then I discovered that there were others, male and female, into which he breathed life. There, beyond the seas, in Florence.

A few days after my birth, men came and swaddled me and then carried me in their arms. They wrapped me in pieces of cloth, paper, and plastic, but I was taken by surprise when they put me in a dark coffin, and I thought that the wrappings were a shroud. I heard them doing the same thing with my siblings. Then we were picked up and they took us in a procession through the streets of the city where I was born. I didn't see it at all, but I could hear the noise of the people in the streets. The sounds of the city faded away and disappeared for an hour or more; then we heard other sounds that suggested we were close to another city. After passing through the streets of this city, the sound of the sea breathing in and out reached my ears. They took us down and put us aboard a ship. I thought they were going to throw me to the bottom of the sea, as in those old stories that I had heard, I don't know where. After some days and nights, the ship handed us over to another port, which in turn handed us over to trucks that took us off.

When I came out of the coffin I saw his face for the first time in many days. His brow dripping with sweat, he asked a group of men to treat us gently. I was the first to be mounted on that vast white tableau. To take my place at its heart carrying this torch that I'm still carrying now. He looked at me anxiously from the ground. He shouted and pointed as he addressed the others. But he disappeared and never came back after that. The rest of my siblings came and took their places one after another on my right and on my left. The horse, the bull, the soldier and the bereft mother who had been crying and hugging her son for four decades. I was crying too, but no one could see my tears.

I was the one who saw everything. For days and days. The days of celebrations and marches in which these people chanted and raised placards, pictures, flags, and banners. Happy, or angry. And the ordinary days when they hurried about their business and most of them didn't look up or notice us. But there were always some who stopped and looked. I saw days when cars and people disappeared and tanks roamed the streets, and other days when bodies were strung up and people cheered at the sight of them, and they were left there for days. I saw days when planes flew around high in the sky and the birds took fright and went into hiding. I saw the day when my only eye was knocked out by a piece of shrapnel and fell to the ground. How was I to bend down to pick it up? Because I'm trapped here. I hold this torch and I can no longer see anything but my past and his face.

One sad, cold, and very ordinary night, I was wandering around the East Village. I saw big white trucks parked on both sides of the street, electricity generators and enormous coils of wire running along the sidewalks, and I knew they were shooting a scene for a movie. In my first year in New York the sight impressed me, and I would stand around enthusiastically with other people who make a habit of watching to see whether any of the actors are famous. But movie shoots were now part of the bigger Manhattan scene that I was used to, no longer "new" to me, especially as you might sometimes have to wait an hour for one scene to be shot and for the stars to come out of the big white cars where they relaxed and slept. But I noticed the face of Julianne Moore that night, and I liked her very much, especially after *The Hours*. I liked everything about that movie, even the music, and I'd made sure to buy the CD to listen to. So I waited, and after three quarters of an hour the shooting started on the other side of the street. Julianne Moore sat smoking a cigarette on the stone steps leading up to the door of a house, and a man came to sit beside her. They talked awhile and then kissed. They reshot the short scene three times. After the last time the director clapped and said "Great!" Moore went back to her car, the lights were turned off, and the crowd dispersed. I went back to my apartment wondering what happened to the character after the film ended. Major actors take on characters and identify with them, and the actor's personality disappears temporarily, but where do the characters go after the acting ends? Do they die? And if they die, do their ghosts hover around us? Or do they remain homeless, looking for a new story to inhabit temporarily?

❧

The catalog was a sapling when I started it years ago and now it's an orchard with branches that reach up to the ceiling. My room is no longer big enough for it. I don't know what I'm going to do. All this and I'm still on the first minute.

❧

I was woken up by her lips brushing over my cheek and then my neck. "Enough, up you get, darling," she whispered in my ear and kissed me. "The weather's wonderful today. Let's go to the sea." Then she got out of bed and went to draw the curtains. I covered my head with the duvet. Before I had time to ask her what was behind all this sudden activity, she said, "Do you have a sea in Iraq?" and then "Come on, get up, you can sleep there on the beach."

"Let me wash my face and have a cup of coffee, and then we can decide," I said.

"Ah, I forgot you're not a morning person. Coffee's ready. I'll wait for you at the table."

I dragged myself into the bathroom, washed my face and brushed my teeth. I opened the closet to look for a clean T-shirt to wear. "The answer's no," I told her.

"Why?" she said, disappointed. "We could have a beautiful day."

"No, I mean we don't have a sea in Iraq. We have lakes and the south of the country has limited access to the Gulf."

"Ah, okay, you scared me a little," she said with a smile.

She had poured me some coffee and prepared a plate with

toast, butter, and the strawberry jam that I like. I sat down across from her. Sipping the coffee, I added, "We had a sea thousands of years ago and the whole country was flooded. But the water receded and what we have left is the two rivers."

She laughed. "'Here we go again. I can't take you to seas that no longer exist. Do you want to go to a real sea? Have you been to Sandy Hook?"

"I don't know Sandy Hook. I once went to Rockaway Beach."

"No, no. Sandy Hook is a really beautiful peninsula. We can take the ferry and be there in an hour."

"Which ferry?"

"There's a ferry every hour and a quarter from Pier 11, close to Wall Street. We can catch the next one if you take a shower and get dressed quickly. I'll get butter and jam sandwiches ready for us to eat on the way."

I drank the coffee and took a quick shower. When I came out she was putting the towels in the backpack. I got dressed and put an extra towel in the backpack, along with the *New York Times* that was on the table.

When we reached the pier the ferry was almost full and some of the passengers had gone up to the open upper deck. We stood in line and bought tickets from a man who was standing at the door. We couldn't find a seat on the upper deck, but we found a corner that would do. I liked the view of Manhattan receding into the distance. When you're in it you can't see it clearly. The ferry passed by Ellis Island, the main entrance point for immigrants to America for the first half of the twentieth century. Immigrants underwent medical tests before they were allowed to go into New York. But immigrants today come by plane, and the customs and immigration buildings on the island have been turned into a museum. I told Mariah that we should visit it. I reminded myself that I hadn't really explored the city and that I kept putting off plans on the pretext that I had to finish my book to get tenure. She agreed, then added, "Yes, of course. There's no harm in knowing more about the history of our immigrant forefathers." She said the last two words in a different, sarcastic tone, and made quote marks in the air with her index and middle fingers.

"If your ancestors hadn't been slaves, you wouldn't be here now," I teased.

"Whatever! If my ancestors hadn't been slaves, America wouldn't be America anyway," she replied. Then she pointed to the west, saying, "Look at the Statue of Liberty and how small it looks from here."

It did indeed look much smaller than one imagines it to be. That's what my brother Naseer said when he visited us in New York and I took him on a tour to the southern tip of Manhattan island and we looked at the Statue of Liberty in the distance. After that the ferry headed across the strait that separates Brooklyn from Staten Island to the west, far from New York and the Upper Bay.

After reaching the peninsula we waited a quarter of an hour to take the bus to the beaches. Mariah said the best and quietest ones were at the northern end because they were more remote. We bought two bottles of cold water.

We reached the northern beaches in ten minutes. The blue that stretched to the far horizon stirred something deep inside me. The water hidden within me rejoiced when it heard the crashing of the waves. I stopped and took a deep breath and I apparently smiled unconsciously, because Mariah laughed and said, "What a smile! If the ocean makes you so happy, we'll come every week. Maybe you were a fish in a previous life."

"Why do you say that?"

"I've told you several times that in your sleep you thrash about like a fish."

"I'm sorry. It's the nightmares. Maybe I was a river."

"Ha ha, that's nice."

We walked along the sand and found a spot where she spread the towel she had brought. Then we took off the clothes we had on top of our swimsuits. Mariah was wearing a white bikini that contrasted with her brown skin. I was about to head into the water when she said, "Wait. We have to put some sunscreen on." She took a tube from the backpack, opened it, put a little on her hands, and passed the tube to me. She started to put it on her face, her chest, and her stomach. I did the same. Then she asked me to turn around so that she could put some on my back. When she'd finished it was my turn. I kissed her on the back of her neck and smelled the fragrance of her body before the smell of the sunscreen overpowered it.

Our part of the beach was relatively quiet. There were no children and no big families. Seagulls and other birds were circling, looking for something to grab. We stayed in the water for about half an hour. We splashed each other with water and laughed. Then we went back to our spot, dried ourselves off, and lay on the towel. She put on her sunglasses and took out *Invisible Cities* by Italo Calvino. The passage in Wadood's catalog had reminded me of the book, and I had given her a copy for her birthday two months earlier, along with a box of chocolates and a bottle of Dune perfume, which I liked. After reading about the perfume I realized why it attracted me, in both its men's and women's versions. It contained the smells that I love—sandalwood, musk, jasmine, and citron, all distilled into a single drop.

I took out that day's *New York Times*. I put the business section back in the bag because I didn't usually read it. Then I began as usual with the opinion page. I was struck by an article headlined "Do the Lives of Iraqis Have Value?" written by a professor of history at a university in California. The occasion for publishing the article was the official indictment of some U.S. Marines for killing twenty-four Iraqi civilians in the town of Haditha in an outburst of anger and revenge, and also of some officers for failing to investigate the massacre. They were charged not with deliberate murder but rather with failing to identify targets or to act in accordance with the rules of engagement. "Shoot first and then ask questions" is what the principal defendant told his comrades. The writer looked back at the massacres that had been committed since the beginning of the war and the incident of rape and murder in al-Mahmoudiya. She quoted General Tommy Franks as saying, when asked about the number of civilians dead, "We don't do body counts." The writer wondered when, if ever, we would find out how many Iraqis had died in this war. She ended the article by saying that the insurance payout to the beneficiaries of an American soldier killed in the line of duty was $400,000, while in the eyes of the U.S. government, a dead Iraqi civilian was worth up to $2,500 in condolence payments to the family.

The subject of the article took me back to Wadood, of course, and I decided to cut it out once we got back to the apartment and to add it to the folder. I tried to read more of the newspaper but I couldn't concentrate, or what I read seemed trivial. I folded up the newspaper so carelessly that Mariah noticed. "Is everything okay?" she asked me.

"Yes, sweetie. I'm going for a little walk."

THE COLLOQUY OF THE CLAY OVEN

I'm from the river. From its clay was I fashioned, one summer long ago, like all my peers, and from red mud and straw. We are born in summer because we need the summer sun in order to come into being. This is what I remember: I was lying in the sun with my siblings, waiting for someone to buy us. They brought me to this house and put me in the back. They held me in place on both sides with bricks and plaster, as if I might run off.

Then my mother came. She said, "In the name of God the Merciful the Compassionate," uttered some ritual invocations, and put a mirror and seven amulets on my forehead to protect me from the evil eye. Yes, she is my mother even though she didn't give birth to me and she's not of my kind. But no one has touched me but her and I haven't seen any face but hers for thirty years. She's the one who cleans my heart and wipes away the ash that sticks there. She's the one who sings to me and gives me water every day. She's the one who feeds me with firewood. She feeds me so I feed her.

She's the one who sits on the ground every morning, drinks her tea, and smokes her cigarette. Then she brings the baking tray and puts it on her lap as if it's her daughter. She breaks the dough into balls that she puts on the plate that she always places on the ground to her right. Then she takes the balls and flattens them one by one. She says "Yallah" as she stands up and comes over to me. She takes each piece of dough and tosses it gently from hand to hand. Then she lays it on the cushion that she's carrying, bends down and puts it close to the walls of my heart. And so on till it's full. After a while she takes them out with tongs and arranges them on the tray. When the loaves have piled up into a little pyramid, she covers them with a cloth, puts the tray on her head, and goes away. She comes back in the afternoon, sits in front of me, and sieves her flour for tomorrow's dough.

I say "my mother" because I claim that she loved me as if I were her son. I remember how her son used to cry in her arms when she fed me. He and his three brothers. But he's grown up now. But even so she told him off when he tried to persuade her to get rid of me and replace me. "But this oven is older than you. It has fed you and your brothers since your father died and it has helped pay your university fees. I won't let it go till I die," she said. She used to swear by me, saying, "By this oven!"

She sat in front of me this morning. She drank her tea slowly, then put the teacup on the ground. She put the tray of dough on her lap. I shut my eyes and heard the sound of the bombs.

. . .

The house is no longer a house and my mother won't feed me this morning.

The first time I saw her she reminded me of Wadood and the scavenger that he had written about. I wondered once again whether my obsession with Wadood and his writings was setting my priorities for me and defining what aroused my interest here in New York. Had his catalog become the frame of reference that overdetermined the way I perceived things? Many of my moments were wrapped up in Wadood's moments or very closely aligned with them, almost like pages of this notebook. This notebook of mine that still complains that many of its pages are blank. Can a life begin imitating another life, or at least some of its details?

One night I left my office on the fifth floor, where I was working on finishing a chapter of the book, to buy a coffee to help me concentrate. I went to the Delion deli and coffee shop on the corner of Waverly Place and Broadway in front of the entrance to the subway. As I was coming out with my coffee I saw her rummaging in the trash bin outside the shop. I was struck by the fact that she was wearing a traditional Asian straw hat and white gloves and dragging a large sack behind her. After that I came across her several times on my nocturnal ramblings and I started to watch her working rituals. She would comb the streets, stopping at every trash bin or dumpster to look for aluminum cans and plastic bottles, which she then put in the large transparent sack that she pulled behind her. When it was full she put it on her shoulder and started to stuff another sack. Sometimes I saw her carrying three sacks. Maybe it was the hat she wore that made me think of rice paddies or other fields I had seen in pictures. I saw her as a peasant in exile in these concrete jungles, harvesting fruits that were empty and depleted.

At the beginning of the spring I invited Mariah out to dinner to celebrate my having finished another chapter. I chose an Italian restaurant in the East Village. We sat down outside at a table on the pavement because the weather was favorable. She wore a white skirt that almost covered her knees and a red blouse, and she was surprised when I told her it was the first time she had worn a skirt since we had met. "Really? I hadn't noticed. Anyway, it's a special occasion that deserves a change," she said. The waiter recommended a bottle of white wine from Sicily, and I ordered it because the variety of grapes was called Damascino and I told her that this was as close as we could get to Abu Nuwas. She proposed a toast to my finishing the whole book. The waiter brought the plate of caprese salad. As we gobbled it down with bread soaked in olive oil, I remembered a line by Abu Nuwas that mentions basil, and I tried to translate it for her:

> Stop and discover wine and basil,
> Since stopping to look at deserted encampments is not my
>   thing.
> Choice wine in an earthenware jug, when mixed with water,
> Has an aroma like that of apples in Lebanon,
> Smooth, tart like musk.
> Spicy, it puts troubled minds at ease.

"Ah, beautiful, but why don't you follow his advice?"

"What do you mean? Aren't we drinking and having fun?"

"Yes of course, but you often stop to look at the remains of the past, weighed down by worries."

I didn't say anything, so she asked if I was upset with her.

"No, not at all. I was just thinking about what you said."

Mariah noticed that I was looking at something behind her. She looked around and saw the Chinese scavenger, who had lifted the lid of the trash bin that belonged to the building next to the restaurant and had started to harvest the glass and aluminum containers.

"That woman's amazing. She works long hours and covers vast areas of the city. I usually see her at night."

"She's not the only one. There are many like her in Brooklyn too. Most of them are old women. They're widowed or their children don't help them and their Social Security isn't enough."

"How come you know so much about it?"

"The woman who was my roommate in Brooklyn for two years worked in an old people's shelter, and every evening she would go on forever about all the things she had heard or seen in the shelter. It's depressing, so let's go back to your friend."

I thought and then said with confidence, "Every age has its deserted encampments. If Abu Nuwas were alive today he would weep often and drink even more. Besides, your army is occupying many of the cities where the poet went to late-night drinking parties and whose names appear unchanged in his poems."

"It's not *my* army, darling. I'm not part of that *we* or else it would be *your* army too."

"I'm sorry."

A month later, after wrestling with insomnia, I went out at half past four and walked south. After an hour, when I reached the riverbank, I saw from afar a truck parked under the Manhattan Bridge. There was a long line in front of it, with men and women pushing shopping carts piled up with bulging sacks. At the back of the truck a man was taking the sacks and then giving each person an amount of money. I watched the scene for five minutes, then headed back.

I'm sitting on the grass in the garden, which is crowded with all the pieces of furniture they have taken out of the house. My sister is sitting beside me, trying to help me put on my shoes. Or maybe I'm helping her. I don't remember that detail precisely. It doesn't matter. It was my mother who threw us out quickly and told us to sit. "Stay here and don't move," she said. I remember that the grown-ups left us alone because they were busy with what had happened. Our neighbor, Abu Zuhair, came running and told the grown-ups that he had called the "fire brigade." "They're on their way," he said, and went into the house. We didn't have a telephone yet and I didn't understand what the "brigade" might turn out to be. Eventually I heard the siren of the vast red truck and saw the firemen in their heavy uniforms dragging hoses into the house. Then I thought about the unusual term for the fire department. The neighbors heard the fire truck's siren and came out on their roofs to watch the scene. Tongues of flame were coming out of the windows of the room where my uncle had been sleeping on the second floor when he came back from Baqouba, where he was given a job as a doctor after graduating. He wasn't in the room at the time, but he had put in it some of the furniture he had bought in readiness to move to his new house after marrying his fiancée.

Umm Zuhair came to take my sister and me to their house. She said we would stay with them that night. I told her I wanted to stay in the garden. "That won't do, my boy," she said. "You have to come."

A few hours later, as we were getting ready for bed in the sitting room in Abu Zuhair's house, Mother said she had to go back to the house to fetch something. I don't remember what it was. But I remember that I jumped up and begged her to let me go with her. "No, stay here with your sister," she said. "What would you come to do?" But I clung on to her and started to cry, and she gave way as usual.

The house had been plunged into pitch darkness because they had cut off the electricity after the fire broke out. I can see it now. It was like a dead house. (It would often be plunged into darkness at night years later, during the war with Iran.) The garden was full of furniture and other stuff and there was the smell of smoke. Mother turned on the flashlight she was holding so that we could see our way. We reached the door to the kitchen. She held my hand tight and said nervously, "Be careful and don't trip." (Did she regret letting me come along?) The smell of burning grew stronger. We waded into the water that covered the floor. We turned right along the corridor that led to my parents' room. Did I go into the room with her? I'm not sure. No, I didn't go in. She put one foot across the threshold and I heard the sound of water. She aimed the flashlight at the floor and said, "Stay standing here. If you come in, your feet will get wet and your pajamas will get dirty. Don't move. I'll just go into our room to get something and then I'll be back." I stood in the darkness on the threshold of the open door. Mother lifted the hem of her gown and went on ahead. The rays of light from the flashlight went with her. I could hear her footsteps on the floor, which was flooded with water. I stood there in the dark in the doorway. I was afraid and regretted coming back to the house with her. I waited, then I caught a glimpse of light from the flashlight and heard her footsteps approaching. The fear subsided but I could still smell the burning. When we got back to Abu Zuhair's house I found it hard to sleep. Their sheets smelled strange. They were clean but they didn't smell like our sheets. In the morning I went to school and told my friends, "Our house caught fire." They looked at me in amazement.

The "burned room," as we called it, stayed as it was for several weeks. Father warned us not to go inside, but I sneaked in several times and stood inside looking in amazement at the blackened walls and the burned pieces of furniture, including the iron bedstead where my uncle slept. The remains of the mattress had turned into black cotton. The smell of fire pervaded the house, especially on the second floor. We couldn't get rid of it until the workers came, took everything out of the room, moved it far away, and then repainted the room. Some years later it became my sister's room and I would frighten her by saying that the fire was still lurking in the room and would wake up one day and burn everything.

Everything shuts its eye everything what I lack and I look for it for me it looks it doesn't find me I find myself where

is everything I'll say I say everything I'll say I shut the eyes
of the sky the hole of the sky is a grave I dig alone I was no I
wasn't there how don't I know I don't believe I believe myself did they go into the hole for who and why they didn't wait
who took the hole who took the house the house didn't wait
for me I shut its eye their eyes my eyes now I don't remember now they are with them I should have been there now the
hole who shut it but not when I opened my eyes hide-and-
seek the hole I ran and ran shut papers and smoke and stones
everything every nothing God where he was he wasn't I shut
his eyes what will he say be is he in the hole I ran and behind
me and in front of me and behind me the hole I am all of
them nothing

I came out through the kitchen door to the fig tree next to the water
tank that sits against the back wall of the house. How I longed to
taste the figs! I was so impatient for them to ripen that summer, as
I was every summer. I stepped off the concrete path onto the wet
ground. Mother would scold me if I dirtied the house with traces
of mud. Standing under the tree I looked for figs that were ripe to
pick. I made sure I didn't trample on the patch of celery and parsley
that she had planted. She had repeatedly warned me not to damage the plants by treading on them, so I walked along the edges. I
caught sight of a fig that was ripe and I reached out with my right
hand to seize it. I could feel it with my hand, on the branch that was
hanging down. It was so soft it was bound to taste sweet. I picked

it and walked to the faucet close to the big water tank. I washed it quickly and then bit off half of it. I looked forward to the soft pulp of the remaining half, which was partly yellow and partly red and gave off an amazing aroma. As I was about to devour the second half I heard the creak of a door opening and then the sound of female laughter. I realized it was the neighbors' daughters laughing. I had recently seen them from the roof of our house, sitting in the side garden. One of them was beautiful, with long black hair and pert breasts. I didn't know their names. Their house wasn't on our street, but on the street behind us. All I knew about them was that they were the Abu Khuloud household and they had moved to the area a month or more earlier. Our houses shared the back wall, which I approached warily to hear more clearly what they were saying. I bent down so that I didn't move the branches of the tree and I walked toward the wall. I crossed the irrigation ditch that ran parallel to the wall and crouched down close to the wall. I tried to put my ear close. I could hear the sound of glass bottles being put in a crate and a voice saying, "Take these too." I noticed a crack in a piece of cement in a corner between two bricks in the courses of the wall, which had been left without rendering or paint. When I touched it with my hand it fell off, leaving a considerable hole, and I could see part of the ground on the other side of the wall. I tried to lower my head to get a better view. I was so busy adjusting my position for snooping that I didn't notice that the soft, wet soil under my feet was sinking. I put my eye right up to the hole. I could see the kitchen door clearly for two seconds before my feet slipped and I fell into the ditch, which hadn't dried out since the last time it had received its share of muddy irrigation water. I could feel the mud in my hair and on my arms and back, and my clothes were spattered with it. I was worried that they might hear me moving and I would be caught out, so I didn't move for some seconds. But the sound of bottles being put in crates continued loudly. I climbed out of the ditch and felt my hair and clothes and tried to scrape off the mud. I went to the faucet, turned it on, and started to wash my hands and tried to clean my clothes as best I could. I thought about what I would say to Mother. I heard the door closing, but I consoled myself with the idea that the hole in the wall would still be there and that I would catch sight of something bigger and more valuable the next time.

I went into the house through the kitchen door, went to the bathroom, took off my clothes, piled them up, and then washed. Mother found the dirty clothes later and scolded me: "Why did you do that? Why did you roll in the mud?" She didn't believe it was from playing soccer.

I began to reconnoiter the back of their house more intensively, from the roof or from behind the curtains in my parents' room when it was empty, just on the off chance of seeing something. Two weeks later I saw the girl filling a bucket with water. I rushed down to the ground floor, went out quietly to the fig tree, and sneaked carefully into my snooping position. The ground was dry and firm. I took a plank of wood I found close to the water tank, put it in the ditch, and knelt on it so that the hole was at eye level. I saw her standing with her back to me, wearing a light blue, partially diaphanous sleeveless dress that she had raised to above her knees, tucking a part of it on both sides into her white underwear so that she could wipe the floor and move more freely. It was the first time I had seen bare thighs. She turned off the faucet and threw the cloth she was holding into the bucket. She soaked it, then wrung it over the bucket. She carried it into the kitchen through the open door and came back a minute later. The wetness had made parts of her dress cling to her body. She wasn't wearing a bra and I noticed her pearlike breasts. She was facing me this time. When she bent down to put the cloth in the bucket for a second time, an ample expanse of her breasts was visible, and I thought that they were fruits about to fall. She wrung out the cloth, went back into the kitchen, and disappeared. Then she reappeared and soaked the cloth again. But this time the area she was mopping was within my field of vision and I could watch her clearly as she bent down and mopped the floor methodically. Her bare thighs and big hips came closer and closer as she walked back toward the kitchen door. My erection grew harder and my right hand had slipped into my pants when I started watching her. I opened the zipper to take it out and play with it, while my left hand rested on a brick in the wall, with my forehead pressed against the wall. For a moment I was frightened someone might come out and discover me, but it was an opportunity I couldn't afford to miss. When she bent over the bucket to wring out the cloth again, I couldn't control myself and I ejaculated onto the ground beneath me. I took my eye away from the hole and looked down. The drops of sperm spattered on the dark soil looked odd. I put my little friend back in his place and did up the zipper. When I looked through the secret hole again I couldn't see her, but I heard the sound of water cascading out of the bucket and then the sound of her footsteps approaching. I saw her put the bucket under the faucet, go into the kitchen, and close the door behind her.

After that I thought that in the future I was going to enjoy various other scenes. I waited impatiently for her but that sighting proved to be a one-off occasion. Three weeks later I saw some builders working on the walls of the house. They scraped them clean and then covered them with a coat of stucco. I was worried this embellishment might affect the peephole I had discovered in the wall. My worry was justified. When I went out two days later and put my eye to it, I couldn't see anything.

But the scene remained vivid in my memory, and afterward whenever I smelled figs I remembered her thighs. Whenever I bit into a fig and enjoyed its softness, I remembered her breasts rubbing against each other.

I go back home.

Often.

Once every two weeks.

I get on the bus at Bab al-Mu'azzam. The number 79A. I always sit on the upper deck. I prefer the front seat on the right so that I can sit in front of the big window and see the city. I feel claustrophobic on the lower deck. Even when I can't find a seat on the upper deck I prefer to stand there, although it's difficult to keep your balance sometimes when the driver accelerates or applies the brakes. I stand and wait for a passenger to leave their seat so that I can take it. I take a book or a magazine with me and read. By the time the bus reaches our neighborhood, it has already disgorged many of its passengers. I prefer it that way, half-empty. It stops at the bus stop near our house, close to the pedestrian bridge. I can see our street in the distance. The door opens and closes. I stay sitting in my place. Our street slowly recedes and disappears. I look at the road ahead and go back to my book. The bus reaches the end of the route and the driver turns off the engine. Sometimes he comes up to the upper deck, is surprised when he sees me, and asks me to get off. When I tell him I want to go back, he says, "Okay, but you'll have to buy another ticket," so I do. Some of them don't check the upper deck and don't discover me. I sit where I am and go back to Bab al-Mu'azzam.

Days later I go back home.

Without getting off.

One of the drivers has grown used to my presence and has come to know me. At first he would ask, "What's up with you, buddy? You never leave?" But then he stopped asking. Once, when we were close to home, a woman called me as she was about to go down to the lower deck. "How are you, dear Wadood?" she said. I turned and saw a smart woman in her sixties, wearing glasses. She had gray hair. She smiled. But she had tears in her eyes as she spoke to me. Her face was familiar but I didn't recognize her. "Thank God you're safe. I heard that they released you. Where are you living now?" she said. I didn't say anything. How did she know all this? "You seem to have forgotten me. I'm Zeidoun's mother. Your neighbors," she said. Zeidoun? Yes, I used to play soccer with Zeidoun. Zeidoun Pajamas. A short guy who wore pajamas all the time. Even when he was playing soccer in the street he wore sneakers but kept his pajamas on. I remember that we formed a soccer team that included a selection of street kids to take part in the local soccer league that played on the dusty square near al-Ghadeer. We called ourselves the Za-youna Cubs and collected donations to buy a real leather football that cost five dinars, which at that time was a massive amount, because the plastic footballs that cost four hundred and fifty fils, less than a tenth as much, were no longer good enough for us. A group representing the club went to buy the ball from Rassam's in Baghdad al-Jideeda. "If you don't mind, I have to get off here. Come and visit," she said sadly. "Thank you," I said, but I didn't utter it. "May God be with you, my dear, may God help you." Zeidoun I remembered but I didn't remember her. She shook her head and said "Oh dear God" as she got off.

On my way back once, I was reading an old magazine and found a translation of one of Cavafy's poems. I was struck by a stanza and images that I still remember. About bygone days that look like snuffed-out candles. Some are still smoking, but others are cold, melted, and bent.

And I rained.

That expression will sound strange to you, so I will explain. There are hundreds of clouds that hide in my body.

Clouds that are formed from the vapor of images and words
and from heaps of things that I don't know and don't understand. Every now and then a wind blows them and turns
them into torrential rain that looks for a way out. The rain
uses my eyes and all the pores in my skin. I shrink and cry.
I sweat and shake and groan in pain. I stay that way for a quarter of an hour and sometimes for hours. Later I calm down
and feel greatly relieved because I've released the clouds and
"cleared my mind." I have read passages that are much sadder
than this one but I didn't rain. Perhaps it depends on the
amount of clouds bottled inside.

"Intense bursts of crying" is the official term that the
doctor wrote in my file. But why are people frightened of rain
inside them? Very well, I'll confess. Sometimes the rain is accompanied or preceded by thunder, which I can hear inside
me and which I let out too—in the form of screams. It's the
cycle of sadness in nature. Don't you remember how we used
to study the life cycles of oxygen and nitrogen and so on? This
is part of the cycle of sadness in nature. I claim that sadness
is a natural compound found in our bodies and in the air we
breathe, and sometimes the levels of sadness increase, depending on the conditions and context.

Anyway, the clouds all gathered in my eyes. The thunder I could hear started to hurt me. I dropped the magazine I
was reading. I clasped my head and my back arched. I could
hear the fear in the voice of the boy who was sitting next to

his mother in the seat nearby: "Mama, what's the matter with that guy?" he asked, and then he started to cry. She tried to calm him down and I could hear the sound of her footsteps as she said, "There's nothing, my boy, don't worry. Come, let's go down."

I started writing the alphabet and words at home early, two years before I went to school. My aunt Suhad, who worked as a teacher, gave me a book and a pencil and taught me how to form the letters and words. I was delighted with the letter *ha'*, my favorite because of its form at the beginning of a word. My obsession with letters and writing was accompanied by a fear of going to school that came from a source I couldn't identify. Whenever my mother said, "My God, you're growing up now and you'll be going to school," I would say, "I don't want to! I want to stay here at home."

"Impossible, my son. How so? Everyone has to go to school," she said. I wasn't convinced that going to school was inevitable until one day we were sitting on the veranda and she said, "You have to go to school to study and become an engineer or a doctor. If you don't go to school, what will become of you? Do you want to be like this kerosene man?" I looked at the young man who was coming back for the second time carrying two jerrycans of kerosene, one on each side to balance each other, to take them to the water heater near the kitchen and empty them into the fuel tank. When he'd finished the job, he came to my mother and took from his pocket a money pouch made of dirty, stained gray cloth with coins rattling inside it. He wasn't more than sixteen years old, and the strong smell of kerosene from his clothes went right up my nose. He was dark and slim with amber-colored eyes and short black hair. He was wearing a pink undershirt that looked as if it had originally been red but had faded with time. He had khaki pants and blue sneakers with gray tips and gray laces. He took the banknotes my mother gave him, put them in his money bag, then took a handful of coins out of it. I saw the dirt under his fingernails. "Keep the change," my mother said, and he thanked her. He smiled as he put the bag back in place. He turned and headed toward the door. My mother walked slowly behind him to close the main gate. The man got on his cart, picked up the reins that were tied next to his seat, made a click with his tongue, and pulled the reins. The old white horse moved off slowly, pulling the green cart. Then the man started ringing the metal bell—*ding, ding, ding*—in search of other customers.

I stood in awe in front of the horse that pulled the cart whenever the kerosene man came. I liked to watch its gestures as it waited for its owner. It shook its head. It whisked flies off with its tail. But what my mother said that day made me forget the horse and made me fear for the miserable fate I would meet if I didn't go to school. My fingernails would always be dirty, I would have to carry heavy jerrycans around all day long, and I would stink of kerosene. I would sit on the cart and smell the horse's shit. I realized that day that I had to go to school.

A few months later I went to the preparatory class in a kindergarten called the Rawdat al-Uqhuwan, which was part of the al-Ibtikar School in Palestine Street. I cried bitterly when my mother left me. And I cried when we lined up in the courtyard. I carried on crying in class, although the girl I was made to sit next to was pretty and tried to silence me in various ways. The teacher was losing patience: "What's up with you? That won't do," she said. She told everyone to be "sensible," then took me to the principal's office. We went through the courtyard to the other building where the big children were. "I want to go home," I said. "We can't send you home. You'll have to wait till the end of classes." "Leave him here for now and we'll find a solution," the principal told the teacher. "Just give me his full name." The teacher told me to sit on the sofa, then went back to her class. The janitor, 'Ammu Warda, sat outside the door watching me and smiling reassuringly at me. The principal looked through her papers, then picked up the phone, dialed a number, and waited. "There's no answer. Does your mother work or does she stay at home?" "At home," I said. "Well, she still isn't answering. I'm going to take you and put you with your sister in the third grade."

I stopped crying when I heard her say that. The principal stood up from her desk, came around, and approached me, saying, "Come on, don't cry. Come, let's go and see your sister." She took me by the hand and we went out to the corridor and then up to the second floor. The principal knocked on the classroom door and opened it. I was wearing the green uniform tunic, while the boys sitting in this class were wearing white shirts and gray pants, and the girls white blouses and blue skirts. I spotted my sister at a desk in the middle of the room. She looked confused and embarrassed. The principal told Miss Wisal, the Arabic teacher, "Sorry miss, this boy wouldn't stop crying and he was disrupting the lesson. Let him sit with his sister and maybe he'll calm down a little." "No problem. Come here, my dear. Who's your sister?" "Wafa," I said. "I can write, miss," I added for some reason. She laughed and said, "You can write? Come on then, if you can write like them we'll put you in this class and you can stay with your sister and not go back to the kindergarten. So go and sit next to Wafa." I believed her and was delighted by the idea. I walked toward the desk at which my sister was sitting with a classmate as the other children watched. At the time I didn't understand why Wafa was behaving strangely. My sudden appearance in class had embarrassed her. "Why did you come here?" she asked me irritably. The girl sitting next to her at the desk was nicer and kinder. She smiled and moved to the right to make room for me to sit with them. I took out my exercise book, pencil, pencil sharpener, and eraser to be ready to write. The principal thanked Miss Wisal and left. "Okay, let's go back to dictation then." I picked up my pencil, all primed to write, but the words that came from Miss Wisal's lips were unfamiliar and very long. I had never heard them before. Before I had written down two letters from the word I thought I had heard she had moved on to another word and then another and the children around me were writing fast. The words piled up and I realized within moments that I wouldn't be able to keep up and I would have to go back to the preparatory class, and another tear fell on my exercise book. I don't remember what happened after that, but I do remember that I cried the next day, though less, and that later I settled in. In fact, I became one of the star pupils. The competition was between me and a Kurdish girl called Viyan. We took turns being first and second in the class. We went on like that for six years until we graduated from primary school. I'll never forget the looks we exchanged in first grade when the teacher gave out gifts for those who had the best grades. The principal came and whispered something in the teacher's ear and the teacher called on Ma'an as one of the pupils at the top of the class. We were surprised because Ma'an was stupid and lazy. But he used to go home in a fancy Toyota Crown with a driver in military uniform. We later found out that he was the son of Khairallah Tulfah, Saddam Hussein's uncle and father-in-law. In second grade they transferred him to another school so he no longer came higher than us in class, but higher than some other children instead.

The first time I fell in love was at al-Ibtikar School. I was nine years old and my beloved was not one of my classmates. No. She was twelve years older than me. Rana. How I enjoyed saying her name. I wrote it hundreds of time on pieces of paper, real and imaginary. Rana was the trainee teacher who taught us history for three months, as was the practice for those at teacher training college. I dreamed of her lips and kissing them. Her breasts, which showed through the relatively generous opening in her blouse, excited me. I was embarrassed by my little erection and felt guilty that I was defiling the pure image of her that I had in my imagination, which was almost innocent at that time. I was bold enough to write her a letter declaring my love for her and my sadness that she was about to leave us.

She wrote in my little autograph book—one of those books with colored pages that we children would pass around for others to write memorable comments in. "To my favorite student. I hope you have a brilliant future. With affection, your friend Rana," she wrote. I was delighted by "my favorite student" and "your friend," but the word "affection" puzzled me somewhat and left my happiness incomplete. I even asked my mother whether there was a difference between affection and love and her answer was ambiguous. I later discovered that affection was not like love, and this was confirmed when I heard at the end of the week that a boy, staying on after classes for his father to take him home, had seen Mr. Sabah, one of the trainee teachers, kissing Miss Rana in an empty classroom. I tried not to believe what I had heard, but I started observing them and I cried when I discovered that she had betrayed me.

I go back home.

I went back home.

Yes, I went back, just once.

I plucked up courage and went down from the upper deck to the lower deck when I saw the pedestrian bridge in the distance. The driver opened the door and I found myself on the pavement. The bus moved off and the people who had got off with me dispersed to their various homes. I hesitated and stood there on the pavement for five minutes. Then I decided that I wouldn't retrace my steps this time, as I used to do in the past. Yes, I would go back home.

I came to our street. I looked for the open area where we used to play soccer on the right. But it was no longer an open space. Its place had been taken by a two-story house with walls painted gray. It had a wrought-iron gate painted white. There were no cars inside. I could smell the citrus blossom on the branches that hung over the wall. A cat with black and yellow spots walked past, looking more emaciated than any stray.

I reached the first intersection where we used to hang out for many hours when we were teenagers and later. We watched everything that was going on and everyone passing by, especially girls who were coming back from school. It was on this corner that I witnessed one of the wonders of the universe. In a matter of just a few months the girl next door had been transformed from a child whose passing I did not notice into a woman whose passing created a magnetic field that controlled the flow of blood in my veins. I even began to pursue her and tried to make conversation with her before she got home. She didn't say anything the first time I tried to speak to her. She looked frightened. The second time she smiled because I joked with her, saying, "What? Can't you hear?" I don't remember what happened after that. Did they move to some other area? Did she disappear from life or from my memory?

The details along the way were the same. Yes, some of the houses looked older than I remembered them and others had been renovated and improved. The street itself seemed narrower. I went past the house of the lawyer, Tuʻma al-Saʻdi. The plaque with his name was still on the gatepost. Then there was the house of the businessman who owned the candy factory in Jamila and whom God blessed with four daughters but no son. He is said to have married another woman who was younger so that she would produce a male heir, but she gave him two more daughters, and I don't remember if he finally succeeded in his endeavor.

I stopped outside our house.

But it wasn't there. I found another house that was completely different. Much taller. I didn't understand how that could have happened. How could a whole house vanish and be replaced by a different house? It had four large windows with smoked glass on the second floor. The palm tree that stood in the corner of the garden had disappeared. The garden wall was relatively high, but you could see the tops of citrus trees that were much shorter than the ones at our house and a mulberry tree of medium height that we didn't have in our garden. The posts at the gate were high and coated in light brown stucco. Between them there was a high black gate. On the right-hand post was the doorbell and next to it a small red light. The house number was still 26 but there wasn't a sign with a name to say who lived there. I felt the heat of the sun stifling me. I pressed the bell and left my finger on it for a long time. I heard a voice shouting, "Where's our house?" It was my own voice but it was coming from far away. "You kept pressing the bell and you wouldn't take your finger off. The people and the neighbors gathered around you." That's what my uncle said when I asked him what happened.

I went back but I didn't go back.

My uncle said, "Wadood, after you gave me power of attorney, we sold the land for a good price and we still have the money. I put it in the bank and whenever you want or need anything, just tell me and I'll withdraw the amount."

I felt stifled and thought I had become a burden on them. I heard my uncle's wife, the fat whore who pretended to care about me, saying to my uncle one night, "How are we going to get out of this mess? Why did you let them discharge him from that place? The boy's not normal. He keeps talking to himself and whenever he screams at night, he startles me."

"Where can he go? He doesn't have anyone but us and I don't have the heart to leave him at the mental hospital. They treat them like animals. I think he's improving."

"Improving? Are you out of your mind?" she replied.

I suspected she was working with them and spying on me. When I told my uncle that, he didn't believe me and said, "May God forgive you. She pouts and whines, but all these things are in your head, Wadood."

I heard her whispering about me to her neighbor.

When my condition improves! Ha ha ha. How many times has my condition improved and then I go back to square one! "How many times are we done for?" They let me go out by myself. I went to al-Mutanabbi Street to buy books and there I met Muhammad al-Sallum, who was with me at university. I hadn't seen him for years and I didn't recognize him at first because in our university days he had been slim and he hadn't been bald. I came across him standing in front of a stall and it was he who called me. "You're Wadood, aren't you?" he said. "Where the hell have you been, man?" As we were chatting and reminiscing about our university days I saw

a handwritten sign on the wall behind him. "Room to let," it
said. My uncle didn't understand why I wanted to live in a
room in al-Mutanabbi Street. "If you're not comfortable here,
find yourself a small apartment close to our place. Why con-
fine yourself to a room?"

But I insisted. "It'll be more convenient there, for me
and for you. You've been very supportive, uncle," I told him.
In the end he didn't raise any objections, because having me
in his house had exhausted his patience and no doubt the
sense of relief he would enjoy after I left far outweighed his
anxiety and his occasional sense of guilt.

I'm mentioning all this to you because you asked me several times how I came to be in al-Mutanabbi Street selling
books. As you can see it isn't exciting or necessarily compli-
cated. It was just a matter of escaping from a little social hell
to somewhere where I had more space. This little room from
which I am writing to you is my real homeland because it is
full of books and every book is like a whole sky. It also con-
tains my catalog, which in its turn will contain everything I
know and can imagine. But I don't want to be unfair to my
uncle or give you the wrong impression of him. He's a kind-
hearted person and he visits me from time to time, at least
once a month, to make sure I'm well and to give me the
monthly allowance that he withdraws from the bank and that
we agreed on after I moved out of his house. Selling secondhand books here these days is not at all a profitable way to

make a living. We always lose out, but I manage to live on very little.

I don't know how to classify it—a dream or a nightmare? I thought that we were one person. A single "I" united us. I saw him when I looked in the mirror and he saw me. We had the same memory, the same voice, and the same body. Our name was neither Wadood nor Nameer. I don't know the name. Then I left that "I," or was taken out of it. I broke away from it. I left Baghdad and traveled far away. When I came back to Baghdad I didn't recognize Wadood because he too had become detached from "I" and had become another person. He became Wadood, in the same way as I became Nameer. And so he didn't recognize me. "I" combined Wadood and me because I wanted to know what happened to Wadood because it could happen to me. "I" says to me, "Go with Wadood to his house to find out what happened, so I can go back to how I was and so he can too. Follow Wadood, who is looking for his house." He goes into a side street and disappears, and I wake up.

THE COLLOQUY OF PHOTOGRAPHIC NEGATIVES

Agfa (24)

1.   overexposed. Mostly black except for a small patch of light in the middle and some haze in one of the corners. (He didn't intend to take a picture anyway. The salesman put the film in the camera, closed the cover, and then handed it to

him. But he pressed the button by mistake, and the shutter opened and saw what it saw at that moment. This was the first time he had held a camera.)

2.   A woman about twenty years old. She has short black hair cut in the garçon style. She's wearing a white blouse and a blue jacket and she has a binder and a book tucked under her right arm and a small purse in her left hand. Her eyes are laughing (there's some dark kohl on her eyelids). Her head is slightly tilted to the right. Behind her is a shop window and we can see a man walking past the shop. To the left there are cameras attached to the wall. (He told her that the first picture he took would be of her.)

3.   The woman is standing next to a young man who's wearing a blue jacket, a white shirt, and gray pants. They are standing right in the middle of the frame and smiling. The background is the same as in picture 2, but the composition is better. (He asked the salesman to take a picture of them.)

4.   A street scene with vehicles (the most prominent is a red double-decker bus) moving toward the lens of the camera. In the median strip there are some shrubs of medium height and a man trying to cross the street. In the background there's a building and a footbridge. The sky is cloudless. (A man who passed them by looked at him in surprise and turned around after walking past. He thought of saying, "What's up? Never seen a camera?" but he didn't say anything.)

5.   A close-up of the woman's face laughing flirtatiously. Her right hand (with a bracelet around the wrist) is raised in front of the lens and seems less sharp than the rest of the picture.

(She said to him, "As you like. You're going to run out of film in five minutes this way." He replied, "Don't I have to practice? And I bought three rolls of film.")

6.   Some large eggplants stuffed in the lid of a cardboard box that's been turned upside down for use as a container. (She said to him, "What? You're making a documentary about the life of eggplants!" He asked her, "Aren't you hungry? I'm dying of hunger.")

7.   A restaurant worker wearing a white apron stained with oil is cutting slices of shawarma with a massive knife. (He said to the worker, "Boss, if it's not too much trouble, could you include some extra tail fat please?" She screwed up her face and said, "Ugh, how can you eat that stuff?" "You're not a serious eater, my dear. It's the best part.")

8.   The woman puts on lipstick and looks into a small round mirror. (She had finished washing her hands and mouth and had come back to the table. Before taking the picture, he said, "You got married and never knew what became of me. While you put lipstick on your lips I bit mine in pain." She was surprised. "What kind of stuff is that?" she said. "That's a folk poet who wrote a poem for his love on the night she married someone else." "Looks like you want me to marry someone else?" "Not now, later!" They laughed together, but her laugh turned into a scowl when she saw him taking a picture of her. "Don't you think you're overdoing it? Enough! If you don't put that camera away, I'll get upset and go." "Okay, that's it. I'm done.")

9.   Her elegant hand, which ends in nails with red varnish,

is holding a plastic cup full of ice cream with "al-Khasaki Sweets" on it. We can see a small watch under the bracelets on the wrist of the other hand, which is holding a small plastic spoon. (He convinced her that he would take a picture only of her hand, that her face as she ate wouldn't be visible in any picture. "So stubborn!")

10.   A fountain in the middle of a square full of bushes and myrtles with cars driving around it. ("Come on, we're going to be late for class if you stop to take pictures all the time." "You should be encouraging me and supporting my talent.")

11.   A wide street and children walking along in school uniform. There are buildings on both sides and eucalyptus trees on the sidewalk. (He said to himself, "This will turn out to be a useless picture.")

12.   A large mural of Saddam Hussein wearing an academic gown and cap, holding a graduation certificate. Under the picture are the words "The pen and the rifle speak the same language." (She whispered to him, "He has enough pictures everywhere and then you take a picture of the picture!" "That's because I'm using him to practice.")

13.   A brass plaque inscribed "Al-Farahidi Hall" in black over a large wooden gate.

14.   A group of students, male and female, sitting in a lecture hall. (They insisted he take a picture of them. He whispered in her ear, "Half of these people are hypocrites and it's not worth wasting a photo on them. But what can I do? I can't pick and choose." "It's your fault. Put the camera away and be done with it.")

15.   Her white blouse and her gray skirt are lying on the floor next to the bed and one of her shoes is sitting a few inches away.

16.   A white bra lying on the floor. (She's in the bathroom washing and she doesn't hear the sound of the picture being taken. He wanted to immortalize this moment. He didn't realize that the floor of the tiny apartment could assume such aesthetic and poetic value.)

17.   The bathroom door is ajar. A side view of the upper half of her body bending down slightly over the basin. The arm washing her face shields most of her left breast but does not hide it completely. (This time she hears the sound of the shutter as it opens and closes. She'll open the door and say, "What's that?")

18.   The eyes are full of fear. Her mouth is gaping in an angry scream. Her hands are covering her breasts. (She'll slam the door closed and sob in the bathroom. She'll refuse to open the door or talk to him.)

19.   She's sitting on the edge of the bed fully dressed. She has covered her eyes with her hands. (She shouted out loud, "Enough. Don't you know what enough means? I've been telling you all day long that I don't want to have my picture taken. Give me the camera.")

20.   A picture that is not clear. She is standing with her hand outstretched toward the lens. ("That's it, I swear. I'm not going to have the film developed." He took it out of the camera and offered it to her. "There you are, take it. No one's going to see the pictures. Burn it. Throw it away if you like.

Whatever you want, do it, but just stop crying." He put the
film on the bed beside her.)
21, 22, 23, 24 darkness (She had intended to destroy the film
but decided to keep it as a souvenir.)

I opened the glass door of the refrigerated cabinet to look for the
milk that Mariah likes: two percent fat. The cold air trapped in the
fridge brushed my face. As I took the plastic bottle of milk and put
it in the shopping basket I was carrying in my left hand, I noticed
that there was a whole row of milk in glass bottles of various sizes.
It was rare to see milk in bottles now that paper and plastic were
dominant. I left the cabinet door open and picked up one of the
bottles. The name of the company was Fresh and the slogan under
the name was "From the Farm to Your Table." Under the slogan
there was more writing in a smaller font: "We Pamper Our Cows
Because Happy Cows Produce Delicious and Refreshing Milk. We
Don't Use Antibiotics. We Use Glass Because It Is Safer than Plastic
and Does Not Pose a Danger to Your Health. Enjoy It with Us." The
bottle I had picked up was whole milk, but there was also milk flavored with chocolate and orange. I put the bottle back in its place,
took a bottle of orange-flavored milk and put it in the shopping basket. The orange-flavored milk and the coolness of the open fridge
took me back to Baghdad in the middle of the seventies and to
our delight (mine and my sister's—Naseer had not yet been born)
when the milkman, driving a large refrigerated truck with the words
Dairy Company written on the sides in large letters, came along

and stopped outside the house. We would help Mother carry the crates of empty bottles to the door so that we could change them for full bottles. The milkman would get down from the driver's seat, turn, and stand at the back of his truck. Then he would unbolt the back door and the cold air would drift down. He checked the number of empty bottles in each crate and made sure they weren't broken. Mother told him about the other crate that had smaller bottles: "Half orange and half banana." The orange was my favorite flavor, but Wafa liked the banana. He pushed the two crates into the truck, climbed into the back of the truck, and pushed a crate of white milk to the edge of the deck. Then he arranged another crate that was half orange and half banana. Mother would take one crate down and he would take the other. Then she would ask him for some big packets of the yellow cheese and some of the small packets of clotted cream that he sold. She put them on the crate of white milk and paid him, and he gave her a receipt. My sister and I would help each other carry the crate of flavored milk into the kitchen. This cooperation was temporary and exceptional, dictated by the need to enjoy the milk as soon as possible. The eternal struggle between us would resume as soon as we had the crate in the kitchen and disagreed over which of us should have first dibs on the bottle opener. She often let me go first, saying, "You're the baby." The milk truck disappeared at the end of the 1970s for no obvious reason. With it the flavored milk disappeared, and only traditional milk remained.

Mariah was surprised that evening when she saw the bottle of orange-flavored milk in the fridge, and I told her the story.

☙❀❧

> People of my time, do you know of secret thoughts?
> I know, but I'm not going to reveal:
> Neither my birth nor my old age are my choice
> Nor how long I'll live. So what choice do I have?
> My life is a torment and death is a relief
> And every son born of woman is a prisoner in the soil

I see myself there.

It's strange that you can't go back to the place you long to go back to. But you go back, under duress, to the place you long to escape. That has often happened to me in my waking state. They wrap me up and jab me with a needle, and when I wake up I find myself there. It still happens in nightmares, of course.

I see myself there.

In my corner, curled up near the window. I am thinking: how can I not be? How can I not be "me"? Can I put an end to my existence? Believe me, I wasn't philosophizing, and these questions were not self-indulgent, but rather expressions of deep pain. A question might occur to you: so why haven't I killed myself? Who told you I haven't tried? I did try in the beginning and it wasn't at all easy. I tried three times and failed. The first time they found me before I had bled enough. One of them screamed and they rushed toward me. The traces of my brush with death are still on my wrist. Then

I followed another method, but all I gained from this battle was a poisoning, a chronic stomach ulcer, and two weeks confined to bed. That's how life (and those who control it) punishes you if you want to leave it and stab it in the back—by sentencing you to more pain. The same pain from which you are trying to break free. Then I convinced myself that killing myself would be an admission that I was defeated and that they had triumphed over me, at least in the last round, and that's something I would never accept. You might make light of what I'm going to say, but I honestly had a real horror that what would follow my suicide would be the same life I had already lived, in all its details and with all its pains. I would be more miserable in it because I would know everything before it had happened and I wouldn't be able to change it. I have to be honest—the credit goes to Dr. Salman, the young doctor who showed unusual interest in my case after he was moved to the hospital. He had only just graduated and had started work enthusiastically and with zeal. The misery of life and the bureaucratic routine in a place such as Iraq had not yet crushed his idealism or his dedication. He listened to me seriously and I felt that he believed everything I was saying. Unlike the others, who had become like rusty machines that treated me roughly and inhumanely. It was he who convinced me that suicide would be a defeat, and it was he who encouraged me to write. He told me he couldn't give me a notebook and a pen. Pens were banned because they might be used to harm oneself or others. But he gave me a small tape recorder with cassette tapes. It was an old machine he had used while at university to record lectures. I was wary and had suspicions that he was in league with them and wanted to spy on me. I didn't record anything of value at first. I was also worried they might confiscate the tapes later. So all I recorded was some words and symbols to remind me of pointers to the material I was recording in my head. From then on, the embryonic idea of the catalog started to take shape, and he deserves credit for encouraging me.

I see myself there.

I'm still standing, clutching the iron bars and resting my forehead on them.

I put my finger in my mouth and wet it with saliva. Then I take it out to check the direction of the slight breeze. That's when the wind comes our way. I'm like a sailor getting ready for a long voyage. I wave at the birds that sometimes pass. I clap for no one. In various ways and through various activities I take advantage of the half an arm's length of freedom made possible by the absence of glass in the windows. They removed the glass because one of the patients in the ward broke the window with his fist and used a piece of it as his passport to oblivion. But this freedom, which allows me to put my arm out and clap my hands outside the ward, comes at an exorbitant price on winter nights when the cold sneaks in and claps in our bones. The extra blanket they give us in winter isn't enough. Everyone misses the windows when a violent sandstorm blows up, covering everything and all of us with a thick layer of sand. Despite the bother of having to clean the place up the next day and despite the taste of the dust, the sight of the sky that day was extraordinary, at least for me. I stood watching it for more than an hour.

The strange thing about that place is that its effect on the inmates is usually inversely proportional to the declared objectives. Those who are mad remain mad, and may even get madder. The sane go mad. I don't believe that the lines between the two states are necessarily clear. The lines that some people think are clear do in fact have overlaps, zigzags, and areas of ambiguity. There are islands, regions, and pockets where madness asserts sovereignty and raises its banners, although they lie in the realm of reason. The opposite is also true, because there are sane people who have been displaced and driven from their homes into the realms of madness.

I see myself there.

In my head I was going over what Beckett wrote, repeating in silence: "Nothing happens, nobody comes, nobody goes, it's awful!" but it is different. Godot doesn't come, of course. But things start coming to me by themselves and addressing me. Yes, things don't happen, but they speak. And my uncle used to come and visit me. To tell the truth, he never stopped visiting me. He might stay away for two or three months, but he would visit me. He didn't say much, except for the usual questions about how I was and his constant assertion that my condition was improving and that he was trying to mediate to get me out as soon as the doctors would allow it. Things spoke more than my uncle, more than everyone. Except for Dr. Salman perhaps. And my Turkoman friend Safaa. Yes, he was the only person who was relatively close to me. Safaa cried bitterly when he said goodbye to me. He studied engineering at the University of Technology and graduated with honors, and then completed a master's degree. He then managed a factory that his family owned. But he had a breakdown and they put him in here, or rather in there (I wonder whether there's a part of me that's still there!). I've often thought about the terms *break down* and *a nervous breakdown*, and the question kept bothering me: "Can someone who has had a breakdown revert to how they were before? Sane and healthy?" I don't know. I often imagined myself as a building that has collapsed and is trying to rebuild itself, stone by stone, wall by wall, floor by floor. It's trying to restore its structure and all the details as far as possible. You have to imagine the time and effort that all this requires. You have to persuade those who were living in the building that they can move back in to bring it back to life and keep it alive. Yes, there were people living in me and some of them will never come back, of course, because they died when it collapsed. Many people will abandon you after you collapse. Ah, I like this image. I'm an abandoned person that is inhab-

ited at the same time. Inhabited by things and spirits. But
how many collapses can the building take anyway? Then,
after hours thinking about this metaphor, I realized that the
difference between the building and the rubble lies in the
way the stones and the other materials are arranged—in other
words, in the form. The content is the same in the building
and in the rubble. The text is written in two ways.

I see myself there.

When I tire of watching the scene from the inside
(a small ward with four beds), I rest my forehead on the iron
bars and watch the scene outside. A piece of wasteland except
for a eucalyptus tree in the distance. It stands alone near the
perimeter wall, as though it's waiting for a visit from another
tree that has promised to come back but is running late, or as
though it's waiting to go back to its family. A few yards to the
right of it there are piles of sand and bricks. To the left there
are some rusty steel bars of the kind used in reinforced concrete. The space between the window and the eucalyptus tree
is overgrown, with patches of grass here and there. Beyond
the wall and the eucalyptus tree stretches the sky, crisscrossed
sometimes by small birds that rest on the branches of the tree
or land on the steel bars. When there's a fair number of them
I can hear them twittering. My heart beats and its wings flap,
without flying off and without me flying. I ask myself: who
clipped my wings? The scene, as you can see, needed something more, so sometimes I used my own stock of images to

add what was missing: a butterfly, for example. And I trained myself to listen to the tree first, and I succeeded. The tree says everything. After that I listened to the birds, and between the two of them I can hear everything. The scene is permeated by an additional logic that isn't apparent.

She told me her mother wanted to meet me and asked whether I had any objection to our visiting together at the weekend and having dinner with her. I agreed enthusiastically. She clapped in childish joy, then added with a smile, "Don't worry, this isn't a test and it doesn't necessarily mean that our relationship is now very serious. She just wants to meet my boyfriend."

"So you don't think our relationship is serious?" I said.

"Of course it's serious. But too much seriousness ruins everything. We're still at the beginning," she replied. I didn't comment.

The next Saturday we took the number 2 subway to Brooklyn. Her mother was still living in Crown Heights in the house where Mariah was born and lived until she finished high school and moved to Pennsylvania to go to college. On the way I asked her about the area. She said her childhood there had been generally happy. But she remembered the unrest and violence that lasted for three days in 1991 after a vehicle in a Jewish funeral procession accidentally killed two black children. Protests broke out, many shops were burned down, and the police deployed in large numbers. She was nine at the time. She was frightened and didn't go to school, staying at home with her mother's husband, who was then out of work. Her mother has been working as an English teacher in a government school in the area for three decades and will retire in five years. Her father is from Georgia, but he left Mariah's mother after she was born and she hasn't heard anything from him. When she was eighteen her mother broke the news to her that the man she had been calling Dad for years was not her father and she told her the name of her real father. She told her that he had abandoned her as soon as he heard she was pregnant and hadn't left an address or ever contacted her. Mariah felt sad of course, although her stepfather had treated her as if she was his own flesh and blood and she had never felt that he discriminated between her and her half-sister Maya, who was born two years later. For a while she was determined to find her father and meet him face to face. She looked for him and found that he was living in Georgia, where he worked as a minister in a parish church, and she learned that he had found God after a life of frivolity, dissipation, and addiction. He was "born again" and married with three children. Under a family photo that he had posted on the church's website he had written, "The family is the source of love and the Christian life. Through it we assert our truthfulness and our loyalty in our daily lives." Mariah wondered whether he felt guilty or, when he wrote that sentence, whether he thought about the daughter he had left in his girlfriend's womb when he abandoned them. She bought a plane ticket to Atlanta and decided to go and listen to one of his sermons in his church and to go up to him afterward and tell him she was his daughter. Her mother didn't object, saying she understood her desire to meet her father and be in touch with him. But Mariah decided against going, since meeting him wouldn't change much and might complicate things. She might be able to forgive him for abandoning her mother because he was afraid of responsibility, and maybe he had been going through a difficult stage in life, but she would not forgive him for his silence all those years, especially after he settled down and found God! She wrote him a long letter saying everything but she never sent it.

"I'm sorry," I said.

"There's no need to feel sorry," she said. "As far as my relationship with my father is concerned, I reached a stable emotional state years ago, or rather I don't have a relationship with him. I'm not sad and I won't be sad. No, that's not true. I do feel sad once or twice a year."

In the first weeks, after she told me about her problems with her father and how the relationship had been cut off, I asked her about her childhood. Her answers were brief and vague and I guessed that she would open up later when she felt more comfortable. I teased her, saying, "Does the fact that you're telling me these details mean that our relationship is now more serious?" She punched me and said, "Enough. Are you going to punish me all week for what I said about being serious?"

Her mother's husband worked as a railroad engineer with Amtrak. He didn't spend all week at home because he worked on the New York–New Orleans line and spent the night in New Orleans before coming back.

I asked her what family name her mother used so that I could address her the way she liked, and she said, "The same name as I use, Dawson. I decided to take her family name and she didn't take her husband's family name."

We came out of the station and walked for some minutes. Then she pointed at one of the houses in a line of three-story brownstone buildings. "That's it," Mariah said. In front of each house there were stone steps leading up to the front door.

Her mother's apartment was on the second floor. Her mother opened the door wearing a blue dress and a white apron around her waist. She hugged Mariah warmly and kissed her, then shook my hand. She was in her early fifties, though she looked ten years younger. She had large dark eyes, a thin nose, short hair, and a warm smile.

I was struck by some pictures on the wall in the hallway. There was a black-and-white photograph of Nina Simone. "Mom really loves her songs," said Mariah. There was another one of a black woman with Martin Luther King. I didn't know who she was so I asked them. "That's Mahalia Jackson," Mariah's mother said. "The best gospel singer." Then there were some family photos showing Mariah and her sister in various stages of childhood and adolescence, a picture of Mariah holding her graduation certificate from the University of Pennsylvania, where she studied history, and one of Maya graduating from high school. "Maya's studying at Brown University now," Mariah's mother said proudly. Then, pointing to a picture of her and her husband in wedding attire, she added, "Marvin, my husband, should have been here but he's late back from New Orleans."

We moved on to the living room and she started asking me about my family and how we came to the States, and about my relatives in Iraq and how they were doing. I told her I had come in 1993 and that most of my relatives had left Iraq in recent years. "I'm sorry to hear it. The war is a crime. I didn't vote for Bush or his racist father before him." I smiled but didn't say anything.

She asked me to sit on her left and Mariah sat on her right, facing me. The fourth chair remained empty. When we were seated her mother gave Mariah and me a hand each, closed her eyes and said, "Let us thank the Lord for this blessing, and for the love that unites us. Amen. Please, help yourself." The plates were neatly arranged—a small plate for salad on top of a larger plate, with a white napkin to the left. Mariah's mother had worked as a waitress for some time before finishing her university education and starting to teach. "We'll start with turnip and spinach salad, then fried okra, and then fried chicken Southern style. Did you bring your appetite with you, Nameer?" she said.

I told her I had all my appetite with me and she laughed. I added that okra was an important dish in Iraq too. She was surprised, raised her eyebrows and said, "Really?"

"Yes," I replied, "it's cooked with tomato sauce and we eat it with rice or with pieces of bread like Indian tandoori bread."

Putting some salad on my plate, Mariah's mother asked, "I know you don't cook, Mariah, but does he cook for you?"

"No, but he takes me to excellent restaurants in Manhattan," she replied.

"If he's a generous man, don't let him get away from you."

We laughed, but Mariah protested: "What do you mean, Mom? You shouldn't say things like that."

Her mother turned to me and said, "This is what we call soul food, which our ancestors cooked."

The food was delicious and the okra was cooked with peppers, onion, and spices. We finished off dinner with apple pie, a little ice cream, and a cup of coffee. We helped her mother take the plates to the kitchen, and Mariah put them in the dishwasher. Her mother pressed us to stay after dinner and watch television with her but I thanked her and Mariah said, "Nameer doesn't like TV."

Mariah's mother raised her eyebrows and said, "He's free to like whatever and whoever he likes and hate whoever he hates."

"I'm going to take him to The Old Crib," Mariah told her.

"That's an excellent idea. He's eaten our food, so he can listen to our music."

I liked the name of the place, "crib." Mariah said it was a small bar where young jazz and blues musicians came to play and sometimes famous people would pass by, and who knows if we might strike it lucky tonight.

Mariah's mother said goodbye to us, and hugged me and kissed me too. As we went down the steps she asked me if I had been bored.

"On the contrary, I enjoyed it very much," I replied.

The Old Crib wasn't far, but it was small. We paid an entrance charge at the door, found two chairs at the bar, and had to squeeze carefully between the tables to reach the bar. We could see the singer in the far corner at the other end of the place, but a pillar meant we couldn't see the others in the band. Mariah ordered a Corona beer and I asked for a mojito. A sign behind the bar said "Whisper. The music sounds nicer than your voices." After two songs the singer said they were going to take a short break. She came to the bar to fill the empty glass that had been on the floor next to her foot. Mariah asked her to sing a Nina Simone song.

"I'd be delighted. Any song in particular?" the singer asked.

"'I Want a Little Sugar in My Bowl.' It's my favorite song," said Mariah. The singer sang it right after the break. I kept humming the tune as we took the train back to my apartment.

Alone in front of it alone a black hole in my heart his heart wreckage a dead sky its stars no alone a sky with holes from which blood is dripping God's blood blood blood blood a sky its blueness a needle sewing I hurt I cry I'll forget I don't want a nail to go in more than one nails a nail in the wall in the piece of wood in my heart holes dust in my mouth his mouth doesn't speak his lip a tree that's dying I stand up and walk shshshshsh it'll end but after a while I'm not walking I see him climb this edge fall here they slept dust closes them don't tell them phew the papers under the cupboard heartbeat an ink pen her wing colors my finger she stops I put her in the book don't say or say say he won't write the moon split open its door and run away the moon's door is broken papa enough

Mariah loves me and knows how to love me. She reminds me of a line in a popular old poem: "She's young and doesn't know how to love and desire has never stirred her heart," because she's quite the opposite. She's young but she knows how to love. And I love her love for me. Without promises or conditions. She knows how to run her fingers over my wounds to discover the contours of my soul. But, intelligently and wisely, she makes do with tending to my wounds and she doesn't want to eliminate them. She never claims or proclaims that she's going to heal them. Unlike that woman who, after the first night we spent together years ago, asked about my relationship with my father. When I told her how I hated him, she said, "I'll heal all your wounds!" All I could say was, "You seem to have started confusing your working hours and your hours of relaxation." (She had studied psychology and had started training to be a social worker.) That relationship ended the next day.

A whole year passed without either of us saying "I love you." It wasn't necessary anyway. Once we spoke about scars, visible and invisible. It was one of the first times we slept together. I ran my fingers down her back and asked about a little scar there on the lower part. She said it was all that was left of an accident when she fell off her bicycle at the age of ten. She added a phrase that I loved at the moment: "I like that scar. It's part of the history of my body and part of my memories." When she asked me about my family and we came to my father, I said, "I hate him." She wasn't surprised. She asked me for details and when I told her the story she said she understood. "White people keep talking about 'peace' and the need for people to make peace with their past. I don't believe in that logic. There are things that can't be accepted and memories that must stay alive."

"Amen," I said.

I want the feathers I want them he has to to stick them one by one these feathers I stick them so that I can go down to them there I can't see anything you won't see a feather fell I'm not a bird no I don't dig by night their names fly a feather fell faces faces faces where are they where is it all they eat the dust an eye flies my eyelash is broken where no address permit travel document sees me the smoke and shuts shuts me Ereshkigal where's my mother where where you have to fall more maybe they where are your feathers I'll find them darkness darkness

"I must learn Arabic," she said seriously one day.

"It's a beautiful language. There's a poet who says, 'He who filled languages with charms placed the secret of beauty in Arabic.' But why?"

"So that I understand what you say in your sleep. You toss and turn like a fish on dry land and mouth things that I don't understand."

"Sorry."

"No need to be sorry. It's sad that we can't be together in dreams and nightmares."

"Yes, in an ideal world we would keep each other company even in sleep. Then I could experience the peace you enjoy when you sleep."

"I always sleep deep," she said with a laugh.

Even the sound of the radio, which I left on at night to hear classical music and the news bulletin every hour, didn't disturb her in the least.

Because she had started to spend most weeknights in my apartment, she had begun to move some of her clothes and leave them at my place. She was like a bird nesting on the branches of my life. I gave her a copy of the key to the apartment and cleared a space for her in the closet and half of the bathroom cabinet.

She slept deep. As if she were lying on the seabed. But even when she's sleeping on her left side and I pull back an arm that's wrapped around her, she'll pull it back and cling to it as if she doesn't want me to move away. But I toss and turn, then try to read a while. She wears an eye mask that shields her from any light. She sleeps on the seabed like a mermaid, while I thrash and turn between the shore and the water. When I fail, I get out of bed, get dressed, and go out for a walk.

Time doesn't move in one direction. I wouldn't believe that unless I had escaped from one of its processions. I fell on the roadway and joined a procession that was moving in the opposite direction. I began to see my life in reverse and I went back to my mother's womb. When I turned to go back, they aborted me.

Insomnia hadn't previously been a serious problem in my life. I suffered from it from time to time for one night and then it would pass. It didn't call for any treatment. But after I came back from Baghdad it imposed itself like an unwelcome regular guest. At first I sought help from mint-flavored NyQuil, which was originally meant for colds and flu but also has a sedative effect. The only problem with it was that it took a heavy toll on my vitality the next day. I would feel lethargic all day long. But even NyQuil began to lose its effectiveness as the months passed. I began to drink two doses and then three, and addiction to it started to cause side effects and an inflammation in the wall of my stomach. After I visited the doctor to have the effects of the inflammation treated, he offered to prescribe me sleeping pills. I tried not to become addicted to them and promised myself that I would take them only if the sun had risen before I was able to fall asleep, if I had an important meeting or work that required that I sleep at least two hours.

THE COLLOQUY OF SHAB'AD

Shab'ad didn't sleep much. She kept tossing and turning, fighting off an anxiety that made it difficult to sleep—the anxiety that she might write the wrong words in the morning. Why should she be anxious when she had been training for years and could write with her eyes closed? She had memorized the poem that she had composed specially for the goddess Nisaba, and the next day she would write it down in front of everyone in the temple. She repeated it aloud dozens of times, and before she went to bed, she repeated it in front of her father, who smiled and kissed her on the forehead. "You will be a great scribe, Shab'ad, like your father and your forefathers," he said. "Great Nisaba will bless you and grant you the strength to be a priestess in her temple."

She repeated the verses of the poem once again in the darkness:

> Glory be to Nisaba
> Daughter of An and Urash
> Sister of Ninsun, mother of Gilgamesh,
> Mother of Ninlil.
>
> Enki, the God of Wisdom, named you scribe of the gods
> and built you a school
> It is you who keeps the records
> And chronicles momentous events
> The gods seek your help, you offer them advice and
> counsel
> Glory be to Nisaba.
>
> Nisaba is bearer of the lapis lazuli tablet
> Nisaba, the oryx that drinks the sacred milk
> That opens the mouth of the seven heavens and kisses
> them
> The mistress who was granted divine powers
> Glory be to her
> Glory be to Nisaba
>
> My mistress
> Mother and goddess of the earth.
> You are the one who soothes the earth with cold water
> The great mountain begat you, wisdom gave birth to you
> Glory to you, O pure one, mistress of scribes
> Keeper of the records of Enlil, keeper of the seals

O sage of the gods
Glory to you
Glory to Nisaba

Shab'ad knelt humbly in front of the wall of the temple
where Enki appeared as he approached Nisaba. He had prepared sacrifices for her and built her house of wisdom for
her. He put the tablet of lapis lazuli on her knees, so that
she could consult the holy tablet in the sky and write down
the names of the stars. She repeated the poem in a trembling voice and, when she had finished, the high priest of the
temple said to her, "Nisaba has honored you and made you a
teacher. May She bless you with a joyous heart and free you
from sorrow." He asked her to recite the scribe's prayer, and
she recited it in a voice that sounded more confident:

Knowledge illuminates every dark place.
Glory to Nisaba, who gave us order
And marked the boundaries
The mistress whose divine powers are unlimited and
        unrivaled
The queen of kings.
The scribe
She who knows everything
And guides our fingers on the clay
She tells them how to press the stylus onto the tablets
And how to embellish them with a golden pen
Nisaba is the one who gave us the measuring rod

And the shining thread of the supervisor
She is the country's scribe
It is she who feeds the gods
And sates humankind.
She has a crown of wheat on her head
House of stars! House of lapis lazuli!
He who reaches every country
And builds a temple in Uruk
The lords look up to you every month
Nisaba draws her divine power from the heavens
The Mistress of Wisdom who reads her tablet of lapis
    lazuli
She draws a map of the sky and places its ropes on the
    Earth
She draws the boundaries
Glory be to her
Glory to the Mistress of Erech
Glory be to Nisaba.

Shab'ad remained a loyal priestess of Nisaba and a skillful
scribe who over two decades inscribed thousands of tablets
documenting life in the city of Umma: sale and purchase
contracts, inventories of harvests and land taxes, prayers and
rituals of worship, magic spells to ward off evil spirits, poems
old and new for the gods. But her first poem remained the
one closest to her heart. Shab'ad died without imagining that
after her death her poem would become the prayer that the

scribes would recite in Mesopotamia during rituals, or that it would creep north and be written on the walls of temples devoted to Nisaba, or that all the tablets she inscribed would be moved to the great school in Shaduppum close to the Diyala River where a temple was built for Nisaba. Taha Baqir's team excavated at the site between 1945 and 1963 and discovered two thousand clay tablets, including Shab'ad's poem to Nisaba. He handed them over to the National Museum, where they remained until April 2003, after which they disappeared into a black hole.

Strolling aimlessly and talking nonsense offer similar pleasures. The feet, like the tongue, have no particular direction or purpose. They cross the street suddenly and veer right or left without reason. There is no clear, straight trajectory, no map or compass. Invisible scribbles on the map of the city. Later the raving is organized, relatively speaking, into particular sentences that are constantly repeated.

When I first came to New York I had an ambitious plan to explore all parts of the city on foot, but time didn't allow for that, of course. Even so, I often walked, in a different direction each time. I began by heading north along Fifth Avenue until I reached the Empire State Building on 43rd Street. Sometimes I would walk on to the edges of Times Square and then retrace my steps. But this route was full of shoppers and tourists the closer I got to Times Square.

Later I preferred to walk west toward the Hudson River. I went through the West Village, which was also crowded with stores and restaurants, but the crowds diminished the farther west I went, especially in the quiet backstreets that had expensive stone houses. To reach the river I crossed the West Side Highway. Then I walked south along the path for joggers and cyclists. I preferred this route because the sight of the river imparts a sense of tranquility, especially just before sunset. There were yachts moored at the jetty of the river port. At night the lights of New Jersey sparkled on the other side of the river.

As the months passed and I took more long walks, I started to roam around in Chinatown. At first I just enjoyed myself and I didn't analyze why I felt relatively at ease there. I looked at the store windows and enjoyed the shape of the Chinese characters, or the Korean characters in part of the neighborhood, on the store windows and the posters, without understanding or bothering to find out what they said. It was often obvious. Restaurants, many of them, stood alongside bakeries, vegetable stores, massage and acupuncture establishments. Maybe it was the liberation from the burden of translating and interpreting that I had to perform every day in various ways. Here I could be a perfect stranger, with no desire to understand anything and happy to let symbols remain symbols.

The end of the walk, or rather its unspoken objective, was always Columbus Park on the intersection of Mulberry and Bayard Streets. I was drawn to this place, where many of the local residents sat, mostly old Chinese people, especially on the weekend. They played cards, chess, or mahjong or sat on the benches watching other people. I found out later that the old women in retirement were immigrants from China or Hong Kong who had worked in the sweatshops that were common in that part of Manhattan in the 1950s. In the meantime, some young people, mostly white, practiced Tai Chi or basketball in the square. There were always some tourists who wandered around inquisitively and took photographs. But my favorite spot was the corner where a cluster of Chinese senior citizens gathered under a cherry tree to play and sing traditional Chinese opera. The whole ritual reminded me of the Baghdadi *chalghi*, except for the fact that there were women performers. The instruments were descendants of the varieties that were common to the countries along or close to the Silk Road. The *yangqin* is similar to the *santur*, with the player hitting the strings with two pieces of bamboo, and the *zhonghu* is a two-stringed instrument played with a bow, rather like the *joza*. The *yueqin* is like an *oud*, but the body is round rather than oval. They also use a small tabla and a wooden rattle. A pipe player sometimes joined the ensemble too. The amateur singers waited for their turn to sing. Some held pieces of paper with the words written on them, others turned the pages of sheet music placed on music stands that the players brought with them, and they agreed on a piece to play. Men and women in their fifties and sixties, and even their seventies, awaited their turns patiently and then sang with gusto.

I didn't need to know the language to understand the words, since they were the same in all languages—the tightropes that stretch between pleasure and pain, which we all walk. We feel dizzy and sometimes we fall, but we keep walking. The words that the racked strings on every instrument know, where sorrow and joy intersect. The pains of longing for another time and place. Anguish at the vast distances between things and people. The vast distances between everything and nothing.

A stranger is someone who is despised wherever his mounts stop.

A stranger is defenseless and he always finds it hard to express himself.

People help each other out, but he has few to help him.

And someone else said:

It was not in anguish at fear of the separation that my eyes started to tear up, but a stranger is a stranger.

O ye! These are the qualities of a stranger who has left behind a home built out of water and clay and moved away from close friends, whether they be rough or smooth in nature, with whom he may have shared a drink among the brooks and the meadows, and who has observed with his eye the charms of sleepy eyes. If all that then results in disappearance and extinction, then where do you stand with respect to someone nearby who has long felt like a stranger in his own country and who has had little luck and gained little from his beloved and his residence? And where do you stand with respect to a stranger who has no way to find a home and no means to settle down? He looked pale when he was in a hut and he was so overcome with sadness that he was like a waterskin. If he spoke, he spoke sadly and intermittently, and if he remained silent, he remained silent in confusion and under constraint.

It has been said that a stranger is someone shunned by his beloved, but I say, "No, a stranger is someone with whom the beloved is in contact. No, a stranger is someone that the observer ignores. No, a stranger is someone toward whom the drunkard shows goodwill. No, a stranger is someone who is called from nearby. No, a stranger is someone who is strange in his strangeness. No, a stranger is someone who has no in-laws. No, a stranger is someone who enjoys no rights." And if that is true, come let us weep over the state of affairs that has made the stranger an outcast and has engendered this ill treatment.

O ye! The stranger is someone whose beauty has faded like the setting sun, who is estranged from a loved one and from those who reproach him, someone who has spoken and acted strangely, someone who has traveled far, coming and going, and who dresses weirdly in tattered clothes.

O ye! A stranger is someone whose appearance speaks of ordeal after ordeal, who shows signs of trial after ordeal, and whose real nature is apparent from time to time. A stranger is someone who is absent even when present, who is present when he is absent. A stranger is someone you wouldn't know if you saw him, and who you wouldn't recognize if you didn't see him. Have you not heard the one who said: "What excuse can be made? No family, no home, no companion, nothing to drink, and nowhere to live"?

This man is a stranger who has never budged from his

place of birth or shifted from where he first drew breath. The strangest of strangers are those who have become strangers in their own country, and the most distant of those who are distant are those who feel distant close to home, because the aim of the exercise is to stop thinking about the world, turn a blind eye to what is visible, keep one's distance from what is familiar, so that one can find someone who can save one from all this by offering a gift, support, a solid pillar to lean on.

O ye! A stranger is someone who is shunned when he mentions the truth and who is driven away when he calls for justice. A stranger is someone who is called a liar when he offers proof and who is tormented when he makes unsubstantiated claims. A stranger is someone who receives nothing in return when he gives and who is not visited when he settles down. O let us take pity on the stranger! He has traveled far without arriving and has suffered long through no fault of his own. He has endured great harm without falling short and suffered greatly to no purpose.

A stranger is someone they don't listen to when he speaks, and if they see him, they don't gather around him. A stranger is someone who, when he breathes, is afflicted by grief and sorrow, and when he holds his breath, is stricken with sadness and regret. A stranger is someone whose voice is not heard when he approaches and is not asked after when he turns aside. A stranger is someone who is not answered when he calls.

O ye! To be a stranger as a whole is agony. He is full of grief, his night is regret, and his daytime is sorrow. His lunch is sad and his dinner is anguish. His opinions are distrustful, all of him is strife, he is made up of ordeals, his secret is public knowledge and fear is where he lives.

Poor man! You are the stranger in every sense.

Although I had left home, I made sure I spoke with Naseer once a month to see how he was. I hung up if my father or his girlfriend answered. At first I was worried that my father's girlfriend, who had become his wife, would mistreat Naseer. But she remained pleasant with him, even after she had two children with my father. Naseer would laugh when I asked, "How are the Indian bastards?" He didn't seem to be as upset as I was about what his father had done. Maybe he was more forgiving than me. In his last year of high school he won a sports scholarship from the University of Virginia after being scouted in the Northern Virginia basketball league. He left home to live in the dorms in Charlottesville, which was two and a half hours south, and he was happy with his independence, his celebrity status at the university, and the travel across the country with the team. I greatly annoyed him when I insisted that he concentrate on his studies to make sure he had a stable profession after he graduated and didn't depend solely on basketball, because the competition was fierce and the chances of playing professionally with a team in the NBA were slight. I was pleased when he succeeded in finding a balance between basketball and his studies, where he majored in business administration. He got very good grades and after graduation found a job in Charlottesville with State Farm, a big insurance company. He shared an apartment there with a friend but later moved to live with his girlfriend. He continued to play basketball on the weekend. I visited him there twice, and he and his girlfriend visited me in New York after I had settled down there.

THE COLLOQUY OF THE CATALOG

In the beginning was the explosion.

Isn't that what the prevalent, accepted theory says? But maybe that massive explosion was the universe screaming and weeping as it emerged from the womb of nothingness into the pain of existence. This universe that expanded at the speed of light. Instead of crawling, it began to fly in every direction with a million wings and stars.

In the beginning was the explosion.

The whole universe is a jungle of fragments flying apart in the cosmic darkness. Some of those fragments have become a star that has settled into a sad orbit. Others are just cosmic dust that floats around. I'm trying to put together the fragments of a little explosion—dust particles from which I can make a necklace I can hang. Yes, hang it, but where? Where can I hang it? Around the neck of the void.

My task is exactly the opposite of the task of the midwife or the obstetrician who cuts the umbilical cord after the birth. I reattach the umbilical cords between things and their mothers. I restring burned ouds. I put the tear back in the eye. It's tiring work that never ends. And I have many enemies. Sometimes I think I'm a failed spider that's hunting the void.

I went to the small Xerox room to copy an article about Ahmad Faris al-Shidyaq and the beginnings of the Arabic novel to hand out to my students. But a man with gray hair wearing a gray suit was standing in front of the copier, which was churning out collated and stapled copies on the left-hand side. When he noticed I was there he turned and said, "I'm just about to finish. It won't take long." Then he put out his hand to shake mine, saying, "You're the guy who was hired last year, aren't you?"

"Yes, that's me," I said.

I remembered his face because I had seen his picture on the department website when I was trying to find out about the place, who worked there and what their interests and leanings were. I remembered that he taught European history.

"Jim Cleary. I'm sorry. I was on sabbatical in France last year and I didn't have a chance to meet you. But I've read the application file and the articles. You're Iraqi. Al-Baghdadi, right?"

"Yes. I'm Nameer."

"Welcome aboard. Have you settled down and got used to the place?"

"Yes, pretty much."

"Oh, by the way, tell me, are you Shi'ite or Sunni?"

I was surprised at how quickly he blurted out this personal question. Other people might ask the question over a cup of coffee or wait until we've been friends for a while. I had been through this before and instead of giving the traditional straightforward answer, I found it was preferable, and more enjoyable for me, to answer with a question: "Why? What does that matter?"

"Because the *New York Times* says that's the cause of the whole problem in your country. Wasn't Saddam a Sunni?"

"And what about you? Are you Christian, Jewish, or Buddhist?"

He was taken aback by my question, of course.

"Well, Christian, but I'm not religious."

"And are you Protestant, Catholic, or what?"

"Protestant. You haven't answered my question."

"My father's Shi'ite and my mother's Sunni."

"And do you follow your father's religion or your mother's?"

"Neither one nor the other. I'm not religious and I don't believe in anything. I'm an atheist, an 'independent' like those of you who don't belong to the Republican Party or the Democratic Party."

"Oh, wow, and are there people like you in Iraq, or did that happen after you came here and studied?"

"I didn't lose my faith at the airport. I lost it in Baghdad, thank God."

"That's really interesting."

"Great!"

He laughed, but rather nervously. I later thought he might avenge my rudeness by voting against me in six years when it was time to decide whether to give me tenure. We'll see.

"What are we going to talk about today?"

"Anything you'd like to talk about. We can carry on with what we were talking about in the last session, or we could talk about what's troubling you."

I was surprised by her answer.

"What's troubling me is the novel I want to write."

"Yes, you mentioned it several times in previous sessions. Why not say more about it?"

"It's about a secondhand book dealer in Baghdad who has a strange project. I met him in Baghdad and we exchange letters from time to time."

"What's strange about the project?"

I told her about Wadood and the sections he had sent me. But I focused on his letters and his garbled ramblings.

"What you say about your friend and his behavior matches the symptoms we notice among people suffering from the effects of extreme psychological shock after a traumatic incident or severe psychological pain or a physical attack. The torture he underwent in prison is no doubt the reason. Has he had any therapy?"

"I don't know. I don't think so."

"And because he hasn't been able to absorb the shock or deal with it or accept that it has happened, or because the shock can't be explained in any logical way, he's still trapped in a vicious circle. He won't completely escape it until he manages to renarrate the details of the shock repeatedly, until they're put in a context or a form that enables him to go on living normally or less painfully. Your friend has to find closure, as we say, and put the incident that caused all this pain on the shelf in its right place so that he can go on living normally."

"He's collecting piles of stories, incidents, and news reports on the shelves in his room. He wants to write an open-ended book. But then no one in Baghdad lives a normal life. Their days are full of violence and destruction."

"I'm sorry. Writing can be therapy! This has been an important development in recent years—but supervised by a specialist, of course. Many of the soldiers coming back from Iraq write as part of their psychological therapy."

I laughed.

"Why are you laughing?"

"Because my friend is still in the throes of war. The troops come back here, while he can't 'come back.' And that's what he's actually writing."

"Yes, but the soldiers are victims too at the end of the day."

"I don't want to get into an argument with you now. The troops here volunteer to join the army. Iraqi civilians don't volunteer. They don't have a choice."

"Let's talk about your novel. Are you making any progress with the writing?"

"No. I can't write."

"What do you think the reason is?"

"I don't know. I feel my ideas are stupid. I have ideas and images, but whenever I pick up my pen, I feel paralyzed. I find excuses to put off writing. I can't start."

"I mean, are you worried that what you write, and what you might publish, won't have any value?"

"Aren't such fears normal for writers?"

"Yes, but. Why don't you try to write about things unrelated to the subject of the novel? About your daily life, for example?"

"I don't like memoirs and diaries."

"Writing about day-to-day things might help solve the problem and move things along."

Carnations scattered in the garden my leaves and roses also circles so you arrive glass and brick hills chasm he picks me he circles around nothing who wiped him out ah I'm not not you I didn't pick jasmine and cactus faucet convulsion the wood piled up we slept on the roof they drowned in the hole softened how no the rest isn't in your life the seal of sorrows the pomegranate tree under the roof underground they're late and at every moment little leaves a lost butterfly how the jasmine thirsty a crow on my shoulder another crow flies off and lands on my shoulder on my heart in my mouth feathers

In my last session with her I told her that reading the news every morning depressed me. "That's simple," she said. "Stop reading the newspapers!" This response struck me as silly and foolish, and unworthy of a psychiatrist, especially after everything I had told her in our sessions about my background. "How so, I mean, just like that?"

"Yes."

"I can't help but read the newspapers or listen to the radio. I've been doing that every day since I was a child."

"You can take control of your life."

We argued about the concept of control and free will in life, and I couldn't control myself and at the end of the session I told her what I was feeling, which was that I honestly didn't see any point in our sessions and nothing was changing in my psychological state.

"These things take a lot of time. It has a lot to do with your problematic relationship with your father and his relationship with your mother that we haven't talked enough about. You're evading confronting many emotions and memories."

"How much time?"

"I don't know. Every patient is a unique case. Sometimes therapy takes ten years or more before we can access what is buried deep and have a breakthrough."

"Ten years!?"

"Yes."

I laughed sarcastically. "Life is too short for that."

"Yes, life is too short, but it's best to live a healthy life and try to deal with our problems."

"I don't know if I can talk and wait ten years to find a solution."

"It might not take ten years, but it certainly won't be solved in ten sessions. Therapy requires commitment."

After that session I canceled two appointments with her, and a week later she sent me an email saying her clinic was moving to another building on the Upper West Side of Manhattan, closer to where she lived. When I found the new clinic on the map I realized the trip would take me about forty minutes each way on the subway, so I decided to look for another psychiatrist.

THE COLLOQUY OF THE *MUNADDAB*, THE DEPLETED

> nadaba al-shay': the thing flowed
> naddaba is used if it goes into the ground
> nadaba fulan: so-and-so died
> nadaba al-ma', imperfect yandubu, verbal noun
> > nuduban: the water sank into the ground and went
> > down
>
> nadaba al-qawm too: the people moved away; hence
> > naadib, remote

Do we breathe to live?

Or do we breathe to die?

No creature is born in this world without fertility, or enrichment as we say in Arabic.

But birth, the birth of anything, looks like a wound. A temporary wound that heals. There is no birth without the mother bleeding, or without placenta. The placenta that the body ejects after it has served its purpose.

Nothing is born in this world without fertility/enrichment.

Even things have wombs and placentas, and they might bleed when they're born. When enriched uranium is produced in nuclear reactors and does its job generating elec-

tricity, it leaves its placenta—munaddab or depleted uranium,
which no longer has enough radioactive uranium. It's like
a butterfly abandoning its cocoon. But this munaddab is no
longer content to hide in containers or in landfill sites, because humans have found a use for it that prolongs its life,
because it has almost twice the density of lead.

DU

One munitions round made of depleted uranium, a
round designed to penetrate steel, strayed off course as it fell
from the AC 130 so it didn't penetrate any armor: it just lay
in the sands of Iraq like a soldier lost in enemy territory. But
a soldier that won't die or be captured. It'll keep breathing.
What it exhales will settle in a lung or a womb. A kidney or a
bone in some body. And it will live in the water and the air for
four million years. It will poison bodies with its stigma and go
on living.

Do we breathe in order to live?

Or do we breathe to die?

One day Mariah heard me singing:

Ghareeba min ba'ad 'aynich ya yumma,
Mihtara bzamani, yahu il-yirham bhali law dahri rimani?

"What's that?" she asked me, and I said, "An Iraqi blues song."
She asked me to translate the lyrics and I started thinking about

how to translate it, and then I said, "You know, there are sorrows that can't be translated." She waved her hand and went back to what she was reading.

THE COLLOQUY OF THE SCAVENGER

Rassoul woke up at five o'clock in the morning. His mother and his little sister Fatma were snoring fast asleep. He tried to get back to sleep but he couldn't. He got up from the mattress, which wasn't thick enough to stop the damp seeping into his mother's bones and hurting her. As if work wasn't enough of an ordeal. But Rassoul's bones were soft, as his mother said to reassure him when he asked whether he too would feel pain from the damp. The night before she had told him that they wouldn't go out this morning because of the war. But he couldn't sleep and he felt trapped. There was nothing for him to do in this tiny place. It had been a horrific night. The drone of planes and the sound of explosions. They weren't nearby but they frightened them. They couldn't sleep for hours. Their mother kept listening to the news on the radio and praying. Whenever he or his sister asked her what was happening, she repeated the same expression: "The war's started. The Americans are bombing." But he couldn't hear anything now. Maybe the war was over. They said it would be short. He went to the big tin container in the corner and scooped up a little cold water in the palm of his hand

and drank it. He scooped once again and wet his face. He
put on his work pants, on top of the sweatpants that he slept
in. Then he put on his woolen sweater with the turtleneck
and his jacket with a hood. He picked up his shoes from near
the door and put them on. Then he opened the door, and
closed it slowly and quietly behind him so as not to wake up
his mother and sister. The morning cold slapped him in the
face, as well as the smell of trash, which sometimes made him
want to vomit. But he remembered what his mother said. We
have to put up with it and work hard so that we can leave this
mud hut and live in a room in a real house with a bathroom
and find other work. This was his prayer and her prayer. He
pulled the collar of his sweater up so that it covered his nose.
He walked to the hole behind the house and stopped in front
of it. He unzipped his pants and started to piss in the puddle
as he looked up at the sky, which was also changing its clothes
to start work. There were no planes or missiles on the horizon. He felt relieved after shaking the last drops off his little
penis. One of them landed on his index finger. He did up his
flies and wiped his hand on his pants. He turned and walked
toward the trash dump that was twenty minutes away.

The trucks hadn't arrived yet to spew out what they held
in their bellies. But he was a hunter and skilled at finding
what others, even the experienced ones, missed in the piles
of trash that they sifted through. Hadn't he once found a gold
ring? He caught sight of it glittering, ran to it, and grabbed it.

He gave it to his mother, who put it on her ring finger after wiping it with her sleeve. It was rather tight. She quickly hid it in her bosom. She was very happy and hugged and kissed Rassoul. "Bravo to the clever guy! A real hunter!" she said. She went to market the next day to sell it. That day they ate a real meal of the kind they managed to have only at Eid time. But the ring was an exception. Since then he hadn't found anything as important or as valuable. They were looking for cans and empty bottles because they provided a reliable and steady income. They wanted as many sacks of rubbish as they could collect. His mother once found a small radio in the heaps of trash and, when she bought some batteries and put them in, the radio worked. She started listening to it at night after going back to their room. So why had someone thrown it away? She often repeated this question without finding a satisfactory answer. Sometimes she imagined who these people were that threw away all these things that could still be used, along with things that couldn't be used.

Batteries, toothbrushes, empty perfume bottles, sometimes with a drop or two left, torn underwear, fruit peel, earphones, broken CDs, juice cans, eggshells, tomatoes, a football with a hole, surgical gloves, plates and cups, diapers, cassette tapes, rotten meat, pieces of paper, newspapers, magazines, wires.

When he pestered his mother with the same question: "Why do they throw all this stuff away?" she lost patience and silenced him with a convincing answer, rather than just "How should I know?" "My son," she said, "we thank God they throw it all away. Let them. If they didn't, how would we eat and live?"

He liked the term *hunter* and preferred it to *scavenger*. Once he found a beautiful picture in one of the magazines he hunted. It showed a handsome man sitting alone on a wooden chair on the shore of a lake, with a fishing rod and a pack of cigarettes beside him. There was one sentence in large letters in Arabic and one word in foreign letters, but he didn't understand what any of it meant. When he asked one of the grown-ups who worked with them what was written on the picture, the man said, "Advertising." "Advertising what?" "Cigarettes." He imagined himself as a great fisherman. He tore the piece of paper out of the magazine, folded it up and put it in his pocket. He began dreaming that he would be a famous fisherman when he grew up. He would catch fish, instead of people's leftovers. And he would smoke a cigarette during his breaks. He would take it out from time to time, touch the glossy surface, and dream.

He was approaching the dump when he noticed that there were three large piles that hadn't been buried yet. Sometimes the trucks came late at night after the scavengers had gone off home and the piles weren't buried until the next morning.

He was alone, just him and some birds circling over the

piles but unable to lift the empty cans. They would fly away as soon as he arrived. He took one of the two sacks from his pocket to be ready to hunt. The smell of rotting grew stronger the closer he approached: he could smell it through the sweater over his nose. He would breathe through his mouth to avoid it. Usually he put pieces of Kleenex in his nostrils, as he had learned from others, but this time he had forgotten to bring a tissue from home.

He reached the foot of a pile and began to dig around as he moved forward. As usual he found several empty cans. This was the easiest thing. He heard the drone of a plane in the distance. He stood upright and looked out to the horizon. He couldn't see anything.

Two hundred yards from the dump there was a building that used to be a small military installation as part of the Ministry for Military Industrialization. It had been bombed in 1991, and the building was abandoned till the end of the 1990s, when this area became an additional trash dump. The scavenger families moved into the damaged building and lived there, but the pilot's information was that the site was a strategic target.

"Anyone who has once started to open the fan of memory never comes to the end of its parts; no image satisfies him, for he has seen that it can be unfolded, and only in its folds does the truth lie."

Is this incessant desire to archive everything a sickness? Can it spread by contagion, or just by reading? For years I've been clipping pictures and news stories out of the newspapers and keeping them, albeit not methodically. The pace at which I archived material picked up when I came back from Baghdad after meeting Wadood and finding out about his project, and after the level of violence and destruction in Iraq increased. But I had never been interested in collecting stamps, documents, or postcards, and it had never occurred to me that I would have this obsession. Once I was leafing through Wadood's manuscript as I sat in my office. When I got to the Colloquy of the Stamp Album, I was struck by the passage where he describes the stamps. I stopped reading and looked for old Iraqi stamps on the Internet. The search results took me to eBay. I had read articles about the strange things that are sold there. I found many old Iraqi stamps, from the time of the monarchy, the beginnings of the republican era, and Saddam's time, of course. Some of them were in excellent condition and on sale at reasonable prices (there was no bidding on the stamps because there wasn't enough demand), so I bought some. After I'd given my address and my credit card number, the site told me the stamps would arrive within three days. The page took me to all the things on sale that were in the Iraq category. Apart from stamps, it was mostly banknotes and coins, old and new. That day I also put a 50-fils coin from 1931 and a bronze one-fils coin from 1938 with a picture of King Ghazi in my shopping basket. I would go back to the site once or twice a week to add more things to my shopping basket.

A tourist map of the Baghdad area in 1962, with the names of the districts and landmarks in English. A Royal Rescue Medal, which was awarded to those who helped save Baghdad from floods in 1954. The envelope of a letter sent from Baghdad to Jaffa from 1939. An official envelope from Mosul University, sent to Holland in 1971. A large box of matches with a picture of the spiral minaret in Samarra. The Iraqi atlas for primary schools, published in 1972. A postcard with a picture of Hafiz al-Qadi Street. One of the strangest things I found and bought was a yellow piece of paper from the clinic of Dr. Abdilqadir Wahbi al-Amir (it gave the address as al-A'zamiyya, The Ship Shop, Near the Bridge, Clinic Telephone: 310 Kadhimiyya, 253 North); on it a message read: "Upon examination of Mr. Abdil-majid Ismail, it was apparent that he was suffering from malaria and anemia, and after giving him the necessary treatment I advised him to rest completely and to take medicine for five days. May 5, 1949." It had two stamps on it with a picture of King Faisal as a child, frankings, and some handwriting saying the patient should receive his salary in full and be given sick leave. There had recently been a proliferation of plates and sets of silver spoons stolen from Saddam's palaces. I examined them in detail, but I wasn't interested in owning them. The site mentions the city and country where the buyer lives, and often these were from southern and central states, so they were from American troops coming home with minor spoils of war.

I arranged the stamps and the coins and framed them into five pictures, as well as two maps of Baghdad, and hung them on the walls of the office and in my flat. The rest of the pieces I had bought stayed in boxes that piled up in my closet and corners of my flat. It was like a dark museum invaded by dust and silence, scowling at the world, and no one could visit it. Sometimes I took the things out of their seclusion. I tried to listen to them as they told their stories. Isn't that what Wadood says? That everything has a story to tell. But I couldn't hear anything. Maybe I was a bad listener. Or perhaps they didn't want to tell their stories to me.

I peel the moment by hand as if peeling an orange, but it's a blue orange, as in Éluard's famous poem. The peel of time gets under my fingernails and the scent reaches my nose. I don't know how to describe it, except to say that I feel like a child discovering everything for the first time with his fingers, mouth, and eyes. Not the child that I once was. Another child that I don't know. With no memories and no language. When I've finished peeling it, I try to break it in half and a vast sea bursts out of it and overwhelms me. I dive into it and breathe like a fish. I grow tired and sleep naked on the seabed. When I wake up I find myself on wet ground, and the fruit-moment awaits on the ground.

"But now the moment has come when you must allow me to shake a few meager fruits from the tree of conscientiousness which has its roots in my heart and its leaves in your archive."

When I was a butterfly.

The butterfly is my mother.

My mother was a butterfly that laid her eggs in a moment. All the eggs died except the egg I was in. When my egg hatched, I started crawling, eating, and shedding skin after skin when the old skin wore out. My mother flew off and didn't come back. I wove my cocoon from my tears and my fear. I hid inside it and waited a long time. The loneliness preyed on me, so I slipped out of my cocoon. I flew off looking for my mother. I saw hundreds of butterflies, but none of them was my mother. I almost forgot her. Then my wings took me to a table in a garden. On it lay an open book with the breeze turning the pages. I caught sight of my mother's body between two pages.

My mother is shrouded in words.

For years I've been eating a bagel almost every morning, but just today I remembered the *simit* incident. I may not have thought about it since the time it happened, more than three decades ago. The first time I stood in front of a bagel store in Virginia, I remembered the simit I liked to eat in Baghdad in my childhood.

The bell rang, setting us free. For the long break we ran to the big back gate, which was made of wrought iron and painted light blue. We reached out our hands to buy simit from the peddler who stood outside carrying a tray with simit piled up on it methodically. When we arrived at the gate that day, the janitor was shouting at the simit seller, warning him not to come close to the school gate. We asked him why and he said, "The principal will no longer let you eat food from outside. Go to the school shop and buy sandwiches from there." "Oh please, janitor," we begged him, but to no avail. Rasim Adnan, my classmate who was with me at the time, told me we could climb over the wall to buy simit outside and then come back, and that he knew how. I agreed enthusiastically. He ran off and I ran after him. We reached the line of trees parallel to the wall and he pointed at one of the trees, saying, "Let's climb this one and jump." That's what we did. We clambered up the branches and reached the top of the wall. Our clothes got dirty because it wasn't easy to get down on the other side. He clung to my hands and let his body hang, then let go and landed on the ground. But he didn't get a firm footing, so he stumbled and fell on his side, but it was a slight fall. I did the same and managed to land on my feet without falling over. We brushed off our clothes and ran to the simit seller, who had moved off toward the main street. I felt a pain in my right foot. Each of us bought two simits. We ate one on the way back to school. We had overlooked the fact that it would be impossible to climb the wall from outside because there were no trees to climb. When we reached the iron gate the janitor insisted we give him our names, class, and section, or else he wouldn't open the gate. I don't know why we didn't lie. We told him our names, class, and section. He took the key out of his pocket, unlocked the padlock, and let us in. In the lesson after the break the principal, Sister Beninya Shikwana, knocked on the class door, opened it, and came in in her loose white gown and her thick glasses. Miss Fatma, the history teacher, greeted her. The principal read out my name and Rasim's name from a piece of paper she was carrying and ordered us to stand in front of the class. She scolded us: "You climb over the wall and go outside school to buy simit? Why are you so naughty? If a car hit you what could we tell your parents? You're our responsibility. This shop here is full of all kinds of food. No one is to go out again. If anyone thinks of getting out again, I'll expel them. Understood?" She told us to put out our hands. She was holding the Chinese ruler of ill repute, and she struck each of us with it five times. My hand was still hurting when I ate the second simit after school. And now I'd be willing to put up with that pain again for the sake of a single simit.

When we met, you asked me if I was a writer. I've written hundreds of short poems, five novels, and a one-act play, but I haven't yet had a single word published. I've completed one novel, but I tore it up and threw it away, just as I've torn up everything I've written, because I wasn't convinced that it was complete. After that I had a severe psychological crisis that lasted many years. I might tell you the details later. All I did then was read and sell books. I hid in a dark tunnel and came out only when I grasped a simple truth: there are no real endings, just as there are no real beginnings. There are just imaginary borders, signs, and marks that we put in place in order to structure our irrational existence in this random universe. We dress it up with meaning to cover its nakedness. They are bridges we build over the eternal river that flows, indifferent to us. This truth set me free and opened a new horizon for me. Ever since I discovered it, I've been working according to a new methodology, with confidence and not a hint of bitterness. And I am writing this book, which may never end, as all books (don't) end. It won't end even with the death of the author. Other writers can go on writing its other parts after me.

I look through the notebook and discover that my words have come to resemble Wadood's words in many places. Did that happen because I copied out his colloquies and letters by hand because I was worried they might get lost or be torn up? Because I had read what he had written dozens of times? Was that a pretext for assimilating his style and inhabiting his persona? I'm not sure. No, I didn't write this part. He was the one who wrote it. These are not my words. They are his words. My words are the ones that sneaked into his eternal minute and his catalog to escape through the black hole. Or to hide inside it. I can no longer tell the difference. How did the goldfinch from my childhood, for example, fly off and end up in Wadood's hallucinations? And the butterflies?

All this is circling around me. All these beings and things have been circling around me for decades. Every being or thing has an orbit that it occupies alone, and its own orbital period, which grows longer and shorter. As for me, at first I thought I was stationary, not circling. But I discovered that I'm turning. I'm circling around myself. Yes, I'm circling around myself, looking for myself. Later I discovered that I'm not only circling around myself, but I'm also trapped in an orbit. I'm turning like all those beings and things. I'm turning around something, but I don't know what it is. It might be a vacuum. It's definitely not a sun. I'm turning and nothing keeps me company in my orbit. Maybe I'm turning around darkness. Invisible darkness. Darkness that hides in the light. I'm circling and feeling dizzy and screaming. I lose consciousness, and when I come around I find I'm still turning and turning. I'm looking for a black hole that will take me back to nothingness.

"The painting shows an angel looking as though he is about to move away from something he is fixedly contemplating. His eyes are staring, his mouth is open, his wings are spread. This is how one pictures the angel of history. His face is turned toward the past. Where we perceive a chain of events, he sees one single catastrophe which keeps piling wreckage upon wreckage and hurls it in front of his feet. The angel would like to stay, awaken the dead, and make whole what has been smashed. But a storm is blowing from Paradise; it has got caught in his wings with such violence that the angel can no longer close them. The storm irresistibly propels him into the future to which his back is turned, while the pile of debris before him grows skyward. This storm is what we call progress."

Endings

An Ending

At the beginning of the fall term in 2006 I received an email from the dean telling me about a course, or a workshop, that the manuscript department in the university library was organizing, with grants for those who wanted to work on restoring manuscripts and valuable books from war-torn regions. "Do you know any-one in Iraq who would find this course useful and would be ready to come here in the spring semester?" she asked. I immediately thought of Wadood. I realized that he didn't have a degree or speak English fluently, and I didn't think he would understand enough to handle the course. Never mind. I could write a letter of recom-mendation, stressing the importance of his project. This would be an opportunity for him to get out of Baghdad, and he could use the time here for writing. And it would be an opportunity for us to meet again. Would he agree? I was enthusiastic about the idea, but then doubts started to trouble me when I remembered his mood swings, his psychological problems, and the bureaucratic difficul-ties he would face in trying to get out of Iraq. But I figured that the pros outweighed the cons. I wrote back to the dean to tell her that I wanted to nominate an extraordinary book dealer I had met in Baghdad. Exaggerating, I added that he was interested in restoring old books. She answered eagerly, agreeing to support the request. I had to act fast, and I realized that the best way would be to speak to him directly. I called Midhat and asked him to go to Wadood's shop and call me from there so that I could speak to Wadood my-self. Midhat called the next day and gave the phone to Wadood. It was the first time I had heard his voice on the phone. I put the idea to him and assured him that the university would cover his travel and housing expenses and would send the U.S. embassy in Baghdad a letter to facilitate the visa process. All he had to do was get a passport. "Thank you, doctor, but you know I'm not into academic things," Wadood said.

"The course is at the university but it's not academic at all. It's training on how to deal with manuscripts and old books. It's down your alley," I replied.

After a brief pause, he said, "Okay, very well, but how can I leave all the files and the catalog?"

"The files can stay where they are and you can lock the door on the catalog, and it will stay just as it is. It's just a visit for a few months and then you can go back to them."

"But my English is terrible," he continued.

"No problem, try to improve it in the months you have left, and they'll get a student here to translate for you."

"Thank you, doctor, but let me think about it a while."

"Of course, I don't want to put pressure on you, but I do hope you'll agree. I'd very much like to see you and spend some time with you. You could have fun here and have a little break from Baghdad and its troubles. But you have to give me an answer within a month because of all the formalities and the bureaucracy."

"Okay, but give me two or three days to think," Wadood said.

I felt disheartened after the conversation and was prepared to accept the possibility that he wouldn't come. But two days later Midhat called to tell me that Wadood had called him on a landline and asked him to tell me that he agreed. Two months later Midhat told me that Wadood had done the paperwork and he sent me an email with Wadood's Iraqi passport number and the spelling of his name in English. The university sent a letter to the U.S. embassy confirming that it was inviting Wadood to take part in the course and requesting that he be given a visa. He obtained it after three months and they sent him a ticket to fly from Amman to New York.

I was elated and started thinking about all the places I could take him. MOMA and Central Park, definitely. The New York Public Library and the Strand to see the thousands of books on the walls and the shelves. Mariah was pleased with the news. "You can finally see for yourself that he's a real flesh-and-blood human being and not just a character in my imagination," I said.

"I'll believe that when I meet him," she replied.

On the day he was arriving, I took the A train from West 4th Street and got to JFK Airport half an hour before his plane from Amman was due to land, in the knowledge that they might hold him up at passport control and customs because of his Iraqi passport. I stood by the arrivals gate, and Wadood appeared half an hour after his plane landed, pulling a small black suitcase behind him. His hair was slightly grayer, and he gave a broad smile when he saw me. We hugged warmly and I took his suitcase from him, though he resisted at first. Before I had finished welcoming him and asking him about the flight, he took a bag out of his hand luggage and said, "This is for you, doctor. *Mannasama*, from Baghdad, pastries from Abu Afif's," he said.

"Thanks, Wadood. Why did you go to all the trouble?" I replied.

I had intended to ask him about his catalog and where he was and whether he had brought any new chapters with him, besides those he had left for me in Baghdad, but . . .

I should describe his meeting Mariah and his impressions of New York . . .

but I'm not satisfied with this ending and I don't think it works.

I have to write another ending.

Another Ending

After Wadood inundated me with more than ten letters that he sent to my address at Dartmouth College in New Hampshire, but which I received after I moved to New York, I heard nothing from him for more than a year. I sent him several letters but he didn't reply. I asked Midhat to drop in on him to reassure me that he was well. He did that several times, and he told me that Wadood was rude to him the last time, saying, "Leave me alone, man, and tell Dr. Nameer to get off my back. Give me a break. I've had enough of interrogations and harassment. We have enough here already, and now those living abroad are harassing us too." I felt that these assignments were beginning to annoy Midhat. I was reluctant to ask him to do anything related to Wadood. I busied myself with teaching and the bustle of everyday life until I received Wadood's last letter, addressed to me at the university. I opened the envelope impatiently when I saw his name written on the back. I found a handwritten letter:

Dear Dr. Nameer,

How are you?

This might be my last letter to you. My mental state has deteriorated in recent months and I've entered a dark tunnel and I see no way out. Since you're one of the very few people who are interested in me and my catalog, and since you're not part of the majority who are conspiring to thwart the project and undermine the morale of the person behind it, I feel compelled to tell you, more than anyone else, what I intend to do. For the last few years, however hopeless it seemed, I have clung to an eternal ray of hope (I don't know where it comes from), and I have felt solace and consolation in my little kingdom and in my catalog. But this ray has disappeared from my life and I can no longer find it. Even my relationship with everything I have written and collected all these years has radically changed. I now feel a painful damage deep inside, and I have decided to write the end myself. We don't choose much in this life. We have no choice in where and when we are born, or in the genes through which we inherit our diseases, our talents, and the burdens we have to bear. We don't choose our mother tongue or our religion. We don't choose our paths in life. Don't we deserve to choose the end, if we can? This is what I have decided. Instead of being an actor performing his monotonous role in this theater of the absurd and awaiting an end whose form and timing is decided by others, I will be the master of my ending. I will write and direct the last act myself and I will be free for one moment in my life. I will take revenge on everyone in my own way. My birthday is a month away and I will celebrate it in an unusual way. I'm going to throw all my files into a barrel and watch them turn into ashes. Yes, I am going to burn the catalog. And since it is an important project and a unique text, it would be unbecoming for it to march to its demise alone. What am I after the catalog? Why should I even exist and for whom? The ideal ending would be for me to burn too. The ecstasy of utter annihilation, leaving this form of existence and going to absolute nothingness. But it would be a cruel ending and I don't think I have the courage to self-immolate. I have to find a less painful way. I'm fully aware that it wouldn't be the first time a writer has burned his writings or stipulated in his will that they should be burned after his death. No doubt you know about Kafka, and al-Tawhidi before him, and many others after. I cannot deny that I was inspired by the letter that al-Tawhidi wrote in reply to one from Judge Abu Sahl Ali ibn Muhammad, who rebuked him for burning his books. Read it—it is my response to your rebuke, and al-Tawhidi is more eloquent.

Yours always
Wadood

When I told Mariah about the letter she said that maybe it was a call for help in some way. Perhaps he was looking for someone to dissuade him and take him by the hand. Suicidal people do hesitate and can be saved. But how could I help him? I could call Midhat or other friends and ask them to look after him and keep an eye on him.

Wadood sent three pages with his letter, three yellowish pieces of paper cut out of some book:

Your letter reached me unexpectedly, although I was impatient to receive it. I thanked God Almighty for blessing me with it, and asked Him for more letters like this one, in which, after saying how ardently you miss me, you describe the anguish you felt when you heard reports that I have set fire to my precious books and doused them with water. I was surprised that my rationale escaped you, as if you had not read the words of God (to whom power and majesty belong), when He says: "All things perish except His face, His is the judgment, and unto Him shall you return," or when He says: "Everything on earth is transient." You seem to have forgotten that nothing is permanent in this life, even if it is of noble substance and glorious essence, as long as it has been subjected to the changes of night and day and has been exposed to the mishaps of fate and the passage of time . . . And I will now willingly explain to you my rationale if you ask for it, or offer my excuse if you seek clarification, so that you might trust me in what I have done and understand the grace of God Almighty in suggesting that I do it. Learning is intended to be acted on, and deeds are intended for salvation. And so, if our deeds do not match our knowledge, knowledge turns out to be a waste of effort on the part of the scholar. I seek refuge in God from knowledge that is wasted effort, that is unworthy, and that becomes a chain around its master's neck. This is a kind of argument that is mixed with apology. You must understand—may God teach you good things—that these books contained many forms of knowledge, some of it secret and some of it publicly known. As for the secret knowledge, I have not found anyone who would willingly adopt the truth of it. And as for what was publicly known, I have not come across anyone who cared to seek it out. Yet I have compiled most of these books in order that people might see me as superior, as a leader among them, and to acquire status in their estimation. But I have been deprived of all that and there is no doubt that God chose well when He decided what would happen to me. For this and other reasons, I hated the fact that my books counted against me and not in my favor. Among the factors which strengthened my resolve to act and removed any disincentive was that I have lost a noble son, a beloved friend, a close companion, an erudite follower, and my principal lieutenant. It would have been hard for me to leave my books to people who would tamper with them, impugn my honor when they examined them, make fun of my errors and mistakes when they browsed through them, or share the view that I am inadequate and at fault because of them. If you ask, "Why do you brand these people as distrustful and rebuke them all for this fault?" my answer is that what I have seen of them in life confirms my distrust of them after my death. How could I leave my books to people who have been my neighbors for twenty years, when none of them has shown me true affection or been protective? Among them on many occasions, after my renown was past, I was forced to eat green plants in the desert, to beg ignominiously from both the elite and from commoners, to sell religion and valor, to engage in hypocrisy, and to do things that it is not good for a free man to describe in writing and that are hurtful to a man's feelings. The current state of the world is obvious to your eyes and evident by both day and night. What I have said is no secret to you, given your knowledge, your intelligence, and the fact that you are so well informed and have few distractions. You should not have doubted that what I did was right, both what

I described earlier and what I have withheld and concealed, either to avoid writing at length or for fear of gossip. Anyway, I have become an owl, today or tomorrow: I am in my ninth decade and, after old age and infirmity, can I have any hope of a pleasant life or any wish that things will change? Am I not one of those of whom someone said: "We come and go every day and night / And shortly we will do so no longer." Or as someone else said, "I drank the pearly milk of youth in his shadow until old age came and weaned me." This verse is by al-Ward al-Ja'di, but there is not enough space here to quote it in full. By God, sir, if I had listened to the advice only of those brothers and friends — strangers, men of letters, and loved ones — that I have lost in this part of the world, it would have sufficed. So how much more so if I had listened to those who were close at hand and through whose closeness I found enlightenment? I lost them in Iraq, al-Hijaz, al-Jabal, Rayy, and other nearby places. Their death notices have constantly arrived, and my memory is clogged with them. Am I not made of the same stuff? Is there any way I can avoid their fate? I ask Almighty God, the lord of the ancients, to take my admission of what I know in conjunction with the fact that I have avoided committing any offenses, for He is near at hand and responsive. Besides, in burning these books, I had the example of imams who are widely emulated, whose guidance is sought and who are seen as sources of enlightenment. These include Abu 'Amr ibn al-'Alaa', one of the greatest scholars and a man of obvious asceticism and well-known piety. He buried his books in the ground and no trace of them was found. There is also Daoud al-Ta'i, who was one of the best of men in his asceticism, his knowledge of religious law and his commitment to worship. He was called the crown of the *umma*. He threw his books in the sea and said to them in a whisper: "You were a great guide, but to stay with one's guide once one has arrived is stupid, lazy, and annoying." Then there was Youssef bin Asbat, who carried his books to a cave in a mountain, threw them inside, and then blocked up the entrance. When he was criticized for this, he said, "Knowledge guided us at first, but later it almost misled us. So we abandoned it for the sake of the One whom we had reached, and we detested it because of the things we had wanted." There was Abu Suleiman al-Darani, who put his books together in an oven, heated it up, and then said, "By God, I did not burn you until I was about to be burned by you." There was Sufyan al-Thawri, who tore up a thousand books, let the wind blow them away, and said, "I wish that my hand had been cut off right here and that I had not written one word." There was also Abu Sa'id al-Sayrafi, our sheikh and the master of scholars, who said to his son Muhammad: "I have left these books to you so that you may eventually benefit from them. But if you think they are betraying you, turn them into food for the fire." What can I say, when the person listening to me believes that the times compelled the likes of me to do what you heard I had done—times that bring tears to one's eyes for sadness and sorrow and that wrench one's heart for anger, passion, and grief? What is to be done with what has been, what has happened and what is now in the distant past? If I should need any knowledge deep inside me, then it would be very little that I needed, for Almighty God is a healer and a protector. But if I should need knowledge for other people, I have enough inside me to fill scroll upon scroll of paper until breath after breath runs out: "That is God's grace to us and to people, but most people do not know."

I think this ending is slightly better than the first, but it isn't the end. I was about to put the *the* in quotation marks but I changed my mind. Isn't it strange how the "real" ending is usually superior to all the imaginary endings? Wadood wasn't destined to have his ending written exactly as he wanted it, nor as I wanted it. We have to admit that the endings we imagine and hope for are only suggestions. Sometimes, when it is kind to us, which is rare, life adopts them. Or life's own endings resemble or are identical to the ones we imagine, and then we are overjoyed.

But our endings do not belong to us.

THE COLLOQUY OF THE LAST BIRD

Here I am approaching the sky over Baghdad. The river wavers and zigzags in fear as it approaches, but it can't avoid coming into the city. Is it afraid of the rising plumes of black smoke? I'm afraid of the flocks of massive metal birds. They might come back, as they have done in the past. To hover over us and pursue us. Their roar is deafening. I don't know how they can fly when they're blind. And why do they excrete fire everywhere?

The last thing my father said before we parted was that he had never seen so many of them or such big ones.

Where did my father go?

Where's my mother?

And where are my siblings?

I'm still flying.

. . .

But I'm tired

The End of the Novel . . . and Its Beginning

The sound of the trash collectors woke me up as they emptied the large dumpsters outside my building in the morning. Mariah wasn't beside me, as she was visiting her aunt in Philadelphia. It took me a while to go back to sleep, and then I dreamed that I could hear al-Mutanabbi speaking English in a British accent. When I woke up later, WNYC was carrying the BBC news, as usual at that time. "The United States and North Korea are preparing to start talks in New York on establishing diplomatic relations after North Korea abandons its nuclear program. China is increasing its defense budget by 17.8 percent and reducing its deficit by 1.1 percent of GDP. The former prime minister of Kosovo, Ramush Haradinaj, who led the Kosovo Liberation Army, appears before the International Criminal Tribunal for the Former Yugoslavia. The Reform Party in Estonia wins 27 percent of the votes in parliamentary elections, raising the number of seats it holds to thirty-one. A suicide bomber blows himself up at a shopping mall in Baghdad close to al-Mutanabbi Street, killing at least thirty people."

I got out of bed, hurried to the desk, and turned on the computer to look for more details. All the sites in Arabic and English repeated the same thing, adding that eyewitnesses said fire had destroyed some shops and a number of cars. As I read, I repeated, "No! Wadood! No! not Wadood, not Wadood," like a spell that would protect him or a prayer that would save him. The image accompanying the news story didn't give me any hope. It compounded my fears and my sadness. A man has covered his mouth with a towel to protect himself from the smoke. He's looking at the debris that covers everything around him. Behind him firemen are spraying water from a hose. The stores don't appear clearly in the picture and you can't make out much.

I called Midhat three times but he didn't answer. I sent him an email asking him to check on Wadood as soon as possible and get in touch with me.

Mariah called me an hour later after reading the news, to ask about Wadood and whether I had contacted him. I reminded her that he didn't have a phone and told her I had left several messages for Midhat and that I was trying to call Baghdad. I sent an email to my students telling them that class that day had been canceled. An hour later Midhat called me and said he would go to the area to try to find Wadood or any news about him. He called me back two hours later, and the first words he said were: "My condolences."

"So I have erected one of his dwellings, with books as the building stones, before you, and now he is going to disappear inside, as is only fitting."

I hadn't wept so bitterly since my mother died. Wadood was twenty-seventh on the list of thirty people killed in al-Mutanabbi Street. Wadood hadn't been able to decide his own end, as he had been planning, even if his ending was somewhat similar to the one he had envisaged. He didn't light the fire himself, but it ravaged that orchard he had been tending and watering in his room and trans-formed it into a pile of ash and a cloud of smoke. The only branch that remained of that mythical orchard was the one he had left for me at the hotel and that he later regretted giving me. I wonder whether Wadood foresaw his ending. Did the catalog contain the signs and seeds of destruction within it?

"Only in extinction is the collector comprehended."

I put Wadood's name into the search engine several times a day in the hope of finding out something new about him. Four days after the explosion I found a short article titled *Al-Mutanabbi as a home, farewell Wadood* on the al-Hiwar al-Mutamaddin website, written by an Iraqi called Muthanna al-Nasiri. Here is the text:

The news traveled the desert before reaching me
In shock I clung to hopes that it was false
But when the truth of it left no room for hope
I choked on my tears until my tears almost choked on me
Tongues stumbled as they tried to say it
As did couriers on the roads and pens in books

For years death and destruction have taken turns slapping us and our cities every morning. They erase all names, the names of places and loved ones, one after another. Sometimes they erase them with the blood red color that leaves wounds open. At others with the black that blocks out the Iraqi sun and makes its long night even longer. Yes, Abu al-Tayyib al-Mutanabbi. You saw Iraq when its night was long and now it's longer than ever. A night that now descends sadly on your street, which they have stabbed with fire, along with my friend who lived in its heart.

Wadood Abdulkarim, another name to be added to the thousands upon thousands of Iraqi dead marching into the twilight of oblivion and silence. But wait! Do I not have the right to stop the procession for a few minutes to bid farewell to my friend? I know this name. We were together in the same unit in Baquba back in 1991. We spent a week in the same trench and miraculously survived the inferno of bombardment. Wadood Abdulkarim, a graduate of the College of Arts, who was dragged, like me, into that ill-fated war, which we thought (how naïve we were!) would be the last. We survived because we decided to run away and go home like the others, after all communications were cut off and we had nothing left to eat.

Wadood went back to his family's home in Zayyuna, but an American missile had arrived a few days before him and turned it into a massive crater. He never recovered from the shock, even after years of therapy in the al-Rashad Hospital. After living with his relatives he chose al-Mutanabbi Street as a home because he had lost his home. And now the destruction has pursued him, destroying his home, destroying his soul, and burning his innocent body, which chose to live and die with books. The last time I saw him was a year ago. I kiss your soul, Wadood, and bid you farewell. Now you are finally going home and back to your family to lie with them in the earth.

I wiped my tears away and printed out the article. I wrote "Wadood's Colloquy" on it by hand, added it to the catalog, and decided to write this novel.

NOTES

Page 93   Amiri Baraka, "A Guerilla Handbook" (1969).

Page 110   Walter Benjamin, *Walter Benjamin's Archive* (2016).

Page 115   Walter Benjamin, *One Way Street* (2016).

Page 134   Benjamin, *One Way Street*.

Page 276   Walter Benjamin, *Berlin Chronicle* (1932).

Page 279   Walter Benjamin, *Letters to Gershom Scholem* (1933).

Page 284   Walter Benjamin, "Theses on the Philosophy of History" (1942).

Page 300   Walter Benjamin, "Unpacking My Library" (1931).

Page 300   Benjamin, "Unpacking My Library."

SINAN ANTOON is a poet, novelist, academic, and translator. He was born in Baghdad and studied English literature at Baghdad University. He left Iraq after the 1991 Gulf War. He studied Arabic literature at Harvard, where he earned his doctorate. He has published two collections of poetry and four novels. His award-winning works have been translated into fourteen languages. His op-eds have appeared in *The Guardian*, the *New York Times*, *Süddeutsche Zeitung*, and *al-Jazeera*, among others. He is an associate professor in the Gallatin School of New York University.

JONATHAN WRIGHT's translations include three winners of the International Prize for Arabic Fiction. He studied Arabic at St. John's College, Oxford, and worked for many years as a journalist for Reuters in countries across the Arab world, including Egypt, Lebanon, Sudan, Oman, Tunisia, and Saudi Arabia. He has translated work by Ahmed Saadawi, Hassan Blasim, Rasha al-Ameer, Alaa el-Aswany, Ibrahim Essa, Amjad Nasser, and many other writers.